Bitter Trumpet

Also by Fred Grove

Bitter Trumpet

FRED GROVE

A DOUBLEDAY D WESTERN
DOUBLEDAY
NEW YORK LONDON TORONTO SYDNEY

A Doubleday D Western

Published by Bantam Doubleday Dell Publishing Group, Inc.
666 Fifth Avenue, New York, New York 10103

A Doubleday D Western and the portrayal of the letters DD
are trademarks of Bantam Doubleday Dell Publishing Group, Inc.

Library of Congress Cataloging-in-Publication Data

Grove, Fred.
Bitter trumpet/Fred Grove.
p.   cm.—(A Double D western)
I. Title.
PS3557.R7B58   1989
813'.54—dc20   89-32503
CIP

ISBN: 0-385-26311-2
Copyright © 1989 by Fred Grove
All Rights Reserved
Printed in the United States of America
First Edition
October 1989

Bitter Trumpet

1

As the head-nodding gray gelding took him along the pike at an easy running walk, the rolling wooded hills of home, ablaze in their vestments of autumn, seemed much smaller than he remembered. But, on second thought, everything was much larger then in a young man's eyes: the blossoming hope that the South would win the war in short order, logically assured because one Southerner could whip ten Yankees any day and twice on Sunday. And spurring you on, the ever-smiling, waving girls and the bands playing "The Bonnie Blue Flag" and "Dixie," and the hurrying fear that the war would be over before you could enlist with your friends. He regarded the rounded huddle of hills again. Indeed, they didn't look the same, didn't because Jesse Alden Wilder had changed. For better or worse, he could not say.

He rode on, still full of musing and recollections, in haste, a late haste.

In the distance a spurt of dust took his eye. A rider coming this way. After some moments, as the horseman approached, Jesse recognized Samuel Hill, an elderly neighbor. A small slave owner back then and a fire-eating secessionist, one who literally began to froth at the mouth when abolitionists and black Republicans were mentioned. Jesse could still hear his ringing voice: "The South can fight her own battles, and if she can't do it inside the Union, by God, she can damn well do it outside the Union!"

Nearer, the remembered features came gradually into focus: the broad face, fleshier than before, the biblike beard, snow-white now. A heavy man years ago, his girth now overlapped the pommel of his saddle.

Jesse's first impulse was to speak, but in the next instant his greeting froze. Except for a slight jerk, a startled jerk at that, Samuel Hill seemed to stare right through and beyond Jesse. Unforgiving eyes set straight ahead, he passed without a sign of recognition. Mr. Samuel Hill, who as a member of the school board had voted to hire young Jesse Wilder, an honor graduate of the Nashville Academy, for the schoolteacher's job on Lost Creek at thirty-five dollars a month. Mr. Hill, one of those hotheads who had helped bring on the war, and that done, could do nothing about ending it.

Jesse felt his bearded face go hot. His resentment flared. Damn him! *But I should have expected that!* he mused. Still, he was left with bitter hurt, for somehow he had hoped for at least a nod of recognition. There would be more of this. He'd better be prepared for it.

Troubled, he rode on some distance. A road angled down from the rocky ridge on his right, and he reined that way. When a narrow lane that looked seldom traveled joined the road, he turned in. A surge of anticipation warmed him as he heeled the gelding into a fast trot. He was almost home now. Concern started to replace his hopefulness when he passed the first empty mule sheds, and the empty main stall where his father had kept Ruben, the potent old jack, and the empty main corral. Nothing moved anywhere. He tried to reason why. His father, an established cotton-mule breeder of many years, with markets in Alabama and Mississippi, had become too ill to carry on and had sold all his stock—that was it. Jesse would find him at the house.

He continued on, more slowly now, his anticipation giving way to a nagging dread, burdened by the emptiness and the near stillness, the only sound the distant voice of a raucous crow on the wooded ridge.

Before him the two-story white house took shape, a stone chimney at each end, but no smoke rose there on this cool fall afternoon. His dread deepened.

He pulled rein abruptly. The house was boarded up. Curtains drawn at the windows. Shaken, he rode around the picket-fenced yard to the rear of the house. The brick kitchen, separate from the house, was also boarded. He dismounted and looked inside the nearby smokehouse. Empty. The lingering smell of hickory-smoked meat released a flood of memories. He gazed off at the shanties where the freed Negroes had lived. At any moment he half-expected to see Old William come ambling out from the first shanty. But Old William did not. The farm was deserted.

A forbidding realization moved through him now. He was too late. His father, alive, would never leave the farm. He crossed to the rocked well. The cedar bucket still hung there. He unknotted the rope and let the bucket down, and when it splashed and filled, he drew it up creaking on the pulley and drank. It was sweet and cold. Then he watered his horse, let the bucket dangle a short way inside the well on the rope, knotted the rope, mounted, and rode away, filled with sad knowing. He was far too late. The letter from the family attorney, waiting for him at Fort Leavenworth, was two months old by the time the 6th Regiment arrived from the Plains for mustering out. The letter was brief and to the point: "Come as soon as you can, Jesse. Your father is gravely ill and can't last much longer. It is my fervent hope this reaches you before it is too late. Your friend, B. L. Sawyer."

Entering the town square, Jesse could not deny a somber conclusion: *I'm a stranger in my own land. It will be that way forever.* After a brief indecision, he headed toward the hitching rack in front of the general store. A man unknown to Jesse glanced at him, stared curiously at the Spencer carbine sheathed in a long leather boot, butt slanting forward, under Jesse's leg. Jesse had forgotten what day of the week it was. It certainly wasn't Saturday—not enough bustle, only a few wagons. Nothing had changed here that he could see. Fortunately, the town was unmarked by war. There was the Planter's House, where meals were served in gracious style. And Clymer's Dry Goods, where his dear mother had obtained the latest Butterick fashions. Balmer's Groceries & Meats. Hanover's General Store. And Hall's Drugs & Sundries. A new sign caught his attention: I. P. Cole's Harness & Saddles. All this memoried sameness. Franklin wasn't many miles from here. Bloody Franklin, where General Hood had virtually gone insane that late November afternoon in the heat of battle, ordering charge after charge, too impatient to wait for his artillery to come up. "The Gettysburg of the West," it was now called. Only bloodier. Pickett's men had made only one charge, after a two-hour artillery bombardment of the Union lines.

Jesse shut out the thought. Although he had learned to do that as a necessary mechanism of self-defense, Franklin would always remain in the background of his mind: inescapable, burned into his consciousness. Even now, after all this time, it seemed terribly real: the shrieking shells, the ripping sounds of musketry, the shrill rebel yells, the cries of men hit, the death grapple of hand-to-hand fighting. Worst of all, the faces of the dead and dying strewn across the battlefield. In the smoke and confusion, a man could not avoid stepping on them. Sometimes bad dreams haunted him, particularly during thunderstorms. Dreams of frustration. He would be struggling to complete what he and others hadn't in the battle: to break through the Union line and send the Yankees fleeing across the Harpeth River. Sometimes they would almost make it, only to fall back. Always it turned out that way: They lost. And always, in the nightmare's end, something would tear at his head and ribs and he would be falling, overcome with a terrible pain that blinded him until he knew no more—all of it facts relived.

As a boy he remembered the old saying: Time cures all things. It must have been a very old person who had said that, speaking of something bad that had happened to someone else, because it wasn't true. Time *didn't* cure all things.

He dismounted, tied the gray, and looked about with some uncertainty, his attention drawn to an elderly woman leaving the store. When she turned to go along the boardwalk, he saw her eyes stray to him casually, move across him and beyond. Suddenly her gaze swept back to him and she stared intently, as if searching the depths of her memory. Jesse remembered her. Mrs. Oliver Land, a close friend of his mother's; his mother had passed away a year before the war. Effie was this woman's name, it came back to him. A sweet-faced little woman who was continually doing good deeds at the Cumberland Presbyterian Church and taking food to sick folks and sitting with them.

Jesse nodded and touched the brim of his hat to her. Her round, amply white-powdered face showed a flash of greeting, immediately replaced. She might have wiped it off, it vanished so fast. Stiffening her short, plump body, she marched by him without speaking.

This he had not expected from her. For a moment he was back in the innocent years. But he felt less resentment this second time today. In fact, he almost felt pity, because he understood perfectly: Southern pride. He would never be forgiven. He was an outcast, his more than three years in the Army of Tennessee for naught.

A mule-drawn wagon was pulled up nearby. A farmer and the aproned storekeeper and a barefoot Negro boy toting a sack of feed left the store and came to the wagon, the men talking animatedly.

The storekeeper's bearded face looked familiar, but Jesse couldn't place the man at once. A moment and recognition followed in a rush. Mr. Hanover, of course—Mr. Yancey Hanover—father of John Hanover, killed at Shiloh. John, a member of Jesse's infantry company, a classmate at the academy. His good friend, John.

Jesse waited. It was coming again. *But damned if I'll look away.*

The Negro boy dumped the sack of feed in the rear of the wagon and vanished into the store, the farmer climbed to the wagon seat, backed up the mules and drove off, clattering. Yancey Hanover watched his customer go; turning, he looked preoccupied. His gaze touched Jesse briefly and he went on, whereupon something seemed to pull at him and he snapped around with a start. He stared at Jesse for several seconds, behind his eyes a certain recognition, but no greeting. His face set like stone, he turned his back and took deliberate steps inside the store.

Jesse looked until he could see the storekeeper no more. His face stung; his breath quickened. This time he was close to losing control. He longed to speak out. But taking himself in hand, he swung down the walk to the corner of the square where Mr. Sawyer's office used to be. It was still there, discreetly stated in small gold letters on the dusty window. Mr. Sawyer, Jesse's father used to say, was always discreet and one of the many reasons why he was considered the best country lawyer in this section of Tennessee.

The middle-aged woman secretary, bustling and officious, showed no response when Jesse asked if Mr. Sawyer was in. But when he gave his name and said he'd come to inquire about his father, Mr. Thomas Wilder, she said, "Oh, yes," and instantly a studied appraisal rose to her curious eyes.

She knows, Jesse thought. *Everybody in town knows, everybody in the county knows.* He guessed ruefully that he was getting a little used to it by now.

"Mr. Sawyer is in. Please wait." Rising, she tapped on the office door behind her and, after a pause, entered and closed the door.

Jesse caught an undertone of voices, broken off as she opened the door and nodded him in, the curious eyes searching him again as if he were a strange object.

Sawyer, a gray and gaunt man behind a dark wooden desk, his almost cadaverous appearance offset by benign eyes, regarded Jesse for a moment before rising and offering his hand without hesitation.

"I'm glad you're home, Jesse, but I regret I've only sad news for you," he said, shaking his head. "Your father passed away soon after I wrote you. You must have received my letter or you wouldn't be here."

Jesse nodded. "I did get it. I was coming home anyway after being mustered out, but I thank you, sir, for writing."

Sawyer considered him at length, with a kind of reminiscent knowing. "I believe you resemble your mother's side of the family, the South Carolina Aldens. You have their fair features."

"I suppose so, sir." It mattered even less to him now who his antecedents were. The fair-haired Aldens, who fancied fast horses and fast women.

"Your father left a will, Jesse, but before we get into its provisions, I must tell you that it will be disappointing, with some hurt in it, and I regret that. Please take a chair." He went to a cabinet, drew out a fat envelope, sat down, took silver-rimmed spectacles from a case on the desk, opened the envelope and removed its contents. Setting the spectacles on his long nose, he began reading:

I, Thomas H. Wilder, of Marshall County, Tennessee, being of sound and disposing mind, memory, and understanding, do hereby make, publish, and declare this to be my last will and testament, and do hereby revoke and cancel all other former wills made by me at any time.

I direct that my just debts and funeral expenses be first paid from my estate. All estate, inheritance, transfers, legacy, succession, and other death taxes and duties of any nature, as well as other taxes or any type of description that may be assessed or imposed upon me personally, or upon my estate, shall be paid out of the residuary of my estate.

I hereby dispose of my estate in the following manner: I hereby give, devise, and bequeath unto my oldest son, Claiborne Lane Wilder, of Corinth, Mississippi, one half of my estate, real, personal, or mixed, to have and to hold the same in fee simple, absolutely and forever, without conditions or restrictions of any kind.

I hereby give, devise, and bequeath to my daughter, Mary Elizabeth Somerville, of Lexington, Kentucky, the other half of my estate.

Sawyer paused, his mien reluctant, and continued reading:

To my youngest son, Jesse Alden Wilder, now serving in the Union Army in the West, I give, devise, and bequeath one dollar.

Sawyer put down the sheet of paper and removed his spectacles. "I'm sorry, Jesse. I urged your father to divide his estate equally among you three children, but he was adamant."

"I understand, sir." *My father,* Jesse thought to himself, *who had freed his slaves three years before the war, yet hated the North, and blamed Northern bankers and tariffs for the financial woes of the South.* Jesse could see why he was left out, but still he was sorely hurt. Mainly because of loss of family, loss of the past, which had been good, and the further hurt of being misunderstood, left without voice in his own self-defense.

"Your brother also is executor of the estate," Sawyer went on in a matter-of-fact voice. "The farm is up for sale. There are several interested parties. One is Mr. Hanover at the store. At the moment land is cheap. The farm won't bring over half its true value."

That struck a spark of anger in Jesse. Was everything to go? "I should hope at least that the farm would stay in the family," he said.

"Claiborne was here some weeks ago and sold the last of your father's stock." An expression of regret crossed Sawyer's pale features. "At an unhappy time like this there is generally a tendency to dispose of property too soon. Grief affects judgment adversely. Heirs should allow time for reason to return. Also, as a matter of fairness, I suggested to Claiborne that he and Mary Elizabeth include you in one third of the estate. In fact, because of your long service in the Army of Tennessee, I stated my view very firmly. But . . . he refused. Claiborne thinks as your father did."

Fire-eating Claiborne, who never fired a shot in the war. Jesse was not surprised; by this time he felt no turn of events could surprise him. He reflected before he spoke, trying to keep his voice level and free of his mounting pain. "I remember Claiborne got a government job in Atlanta. A major's commission along with it. I'm glad he survived the war, same as I did."

Sawyer's voice hardened. "You could contest the will, you know."

Jesse's gaze jumped to Sawyer. "If I did, I couldn't win in a Southern court, the way things are."

"You could delay matters."

"I have no desire to. The holdings belonged to my father and he had the right to will them as he chose. I respect his wishes." Jesse rose to his feet. "Well, sir, I thank you for explaining everything—

and for interceding in my behalf. I appreciate that very much." He
held out his hand. Sawyer took it and Jesse turned to leave.

"Jesse, may I ask your plans?" Sawyer asked, offering a tired smile.
"I am a longtime friend of the family, as you know."

"Yes, indeed, sir. I well remember. Those were good times. My
first wish was to put the cold Northern plains behind me. I had
hoped to see my father before he died, but even if I had, I see now
that he would've turned his back on me." His footsteps led him to
the door, old memories darkening his thoughts, and he realized that
he hadn't fully answered the question.

Before he could, the attorney said, "There's a pressing thing,
Jesse. I should warn you what you will encounter here from people."
Sawyer's thick brows bunched in a frown, and he hesitated.

"Afraid I have already, sir. From Mr. Samuel Hill, when I rode
out to the farm, and from Mrs. Land and Mr. Hanover, on the
street just before I came here. I realize it was to be expected."

"The war is still keenly felt, Jesse. There is no forgiveness, no
understanding, even though the war is a year and more behind us. I
doubt there will be a coming together in my lifetime or yours. I
hope you understand that and why."

"I do up to a certain point. But why can't people who've never
known how terrible war is, who've never smelled the stink of a
prison camp, who've never seen starving men fight over a fat rat—
why can't they try to understand the choices a man has to make
sometimes whether to live or die? But that will never come to pass, I
feel, after what I've seen today. It's pride, Mr. Sawyer. Blind,
bloated Southern pride." He lifted one hand, a staying gesture of
apology. He bit his lip. He'd said too much to a kind and sympa-
thetic man. He opened the door.

The older man's voice, still healing of tone, drew him back.
"Where do you go from here, Jesse?"

Jesse turned his head, an arid smile playing along his mouth.
"They say in Texas folks don't ask what a man's name was back in
the States or why he left or where he's headed."

"You should stay in touch with somebody back here. You still
have a brother and sister."

Jesse had a sudden wrench of further loss. *Family. Family used to
mean everything to a Southerner. There was some understanding even
when a family was divided. Even when it was brother against brother*

on the eve of the war. "In view of what's happened, Mr. Sawyer, and
selling the farm, I can see no use of that, I'm sorry to say." He shook
his head.

"At least let *me* know where you are from time to time."

Jesse was touched. He looked down and up. "I will, sir. I just wish
Claiborne wouldn't sell the old homeplace. Leaves even less to come
back to." He nodded his thanks, shook hands, and left the office.

Downcast and left without purpose at the moment, he stopped on
the boardwalk to arrange his thoughts. His anger over the pending
farm sale bit again. At that, he made for the saloon at the end of the
block, located there, he remembered, out of the way, so its den of
debauchery would not be so noticeable. A location that also permit-
ted teetotalers of public witness to slip in unobserved for morning
phlegm-cutters. His father used to laugh when he told that.

The saloon was crowded at this hour. He needed quiet, a place
where he could think. He found an opening at the long bar and
ordered whiskey. Sipping, he caught the murmur of local talk, none
of which concerned or interested him. Already, he realized, his
thoughts were projecting him far away to the haven of the Southwest. Already he was virtually gone from here, and not without
sorrow, because this had been home, rich with love and friendship,
and like so many others, he had fought for defense of home and the
rights of his state. Starting with Shiloh, the war had taken a deadly
toll of boyhood friends who had volunteered together, till he knew
not one who was alive. He'd seen Jim Lacey and Todd Drake die in
the charges at Franklin. He was a survivor, maybe the only survivor
of his circle of friends. At times he experienced a sharp sense of guilt
when their dim faces passed before him.

The whiskey was excellent. He had another.

The coarse-voiced man on his left talked loudly to another of
business conditions. Things were down now, but they would get
better, he said.

"When?" the other asked dubiously.

"When Northern capital comes in."

"And why should it?"

"Because the South still has the raw materials."

"You're barkin' up the wrong tree, Ike. The North ain't never
helped the South. Never will. It aims to keep us underfoot. It was

economic conditions that brought on the war. It warn't all slavery. The South furnished the raw materials at prices the North dictated; in turn the North produced and sold the finished products at prices the South had to pay. I tell you I don't want no Northern capital in the South. I want the South to dig up its own."

"Jest how? The South's never had much capital. It's got less now. We're all broke or near broke."

There was a sarcastic laugh. "I don't see you goin' around barefoot, beggin' for handouts."

"I've had my hard times, jest like ever'body else."

Another laugh. "At them Yankee prices you charge us?"

As the man called Ike grumpily turned his head to order more whiskey, Jesse recognized him: Ike Cole, who'd been a horse and mule trader before the war, known for sharp dealings. He'd weathered the war right well, judging by the stylish plaid coat and the gold watch chain looping across the vest of his melon-size paunch, and the glittery ring on the hand holding the whiskey glass. Jesse looked away to avoid him.

From the rim of his vision he saw Cole glance at him, put down his whiskey glass, turn and stare at him with that horse trader's sizing-up look. "Say," he said, "ain't you the Wilder boy?"

Jesse was trapped. "I'm one of the Wilder boys. I'm Jesse."

"I knowed you right off, I did. I never forget a face, same as I don't a horse's conformation. I remember you as a boy." He appeared to catch himself, to hold back. His canny eyes bulged with a new and sudden insight. His toothless mouth in the scraggly bush of the tobacco-stained mustache fell ajar. He straightened and moved back from Jesse with high affront. "I was jest about to offer you a drink, but damned if I will a blue-bellied Yankee. No, siree!"

Jesse became conscious of a descending quiet around him. A glass tinkled. A foot shuffled. He overcame the jolt of his surprise, shifted and looked at Cole, who was trying to pass it off with an air of puffed-up patriotism.

Then something snapped within Jesse, a buildup, and the next he knew he had grabbed the horse trader by the front of his vest and slammed him so hard against the bar that it shook and glass rattled. And a voice he hardly recognized as his own was shouting into the startled, fearful face, "Shiloh!—Perryville!—Murfreesboro!—Hoover's Gap!—Chickamauga!—Missionary Ridge!—Atlanta!—Franklin! Were you there?" He shook Cole again and again. "You're not too old to carry a rifle. Goddamn you, answer me! Did you fight for the South? Speak up!"

Cole's lips moved, but he couldn't speak. Fear contorted the shifty face.

"Tell me!" Jesse demanded. "Were you there with General Cheatham's Tennessee boys?"

Another moment and he knew there would be no answer. In disgust, he released Cole like something unclean. The trader slumped against the bar. Jesse turned, aware that he had lost his poise, so carefully guarded all day. Somehow it was a good feeling, a needed release. He looked around and faced the crowd, his jaw set, waiting for more. No one moved. No one spoke. They just stared at him. They seemed shaken. Some averted their eyes.

He was making his way to the door when an even-toned voice of a stranger broke the uncomfortable stillness behind him. "Never mind, Jesse. Ike's not gonna answer you because he went an' got his front teeth pulled so he couldn't bite ca'tridges an' not have to serve —that's why."

There was one last thing.

The great white house stood on the rounded hill like an impregnable citadel, frowning over the plebian countryside, its many-windowed, two-story face like so many unblinking eyes that saw all, knew all, it had seemed to Jesse in those innocent years, when riding up the graveled lane to call on Miss Sally Jameson, and so it still seemed today. Nothing had changed here.

Old scenes crowded into his memory, particularly the good times the young people had enjoyed there, though somewhat always ill at ease around Sally's mother, who had come from a Virginia family of considerable means, it was said, and who was related to the Lees on her father's side, no less, it was said, and who stood guard like a mother hen over her pretty daughter, making certain that everyone behaved properly.

Jesse had more pleasant memories of Sally's father, the postmaster, whose warm friendliness was in contrast to his wife's stiff Old Dominion formality. Jesse had loved Sally Jameson, but was too shy to tell her, and then the war came along. Whether she had returned his tender feelings, he never knew for certain, although he thought she had. The main obstacle between them, he had sensed, was her mother, whose concept of marriage for her only daughter did not include the son of a Tennessee farmer and mule breeder.

So now, years later, and so much in the past, why had he come here today? *I have to know,* he told himself. And, like earlier today, his anticipation, while yearning, was not sanguine.

He tied the gray at the iron hitching rack in front of the house, gazing about as he did so, opened the gate in the white picket fence and followed the stone walk to the long porch. Hat in hand, he rapped three times on the door, seeing again the floral design in the stained glass.

After some long moments, hearing no sound within, he rapped again, more distinctly than before. Ill at ease, he looked about. Was that a flutter of movement at the curtained window on his right?

He rapped again, distinctly, but not pounding. His heartbeat quickened when he heard footsteps on the polished oak floors he so well remembered.

The door opened and a firm-jawed, formidable face, older and fleshier, a face that again placed him at a proper distance, met his gaze. Mrs. Jameson, of the Virginia connections.

"I'm Jesse Wilder, Mrs. Jameson. Remember—"

"I remember you, Mr. Wilder," she interrupted. No warmth in that grainy voice and he had expected none. Her hair was a mound of gray. Age had not mellowed her manner or laid a gentle smile on her strong features. Fortunately, he thought, Sally resembled her father.

"Is Miss Sally in, ma'am?"

"Miss Sally, I'm pleased to say, is happily married and living in New Orleans. Furthermore, I'm honored to say, married to a true patriot of the Confederacy who served his country without turning traitor. Good day, young sir!"

Stepping back, head arched high, she shut the door firmly and finally.

He stood there still longer, not actually surprised, his mind sweeping clear to Miss Sally, wondering what might have been between them had things been different. *Well, I wish her happiness. A mighty sweet girl.* He settled his dusty hat on his head and walked off the porch to his horse, hardly aware that he untied the reins and mounted.

Riding down the lane, he could not escape the feeling that he was leaving home for the last time, and a rush of memories drew him back to the beginning of his dishonor.

2

He woke to great pain and raging thirst. Blinding pain hammering his head and clutching his ribs. And the familiar foul odor of death. And a low chorus of moans; now and then a shriek of rending pain. And, nearby, a boy's plaintive voice calling over and over, "Mother . . . Mother."

With effort, Jesse turned his head a trifle to see. The move brought a new surge of pain. He set his teeth against it. On the cot on his right lay a pale-faced boy. "Mother . . ." the boy called again. His lips stirred again, but there was no word. Jesse heard him gasp.

Before many moments a dumpy, bearded little man in a nurse's stained white jacket came to the boy's bed, observed him in silence, then crossed himself; frowning, he drew a blanket over the ashen face. The nurse left and returned with another white-jacketed man, who muttered, "The fifth stiff this morning. You sure he's dead?"

"After all the poor divils I've seen croak? Get the stretcher."

"Get it yourself. I'm all wore out."

Casting the other a look of disgust, the first nurse went away and fetched a stretcher. Together they lifted the boy's slim body upon it and took it away.

Jesse shut his eyes against his pain. *That poor boy.*

After a time he opened his eyes for a view of his surroundings. He was in a long wooden building that housed row after row of wounded. In the distance a few doctors and nurses moved among the cots. Overall hung the foulness and the sickish stink of carbolic acid and in his ears the constant din of voices; a bedlam, it was, a madhouse of moans and ravings and cries and screams.

He lay back groaning, terrified, staring hopelessly at the low ceiling. *I'm going to die just like that poor boy calling for his mother.*

A long time later the first nurse stood over him, holding a glass of milky liquid. "Drink this, laddie. Might make ye feel better." He held the glass to Jesse's lips and, shortly, Jesse knew broken, blessed sleep.

When he woke up again, he felt a tightness about his body. Fumbling, touching, hurting, he discovered that his head and ribs were swathed with bandages. Also, a new patient lay groaning on his right. The left cot was empty. He guessed it was nighttime because the only light came from flickering oil lanterns hanging on posts, casting a ghastly yellow glow. He could still hear the moans, though lesser in volume now. On that perception, he went back to sleep.

Morning. There was no end to his pain, and his moans joined those of the others, as if in concert. He blinked when a goateed face bent over him, an older face lined with fatigue.

"Where am I?" Jesse asked.

"You're in a Union hospital in Nashville."

He supposed it scarcely mattered where he was, the way he felt. "Reckon I'm gonna die like the others?"

"Maybe not. A minié ball plowed a furrow along your scalp, and you took a shell fragment in your side. Broke some ribs. But as best I can tell, your lungs are not damaged. You're not coughing blood. Better rest now, son."

Sleep possessed him again.

The next he knew there was a tug on his arm, and he looked up into a rust-bearded face whose hound-dog eyes regarded him tiredly. Nurse Number One. "Ye'd best give this soup a try, laddie," he said, with a thick brogue, "if ye expect to gain any strength an' ever git out of this pesthole. Come on."

Slipping a stout arm around Jesse's shoulders, he eased him up to a sitting position, pausing only when Jesse jerked from the pain. The nurse left. Jesse could feed himself. Bean soup and hardtack. It tasted good. He finished it. Then, spent, he lay back.

When the nurse returned, he set a chamber pot beside the cot and, taking the soup bowl and spoon, said, "That wasn't so bad, now was it?" All the while the mournful eyes observed him intently from under shaggy dark eyebrows. The way, Jesse thought, he'd looked at the boy taken away.

"I don't like that look," Jesse told him. "Am I that close to the stretcher?"

The nurse was evidently too done in to laugh, but the eyes twinkled and the mouth pulled apart in a toothy grin. "Now ain't ye the one to look on the dark side, just when ol' Pat is notin' signs of improvement. Ye don't cough an' there's no fever in yer face an' tomorrow ye'll be beggin' for the speciality of the house."

"What's that?"

"Beans with hog fat, laddie. Beans an' more hardtack." He took a step away, then turned. "Ye don't know it, but ye was all the talk around here yesterday when they brought ye in."

"How's that?" Jesse asked, puzzled.

"When the army lads was loadin' up the wounded at Franklin, somebody mistook ye for a Yankee an' loaded ye on."

"I'm no goddamned Yankee."

"It might've saved yer life, if what I hear is true about the reb medical corps, that it's even worse than ours. In this pesthole every man's the same, laddie, dead or alive. Rank don't count."

That night the bad dreams started. His company was charging the Yankee trenches again. How many times had they charged on this mad afternoon? Time and again. He hadn't counted. He'd lost his pistol and picked up a muzzle-loader. Acrid powdersmoke filled his lungs. He let go a long yell—"Yee-haaa! Yee—haaa—haaa-haa!" and jabbed his bayonet at the frightened face before him. The man went down. Jesse leaped over the trench. The Yankees were skedaddling now, by God they were! Now it was hand-to-hand there in the yard of the farmhouse. Bayonets, rifle butts. Then something slammed into his head and side, and he was falling into utter darkness, falling . . .

Again the bed on Jesse's right lay empty.

In the afternoon a patient whose left arm had been amputated above the elbow was brought in. A man Jesse judged to be in his forties, he was in evident pain and kept his eyes closed most of the time and suffered in silence.

Soon after, an anxious young first lieutenant approached the bed and saluted smartly. "Major, sir, Colonel Dearbon sends his regards and asks if you wish him to notify your family now or to wait?"

"Tell him I prefer to wait. No need to worry anybody. Give my respects to Colonel Dearbon."

"Yes, sir. Is there anything I can do for you, sir?"

"I guess time is the only thing I need now, Lieutenant. Thank you." He lay back and closed his eyes, moaning softly.

On the third morning the nurse Pat stood at the foot of Jesse's cot, a possum grin on his melancholy face. "Well, Johnny Reb, the sawbones says it's time ye got up an' around instead of lollin' in the luxury of the establishment."

"I'm willing."

"Truth is, laddie, we need yer bed, but ol' Pat won't let 'em take it till yer on yer feet an' fit to stand on yer own."

Bent over, with Pat's help, Jesse started hobbling past the row of cots, surprised at his weakness and shortness of breath. A brief distance and Pat turned him around. "That's far enough today. We'll try it again tomorrow."

Back on his cot, breathing heavily, grimacing against the pain in his side, Jesse noticed the Union major looking at him with close interest. The man no longer moaned incessantly, just sighed now and then. Thick muttonchop whiskers lent a broadness to his craggy face. Jesse got the impression of a man accustomed to command and a man in charge of himself. The straight, stern line of the major's mouth eased as he spoke.

"I couldn't help overhear, young man. So you were at Franklin?"

"Yes, sir."

It was strange, conversing with an enemy officer, and Jesse felt he ought not say much. Yet the major had a kindly voice.

"What corps, may I ask?"

"General Cheatham's, sir."

"Cheatham's Tennesseeans. Ah . . ."

"Yes, sir."

"Your rank?"

"Captain."

"I'm Major R. B. Adams, Captain. I'd like to know your name."

Jesse felt at ease now. "Jesse Wilder, sir. My home is Petersburg, Tennessee."

"My compliments to you, Captain. You men fought like tigers. It was an unforgettable sight from our works to see you forming for the assault across two miles of open ground. Battle flags flying. I'd never seen such grandeur before and don't expect to see it again. We were well entrenched, some battalions with repeating rifles, and we knew before long there would be a terrible loss of life. I believe it was your corps that broke our center for a while."

"Yes, sir. It was hand-to-hand there in the garden behind the house."

"The Carter house. My brigade was posted in reserve behind the house."

An interval of silence followed while Jesse relived that frightful November afternoon, and sensed that the major was doing the same, the fight at the house settling down to a bloody stalemate. The Confederates holding the breastworks they'd won, unable to advance, the Yankees unable to dislodge them—it was there that Jesse had received his wounds. He remembered nothing after that.

A sudden insight dawned on him: He didn't know the outcome of the battle. "Major, sir, tell me what happened. I came to in the hospital here. The last I remember was the fighting at the house."

"I would say it was neither victory nor defeat for either side. General Schofield took his command across the Harpeth River and on into Nashville. General Hood followed. Your Army of Tennessee is now in the hills south of Nashville. Another battle is pending."

"I see," Jesse said, visualizing that.

"Hood is still eager to attack, almost in as big a hurry as he was at Franklin."

"That he was, sir. Something happened the night before at Spring Hill. There were rumors in the ranks. Something went wrong." Why was he telling a Yankee officer this? Yet why not? Nothing he had said would change the outcome at Franklin or affect the future. This was man talk. If he got well, he would finish out the war in a Yankee prison camp; that is, if he survived. On the other hand, if General Hood took Nashville he could rejoin the corps. If . . .

"I believe I can tell you what happened, Captain. A single brigade posted across the turnpike, north or south of Spring Hill . . . during the night or just before dawn . . . would have trapped us, and there would have been no bloody Franklin, though probably defeat for General Schofield, cut off from Nashville. As it was, he marched his command on into Franklin and entrenched. Some breastworks were already prepared. It was a critical error by General Hood's staff."

So that was what had happened. More poor staff work, which had plagued the Army of Tennessee as far back as Shiloh. A great sadness came over him, a great sense of futility and loss. It had all been for nothing. Now his exhaustion and pain took hold. He was sinking into sleep again when he heard the major's atoning voice. "I'm glad that you survived it, Captain. I pray that this will all end soon. It can't go on much longer. We're killing off a generation of fine young men on both sides."

That afternoon Pat brought Jesse clean underclothes, a clean cotton shirt, a pair of worn shoes, and a pair of blue socks with holes in the toes. "Best I could do, but they've been washed. Ye came in here barefoot an' that's foine for strollin' around inside, but before long ye'll have to stretch yer legs an' go outside for fresh air."

Jesse thanked him, adding, "I marched barefoot all the way from the Tennessee River to Franklin and made it all right."

"Sure ye did an' ye was used to it. Go outside barefoot now, as weak as ye are, an' pneumonia will get ye first thing."

"I'm sure obliged to you, Pat."

"No need to thank me, laddie. I just want to rest me back from takin' out stiffs."

In the days that followed, Jesse gained strength and joined the wounded walking between the long rows of cots. Sometimes, wrapped in a blanket against the biting December cold, he would go outside and stroll back and forth on the path beside the building past the watchful guards, his eyes ever south, scenting the wind like a hunting dog, images of friends and home crowding his mind. He wondered how many in his old company, now waiting in the hills under Hood's reckless command, had survived Franklin. His own fate, he knew, was sealed unless Hood captured Nashville. He'd considered slipping away and joining his comrades, but the hospital was tightly guarded day and night. There were other rebs here from other battles, he'd learned from Pat, but he was not allowed to converse with them. He could only wait, yet grateful for the good Yankee care he had received. He was going to get well.

It was the middle of December when Jesse heard the roar of cannon and the rattle of musketry south of the city. He felt a surge of hope. Was Hood attacking as usual? But a guard told him General Thomas was attacking the entrenched Confederates. He listened keenly to the sounds, trying to assess their meaning. Late that

afternoon the chortling guard reported the Army of Tennessee was
giving ground.

The firing tapered off as evening fell, to be renewed early next
morning with greater fury. Gradually the cannonading grew more
distant. The Confederates were now in retreat toward the Harpeth
River, said the jubilant guard, who had sought Jesse out to tell him
the "good news."

It's over. Glumly, slumped on his cot in the foul-smelling ward, he
viewed his future. He was just about well. Any day now an order
would come to send him off to prison. Horror stories of pestilence,
disease, death, starvation, and brutality gripped him. The only question was what prison camp. He'd asked his friend, Pat, but the
Irishman, with an evasive shake of his head, had told him to worry
first about getting well. In his lowest moods Jesse wished that he had
died at Franklin with his friends. His emotions alternated between
guilt at having survived and gratitude for his life.

"Good afternoon, Captain Wilder. I trust you're feeling much
better."

Jesse, dozing, sat up blinking. Suspicious at hearing a stranger call
his name, he said nothing, just nodded. It struck him that this
ramrod-straight man was the model of how an officer ought to look.
Polished silver eagles bright on each shoulder strap. A clean-looking
man of medium height who couldn't be more than thirty, say, his
brown beard neatly clipped, his blue uniform brushed spotless, his
well-shaped face and wide blue eyes inviting confidence. He smiled
with assurance.

"I'm Colonel Paul Scott," he said, his voice clipped. "On de-
tached duty from General Wilson's cavalry."

He stepped forward and extended his hand. Jesse took it warily.
Scott's handclasp, fittingly, was quick and strong. When Jesse
moved to rise, Scott raised both restraining hands. "Don't get up.
You need your rest, although I understand the doctors are about to
take you off the sick list. You are indeed fortunate to have survived
the slaughter at Franklin."

Jesse didn't answer, resenting the term "slaughter."

Scott went on matter-of-factly. "As a courtesy, I feel that I should
fill you in on what has happened, Captain. General Hood has been
driven across the Harpeth River. The Army of Tennessee is now

retreating toward Pulaski. Hood's apparent intention is to get across the Tennessee River. Failing in that, he is expected to surrender."

Stung by the assumption, Jesse snapped up from the cot and stood erect. "General Hood will never surrender, Colonel. He's a fighter to the end."

"He is that, I grant you, Captain. More than six thousand dead and wounded at Franklin." He let that sink in.

Jesse flinched inwardly. *So it's that bad.*

"However," the colonel said, "I didn't come here to discuss the fortunes of war, which have been dreadful for both sides, and extra so now for the South in Virginia, with the continuing stalemate around Richmond and Petersburg." He flashed an engaging smile. "Captain, I've come here to talk about what choices you have as a prisoner. Also, personally, what I can do for you, a fellow officer."

Jesse's suspicion returned. He forced a smile, knowing the answer to his request before he voiced it. "As a personal favor, Colonel, you can have me exchanged."

Scott's mouth formed a protesting *O*. "I should like to be able to accommodate you, Captain, but the North doesn't do that anymore. Hasn't since Vicksburg. Nor any paroles. Too many Johnny Rebs violated their paroles and took up arms again."

"But you just said our cause is hopeless. How could one man make a difference in a war that's lost?" Jesse was deliberately guying him now, and he saw that the Yankee knew it.

Scott made a mocking bow. "You bestow upon me authority I hardly possess. True, one man wouldn't make any difference unless he was a Lee or a Grant. But as I said you do have choices."

Jesse began to wonder, though still suspicious. "What are they?" When Scott glanced about for a place to sit, Jesse gestured him to a stool and seated himself back on the cot, more curious than anything else.

"Now I suggest that you think about these, Wilder, before you answer, because I realize the choices are hard. You have two: either going to a prison camp with high prospects of dying, or serving in the Union army on the western frontier and staying alive."

Jesse sighed. "I see little choice, Colonel."

"There is one very important choice—survival. Your life. Our prison camps, I regret to admit, are almost as bad as the South's Andersonville."

"In the Army of Tennessee we never heard much about Andersonville, only your camps. Douglas in Chicago, Camps Rock Island and Morton."

"They are all horrible places, I assure you. The death rate is high."

"So is it on the battlefield, Colonel."

"I don't want you to decide today. I want you to reflect on it. You would be a volunteer, recruited to guard surveying parties for the Union Pacific Railroad, escort supply trains, protect stagecoach routes, and you would be stationed at frontier posts. Very likely you would fight Indians. Doesn't that strike you better than dying in a Yankee prison camp of typhus, typhoid, or consumption?"

"What if we came up against a Confederate force? I've heard there are Confederates operating in Colorado."

"A good point, one I was coming to. Under no condition would you be expected to bear arms against your own people. That is set forth when a man volunteers and swears allegiance to the United States. In fact, we have volunteers on the frontier now, and they have yet to run into any Confederates in Colorado or elsewhere. That was true, perhaps, on a small scale early in the war, but so far as the army knows now, no such force exists in the West."

Unconvinced, Jesse cut him a suspicious look. "Why does the North, with all its resources and men, need Confederate volunteers on the frontier?"

Scott smiled readily. "There are several very good reasons. Thousands of our Union soldiers are nearing the end of their three-year enlistments. Draft calls are no more popular in the North than they are in the South. There have been draft riots. The North also has deserters. I'm sure you're acquainted with that problem in the Army of Tennessee."

Jesse would not give ground. "When a man goes barefoot and hungry and he's needed back home to put in the crops so his family won't go hungry, he'll take off sometimes. But I can tell you that Hood's army came back to Tennessee with high hopes."

The colonel nodded to that. "There's another reason, which may seem remote to you, why the Union needs troops in the West. As you may know, Napoleon the Third has set up Maximilian as Emperor of Mexico."

Jesse's response was a dry smile. "For some reason, we rebs haven't been kept informed about foreign affairs."

"Well, the French, also the British, see the North as weakened because of the war. True. There is also fear that European adventurers who've gathered around Maximilian have expansion dreams in the American West. We can't let that happen. So you see why more volunteers are needed, in addition to our undermanned troops."

"I do and I don't. But I can't see myself wearing Yankee blue. Goes against the grain. I'd feel like a traitor, like a Judas."

A stillness fell between them. There was understanding in Scott's eyes and voice when he said softly, "I know how you feel, Captain. We are both Americans, we are both soldiers. I honestly believe I would feel the same in your position."

"Neither could I swear allegiance to your government."

"I can understand that as well."

"Just thinking about it makes me feel sick at heart. Like I'd be turning against my own kind, my state, my country." Jesse looked squarely at him. "No, I can't do it, Colonel."

"I understand. But what you fail to see is that this is an honorable way out for you. You wouldn't bear arms against the South. And it means your life, Wilder. That is the one issue here—life or virtual death." The colonel stood and, smiling in that persuasive way he had, held out his hand. Jesse got up and took it. "You sleep on this," Scott said, "and I'll see you tomorrow." He turned to depart, then swung back. "I'll have some tobacco sent to you."

"I reckon not, Colonel."

"You sure? You're welcome to it. I mean that."

"Yes, sir, I am sure. But I thank you." He'd longed for tobacco for some days, now that he was feeling good again. His pipe had been lost when he was loaded in with the Yankee wounded and hauled to the hospital. Tobacco, he mused. A small thing. One of the few little enjoyments a man had. Confederates usually had plenty of tobacco and little coffee, whereas the Yankees had plenty of coffee and were short of tobacco. They'd swapped back and forth between the trenches around Atlanta. Tobacco, here, was one way the North had of getting to a reb when he was weak and vulnerable. Clever. Jesse Alden Wilder would do without.

Coming by on his rounds, Pat said, "I see Colonel Scott paid you a recruitin' call. What will you do?"

"I can't do it, Pat. Goes against the grain."

"Sure it does, laddie, but this whole terrible war's like that. Even so, it beats dyin' in a stinkin' prison camp."

"The colonel said the Confederates are called volunteers."

"That an' there's another name—galvanized Yankees. I'd ruther be called a volunteer. Whatever, ye'd get a chance to go home when this mess is over. Think about it."

The next day dawned bright and clear and somewhat warmer, a pleasant change from the miserable cold of the previous days as the Army of Tennessee retreated southward. Jesse strolled outside, feeling the sun, the kindly wind, his somber thoughts with the marching gray columns. Just remnants now of what had been a proud army, Cheatham's men singing as they passed through Pulaski, marching to their doom at Franklin.

He went inside to find Colonel Scott waiting for him. "Well, Captain, I hope you've slept well and decided to be a soldier again?"

"My answer is the same, sir. I can't do it."

Scott pursed his lips. "I'm sorry. Truly sorry. I can allow you more time, say several days, if you'd like to ponder this further?"

"I've made up my mind, Colonel. Can you tell me where I'll be sent?"

"That disposition is out of my hands, but I think it will be Camp Morton in Indianapolis. It may be less of a hellhole than Douglas or Rock Island. Then, again, it may be worse." He held out his hand. Jesse took it. "I'm sorry," Scott said again and paused, a significant pause. "Good luck."

Reflecting on his decision, Jesse found his conscience was clear. He had acted from the heart; there was no other way. But now, in its place, he was left with dread.

Not long afterward he saw Pat slowly approaching. There was a kind of reluctance about the little man, the expression of an older man disappointed with the young. "So ye didn't volunteer, eh, laddie?"

"I couldn't."

"Ye could tomorrow, ye know. There's time."

"I won't."

"There's the day after that."

"I never will."

"Don't say that."

"I can't bring myself to wear the blue."

"I know, I know. That's the rub. Where'll they be sendin' ye, did the colonel say?"

"Camp Morton, likely, at Indianapolis."

Pat made the sign of the cross, a resignation rising to his woebegone face. He sat on the stool and took Jesse's hand. "Let ol' Pat tell ye somethin', laddie. Ye're a proud one an' it's all right to have a measure of pride—keeps a man clean an' straight. But too much pride can also blind a man. Can cost him his life, an' we only get one chance here, ye know. So don't let pride stand in the way when yer life's at stake. Swallow it an' go ahead." He dug inside a pocket of his stained white jacket. "I've got a little somethin' for ye," he said, placing an object in the palm of Jesse's hand.

Jesse looked down. His mouth fell ajar. It was a coin of golden color. An eagle on it. A twenty-dollar goldpiece. He'd seldom seen that much money at one time, less seldom a goldpiece, and the Army of Tennessee hadn't been paid in months. "No, Pat," he said, protesting. "You shouldn't do this. You work like a mule here. You keep it. You'll need it sometime."

"Oh, I've got me work. There's a shortage of nurses."

Jesse was both puzzled and grateful. "You mean use it for food in prison?"

Pat leaned in, his voice low and earnest. "More than food, laddie. The color of gold can turn a man's soul sometimes, if he's greedy, an' there's plenty of that ilk about. There may come a time when ye need a special favor, a favor that means life or death in that divil's hellhole they call a prison camp. When it comes, use this. It could be the last chance ye'll have." He closed Jesse's hand over the coin, stood and swung rapidly away.

It was too much. "I thank you, Pat. But, no, you keep this."

Pat was striding away, already past the row of cots.

All at once Jesse's eyes clouded. He brushed at them. Thoughtfully, humbly, he examined the handsome coin, then thinking of what might lie ahead of him, he tore a piece from his shirttail, wrapped the coin in it, knotted the cloth and tied it in his hair, which fell fair and thick to his shoulders.

3

The day soon arrived when Jesse and other prisoners marched under tight guard to the Cumberland River, where they boarded a steamboat and were herded like cattle into the dark, cramped hold. As the vessel cast off and turned into the stream, Jesse closed his eyes, and it was as if he were drifting on an endless sea, leaving behind every vestige of life he felt dear.

When evening came, somebody murmured, "I believe this is Christmas Eve, boys," and another said, "That's my calculation, too." And from back in the hold a haunting tenor voice began singing "Silent Night," and some wept.

Guards issued hardtack, some buckets of water, and buckets for slop. The air in the hold soon turned stifling. Rats scurried. Jesse and others who had shoes tried to club them. Now Jesse sat with his back against a wall. It was time to endure. *This will pass.* He fingered the goldpiece in his hair like a talisman, his one link to the other world.

Yet time did not seem to pass; instead, it stood still in the packed, stinking hold. He clamped his mouth against the stench, breathing through compressed nostrils. Little by little the dimness grew less. Finally he knew a fitful sleep.

He came to in complete darkness, aware of a jerking as someone tried to take his blanket. He struck out. His right fist hit a face. The face cursed and Jesse took a blow to his tender right side that shot knives of pain through him. Rising, clutching the precious blanket with his left hand, he struck out blindly with his right. His fist found the face again. The hand yanking on his blanket let go abruptly. Jesse grabbed the blanket closer about him and waited for the thief to try again. Nothing happened. Jesse sat back down.

When the first dim fingers of daylight reached the dank hold, Jesse looked around and identified at once the face he sought, marked by a swollen right eye and a knot on the left cheekbone. A scrubby black beard covered the bony face, which had a querulous cast, and the mouth was small and mean. The one undamaged eye was now fixed accusingly on Jesse.

"You're a poor excuse for a Johnny Reb. Wouldn't share your blanket with a fellow soldier." His complaining voice had a whine.

Faces, sallow in the poor light, turned toward Jesse.

"Share, hell!" Jesse shot back. "I caught you tryin' to steal my blanket. I won't share anything with a damned sneak thief, and that's what you are. A low-down sneak thief who steals from a man when he's asleep."

"I won't be fergettin' that, soldier boy," the thief said between gapped, broken teeth, putting on an injured air. "You'll see."

Jesse had no doubt of that. He read that in the yellowish eye, which gave off remembering glints. "Just stay away from me. Hear?" Later in the day he heard a man call the thief Soggins.

In the days after, Jesse learned by word-of-mouth, they steamed on down the Cumberland to the Ohio, and days more, up it until on this morning he noted a new tone in the endless clanking of machinery, an easing, a lessening of power as the vessel slowed, turned, and they docked at last. Overhead he heard shouts and hurrying sounds. A guard unbarred the door to the hold and shouted, "Up on deck. Every man. Single file."

They filed out like so many stumbling drunks, weaving weakly, unsure of their footing, blinking. Some men fell and had to be helped up. On deck the glaring sun struck with blinding swiftness. Jesse shaded his eyes while breathing his first clean air in days, sweet and cool. He'd never seen so beautiful a day, so clear and bright and peaceful.

"Where are we?" a reb asked.

"What the hell do you care?"

"We got a right to know. This a secret?"

"You mangy rebs ain't got no rights. But I'll tell you. You're across the river from Louisville. From here you go to Camp Morton."

"Where's that?"

"Indianapolis."

"Where's that?"

"Ain't you rebs got no learnin'? It's in Indiana, where you are now."

Camp Morton, Jesse brooded. The prisoners had discussed it and other likely camps. Morton, so the rumors ran, was among the worst, maybe the worst. Jesse had found it wise not to let every wild rumor tear at him. Food was the immediate need. Just something to eat. All during the days in the fetid hold the only rations had been hardtack, water, and, infrequently, skimpy issues of dried, stringy beef, which the men had devoured like wolves, sometimes fighting over it, until the few officers aboard had established an imperfect order.

The guard barked a command and the prisoners, in a column of twos, marched over gangplanks to the shore and, flanked by more waiting guards, trudged along narrow streets to a depot. There a jeering, spitting crowd awaited them.

"Hang the Secesh! Hang 'em!"

Jesse ducked when the crowd started throwing rocks. Guards forced them back at bayonet point. "Hang the goddamned rebs! Hang Jeff Davis's horse thieves!"

Horse thieves? Jesse didn't get it until a reb said, "Hell, they must think we're some of General Morgan's men."

Jesse's thoughts fled back to John Hunt Morgan, whose raids into Kentucky, Indiana, and Ohio earlier in the war had made him either notorious or famous, depending on which side you were on. General Morgan and his fast-moving cavalry, also noted and hated for stealing blooded horses, an offense equal to murder in horse-loving country.

The prisoners, still not fed, were jammed into filthy cattle cars, Jesse with some forty men in one. He saw more reb prisoners assembling from elsewhere until a string of cars was loaded. He drew his blanket around him, cleared a place on the foul floor with his foot, and sat down, in his ears the grumbling of hungry, thirsty men. Guards brought two buckets of water and closed the side door of the car. No rations. Not even hardtack. Jesse's anger flared, then eased. Nothing could be done about it. *This will pass.* The thief Soggins moved about. A wheedling, whining man, he hadn't bothered Jesse since that night. The locomotive emitted a great burst of steam, and the car jerked, bumped its forward neighbor, and they were off, heading north.

Two days later, under a wolf-gray sky, Camp Morton stood out on the prairie before Jesse's dreading eyes as a miserable collection of weathered wooden buildings surrounded by a stockade and guard towers; up close, it loomed even more depressing. He could already smell the latrines. In the near distance a wooden sign arching over a gate read: CAMP MORTON CEMETERY. In there Jesse could see row after row of mounds without even a simple wooden headboard. Hundreds of mounds of raw dirt. A shiver went through him, compounded of shock, fear, and dull anger. *Not even headboards for those poor fellows. Their identities lost forever.*

Marching through the gate, he heard a shout that carried rapidly throughout the enclosure. A shout of "Fresh fish, fresh fish!" Men appeared as if by magic, drifting toward the entrance. The column of new prisoners halted on command and faced left.

Jesse's spirits hit bottom when he saw the gathering prisoners. This was what he and the other newcomers would become in due time. A scoffing, hissing mob of ragged, shoeless, long-haired, bearded wraiths, some mere walking skeletons. He had survived bloody Franklin for this.

A hooting voice sang out, "Show the gentlemen to their suites, James. Hurry now."

Now a louder, mocking voice. "Somebody take our guests' baggage. Be prompt. Be nice."

"Open the champagne, boys."

"Tell the dancing girls to get ready. Tune up the band. The gentlemen have arrived."

"That feller there in the front rank with the clean shirt. Show him up to room number twelve where the sheets are changed every day. Careful you don't put a louse on 'im."

"That good-lookin' bird on the end. How'd you like your tea, sonny? One lump or two?"

Broken up into companies, the prisoners marched to a row of low, barracks-type buildings and halted. The apparent commandant of the prison, a colonel, black jackboots glistening, trailed by a large black-and-white dog, strode from his office to address them.

"At ease. . . . You men will get along all right if you obey orders and observe the rules. There will be no preferential treatment for officers. None of your Southern class distinctions." He had an underthrust jaw, a bulldog face, thick, sloping shoulders, and his blunt voice seemed to punch out each word. He pointed to a line of lime wash drawn between the barracks and the stone office. "That is the deadline. Any man who crosses the line will be shot on sight. No man should approach within six feet of a sentry or try to engage the sentry in conversation. Do that, you'll be placed in solitary confinement. Rations will be issued every morning at the commissary." He pointed to a building that sat apart from the others. The bulldog visage appeared to change, to relax, to undergo an attempt at camaraderie. "Now, men, there is something you can do for yourselves, though at first I know you won't like the idea. You can volunteer to serve in the United States Army in the West. You would not be required to fight the South. Certainly not. As soldiers once again, for example, you would do garrison duty, guard wagon trains, and you might even fight a few Indians. You would draw regular army pay. I ask you to consider this opportunity only because it is honorable. Keep that in mind. That's all." He right-faced, boot heels clicking. "Sergeant Vose, assign the quarters." Followed by the dog, he strode back to headquarters.

A muscular man stepped quickly from a platoon of riflemen and began ordering the companies to quarters. His militant stride and decisive manner and tone were imitative of the colonel.

Trailing into A Barracks, Jesse found a drafty, one-story affair with iron bars on the windows. Two wood-burning stoves provided scant heat. Double-decker wooden bunks lined the walls. A mingling of strong smells rose: unwashed clothing, sweat, dust, woodsmoke, and tobacco smoke. Other prisoners occupied about half the barracks. Jesse held up, undecided where to go.

"Move, reb, move!"

Jerking, Jesse glanced behind him. It was Sergeant Vose. The ramrod image of the disciplinarian was there in the short muscular frame, in the square-faced head that sat like a rock on the powerful neck column, but the appraising gray eyes, Jesse saw, were openly venal. Vose's voice dropped a notch. "I see you've got the three bars of a captain on your jacket collar. Your name?"

"Jesse Wilder. Cheatham's corps of Tennesseeans."

"You sound like you're proud of that?"

"I am."

"Won't do you no good here, Captain, like Colonel Burnham just told you boys."

"I don't expect any privileges, but as prisoners of war we do deserve to be fed decently."

"You Secesh don't deserve nothin'. You rebelled against the U.S."

"We fought for our rights and deserve to be treated like human beings. All we've had since Nashville is hardtack and stringy beef. Damn little of that."

"You was lucky—damned lucky to get that. You won't fare much better here. We're short on supplies. There's a war on, y'know. But there might be a way to remedy that."

"How's that?" Jesse's voice betrayed instant distrust.

Vose cocked a speculative eye. "Got any contrabrand on you, Captain?"

"Contrabrand?"

"Y'know, watches, rings . . . silver, gold?"

"Nothing."

"That's what they all say at first. Now get over there to bunk number eighteen and stay out of trouble."

Jesse obeyed without comment. An extremely emaciated man, his eyes a dull blue, lay on the lower bunk. He held out a thin hand. His voice, however, was surprisingly strong. "My name's Willie Reed. You'd be welcome to this lower bunk, but I'm too weak to get up there."

"I can climb," Jesse said, gripping the hand and giving his name. Reed's condition shocked him. He was no more than skin and bones.

"Call me Willie. Where's your haversack?"

"Don't have one."

"You come in with even less than most boys."

"I reckon there wasn't much in it when I had one."

They both grinned. Jesse seated himself on a small nail keg.

"I heard Vose make his usual approach," Reed said. "He tries to shake down every new man that comes in. Promises better rations if you got what he calls contrabrand to trade. What little I had went long ago. Or sometimes he'll just up and take it." Reed coughed, a deep, racking cough, spat into a bucket by his bunk, and stopped for breath. "Man's got a nice gold or silver ring, say, Vose will trade back an extra smidgin of cornmeal and a little piece of moldy bacon. I'd be glad to stand in front of a firing squad for the one chance to shoot the son of a bitch, and maybe I will yet." He coughed again.

"You'd better rest," Jesse said.

"Glad to make a new friend. That's all that counts in this hell-hole. What's your outfit and how'd you get captured?"

Briefly Jesse told him.

"Guess you're lucky at that." Reed pulled himself up, a hollow-chested man, breathing raggedly, as two men came in and sat down dejectedly. "Want you to meet Lem Horner and Abel Kemp. Boys, this is Jesse Wilder from Tennessee. He was in the big doin's when Hood played hell at Franklin."

They shook hands. Horner was a small, wiry man whose quiet dark eyes and placid face showed patience and steady determination. Kemp was the opposite: A once-powerful body went along with restless brown eyes flicking out of a rugged, hawklike face. Both were emaciated, but not yet close to Reed's skeletal state.

"We's all with General Morgan when he surrendered after the Ohio raid in July of sixty-three," Reed explained. He was the oldest of the three, and Horner and Kemp seemed to look up to him. "Been here ever since. Most of the prisoners ended up in Columbus and Camp Douglas." He made a wry face. "Guess there wasn't room for us. No place could be as bad as this." A fit of coughing seized him before he could continue. "Our raid went bad when the Copperheads failed to help us like they promised. All they ever amounted to was talk and promises."

"Copperheads?" Jesse questioned. "Afraid I'm in the dark. What's a Copperhead?"

Reed returned a tired little smile. "Let Lem tell you. He's a student of the Copperhead movement."

"You mean what was supposed to be a movement," Horner said, with sarcasm. "A Copperhead is a Southern sympathizer in the North, but sympathize is about all they've done. They're also supposed to be for peace. Oh, they held secret meetings in abandoned barns and swore oaths and worked on secret grips. All that put-on. And when the South furnished arms, sent in from Canada, they cached the arms in haystacks and more barns. When Morgan took us into Ohio, they's supposed to rise up and help us take over. But they didn't turn a hair. It was all talk."

"For one thing, they lacked military leaders," Reed said.

"They could've done something. They didn't turn one hand. Didn't fire one shot."

"That's the way it's been from the start," Kemp added bitterly, moving his wide shoulders. "Things supposed to happen didn't. Believe me, it's been a rich man's war and a poor man's fight all the way. It's the planters that got us into this. The slaveholders."

Jesse nodded with them, thinking of Mr. Samuel Hill.

"Another thing," Horner said in a reminding voice. "Besides arms, we heard Richmond sent money to the Copperheads. What happened to it? It went somewhere. Into somebody's pocket."

"Would you-all enlist again?" Jesse asked them.

They all became thoughtful. "Why, I reckon I would," Reed said after a time. "If we could follow John Hunt Morgan again. We worshiped the man. We'd go to hell for 'im. A lot of us did."

Horner and Kemp jogged heads in agreement, and Kemp added, "Funny. All us poor peckerwoods, who didn't own ary a slave, fightin' a war over slaves." He shook his head in bewilderment.

"There's another reason why I enlisted," Horner recalled. "I got mighty tard helpin' my father work that hardscrabble farm in eastern Tennessee. It was dull and times hard as usual. That's all we knew, and when General Morgan issued the call, I took off like a scalded cat." He slanted Jesse a look. "How about you? Would you do it over again?"

Jesse had to weigh that. "Would, I reckon, even if I knew what I know now about war. How terrible it is, what it does to a man. Would, if all my friends volunteered again. Hell, we couldn't wait." A dim smile came to his lips at the memory of so much innocence. *Better that we didn't know what was ahead of us.* His next thought, fresh and nagging in his mind, he cast out warily among these veterans. "When we came in, the colonel gave us a big pitch about volunteering for the Union army in the West. Told us how nice it would be." He was waxing sarcastic. "Do garrison duty. Guard wagon trains. Fight a few Indians, maybe. Draw regular army pay. How do you-all look at that?"

Kemp didn't hesitate. His eyes flashed. "The fact that we're still prisoners is answer enough. Me wear Yankee blue? I'd die first."

Horner was slower to speak, and suspiciously. "It might be a Yankee trick."

"I don't think so," Jesse said. "They're hard up for men. Three-year enlistments ending. Yankees don't like the draft, same as we don't. The proposition was put to me in Nashville when I was ready to leave the hospital. I felt the same way you men do. I turned it down. Yet, if it meant a man's life and he didn't fight the South . . . ?"

Kemp flung him a hard look. "I said I'd die before I'd wear the bastard blue. You aim to volunteer?" he accused.

"Didn't say so, did I?"

"We've learned to wait," Reed said, his older man's voice oil on the waters.

"Have any men gone out of here as Union volunteers?" Jesse kept on.

"A few," Reed said. "Not many. Yet maybe more than we know. There's right smart of prisoners here. Some might volunteer on the quiet. Not when we're in formation. I figure part of the idea behind these starvation rations is to force us to volunteer."

Jesse said no more. The question wearied him, depressed him as an alternative. His hunger growled within him, and that ever-present need raised his query, "Will they feed us any supper this evening?"

Horner loosed a cackling laugh. "You are a hopeful cuss, Wilder. Tomorrow morning, after Vose counts noses, we'll march to what they call the commissary and they'll issue our smidgins. That's all we get. No supper. We do our own cookin', what little there is to cook."

When taps sounded, the sad notes sadder than he had ever remembered, Jesse lay on the upper bunk, listening to the shuffling and coughing and the rise and fall of hungry voices. A blast of cold wind tore through the warped siding of the barracks, chilling him through the thin blanket. A double purpose occupied his mind: food and escape. Poor Willie Reed was dying of consumption brought on by starvation, dying without complaint. A truly brave man. The knowing angered Jesse, saddened him. And his old guilt assailed him. Why had he survived? Why hadn't his friends? Was it preordained that he survive? Was it luck? If so, it was an ironic luck that had saved him, only to bring him here to this chamber of slow torture and sure death.

During the night, as the voice of the wind grew bolder, howling and slamming against the barracks, the nightmares returned to haunt him. This time with a new twist. The Army of Tennessee was retreating. Jesse and his friends, caught in a crossfire, were running for the safety of a stone fence, the Yankees close behind. Jesse ran faster, but he couldn't get away. The faster he ran, the faster the

Yankees ran. Hearing hoofbeats, he glanced over his shoulder. A giant of a man on a big gray horse with its teeth bared was bearing down on him. The bluecoat was swinging a saber that flashed in the sun. Jesse yelled as he saw the blade slashing down at him.

He woke up in a cold sweat, and he was yelling.

"You all right, Jesse?" It was Willie Reed calling from below.

"Just a bad dream. Sorry I woke you up."

"You didn't. I don't sleep much anymore."

At dawn they formed companies on the windswept jail yard in front of the barracks for roll call, men in worn gray jackets, many without shoes, humped against the biting cold, coughing, hacking, spitting. Reed hobbled out, assisted by his two Morgan comrades.

Sergeant Vose was there with a bevy of guards. Roll call finished, Vose reported to a captain. "All present and accounted for, sir." In the distance Jesse could hear other noncoms reporting. The captain reported to a major, who reported to Colonel Burnham, standing in the center of the parade ground, the fat black-and-white dog sniffing at something on the ground behind him.

Just then Jesse heard a drawling voice from the rear rank. "That dog's about the only thing around here that ain't been et. Hmmm."

Burnham raised his voice. "At ease, men. Are there any volunteers this morning for the Army in the West? Report here to me. Remember, you'll draw regular army pay." He waited, ranging his gaze back and forth.

No man stepped out, but Jesse caught a distinct hissing from the ranks.

Ignoring that response, Burnham called the prisoners to attention and they marched double file to the commissary building. Jesse, as a new prisoner, received a half pound of sacked cornmeal, a tin cup, a tin spoon, a tin plate, and a battered frying pan.

"Where's the coffee?" the man behind Jesse growled.

"Ain't none. Move on."

Grumbling, the shuffling line moved on. In the barracks the prisoners took turns cooking on the wood-burning stoves. Jesse mixed water with half the cornmeal and fried it in the pan. As crumbly as it was without bacon grease, it tasted delicious. Ravenous, he was halfway through when he noticed that Reed wasn't eating; in fact, had no food.

"Here, Willie," Jesse said, feeling guilt at sight of his emaciated new friend, "take this. You're welcome to it."

Reed shook his head. "Much obliged. The boys offered to fix mine, but I said no. You won't believe this, but I've lost my appetite. Maybe so I'll eat later."

"You need to eat to keep up your strength."

"I know." A fit of coughing seized him.

"Willie," Jesse said earnestly, "I'm gonna get you some decent food. I've got a twenty-dollar goldpiece hidden on me."

"Don't." Reed's waxen hand was firm on Jesse's. "Be a waste. I'm a goner. I know that. Save it for yourself. Besides, you'd have to trade with Vose. He'd take your money and all you'd get back would be smidgins. No, Jesse, I won't let you do that. Be a waste."

Jesse sat back, discouraged and angry. He picked at the remains of the cornmeal, still feeling guilty.

Prisoners were passing between the rows of bunks. Several, who seemed to be in a group, appeared downright fleshy. Soggins, the thief, trailed them like the tail of a kite, a wheedling grin on his seeking face. One of the group turned and waved him away. Soggins smiled all the more, fawning, bowing, scraping, obliging hands before his face.

Jesse turned in question to Reed, who said, "Look fat enough to butcher, don't they?"

"Recent fresh fish?"

"Been here as long as we have. We call 'em the Copperheads. Claim-to-be Southerners. Came out of the slums of New Orleans. They work for Vose. Snitch and prey on other prisoners. If a new man has something they want, he's got two choices: give it up or get the hell beat out of him." Reed had to stop. His breath leaked noisily. "Some Alabama boys had a tunnel goin' good. Before they could get it finished, the Copperheads snitched. The 'Bama boys are still in solitary. The Copperheads bunk at the other end of the barracks. You ought to see their provisions: coffee, dried fruit, flour, bacon, potatoes. Sometimes they even have ham."

"Does Colonel Burnham know this goes on?"

"Know it? Helps him control the prison. Why bother? He stays in that little stone office most of the time. Him an' his big fat dog. Oh, now and then he'll take a quick walk around the barracks area. Lives outside. Vose runs the prison for the colonel, kowtows to 'im."

"I saw other officers at roll call. Don't they have any authority?"

"They show up at formations and serve as officer of the day. That's about it. I've yet to see an officer inside this barracks. They let Vose do the dirty work, and he cottons to it. Next to the colonel, he's the most powerful man here. Remember that."

Jesse clamped his jaws. A scrambling broke his chain of thought. Looking up, he saw a rat scuttling past the bunks, after it a rail-thin individual with a wooden club. He swung the club, missed. Swung again and caught the rat a glancing blow—stunned it. Gleefully, he grabbed the rat by the tail and held it high, triumphant. Another prisoner, close behind, made a grab for the prize, but missed. The victor came around with the club. In doing so he lost hold of the rat, which scurried free. Then the two men fell to the floor, slugging, clawing, cursing. As if realizing the booty had escaped, they got up, and the man with the club snarled, "Goddamn your hide—you cost me my supper!" and flung away.

Some men laughed.

Willie Reed hadn't laughed. He just moved his head from side to side and looked down.

The Copperheads were coming back, walking slowly past the bunks, their manner appraising.

"Look out, Jesse," Reed warned. "They're comin' for you. Hope you've got that goldpiece hid good."

The Copperheads stopped three bunks away, said something inaudible to Jesse's ears, and a man stood up protesting. They grabbed him, pummeled him, and searched him. Apparently finding nothing of value, they dropped him and came on.

Now they stood at the foot of Jesse's bunk, blocking off any escape. Four of them.

"Believe you're all wintering well," Jesse said, rising.

"What does that mean, Fresh Fish?"

Jesse knew taunting them was dangerous, but his ire continued to build, overriding his caution. "Means you dine well and get fat while other men starve and die. Means you're on a different rationing system. Means you get special privileges at the expense of your comrades." Now, he'd said it!

"Ain't you the smart one." The speaker stepped forward, a burly man with a beer-keg belly and small eyes set narrowly in a face formed of thick layers of flesh, lips so thin they seemed lost in the pinkish folds. This surrounded by a reddish beard. He made a motion.

Suddenly they rushed Jesse, forcing him against the wall. He fought back, striking blindly. They pinned him there, beating him about the face and body until, weakened, his head hung and he could struggle no more. Quickly, practiced venal hands searched him all over, even to crotch and armpits. Growling disgust, they dumped him like an empty sack and strode on.

Someone was splashing water on his face. He blinked and looked up. It was Willie Reed, and he said, "You shouldn't have fought 'em, boy. You shouldn't have. I wanted to help, but I couldn't."

Jesse put an understanding arm around the bony shoulders. "Where are Lem and Abel?"

"Vose put 'em on wood detail."

Jesse felt of his face. "When they come in, we'll talk." He climbed drunkenly to the upper bunk and flopped down, groaning, but the part of him that remained lucid and unhurt said, *This can't go on. Tonight. They won't expect trouble tonight.* In his matted hair he searched for the goldpiece. It was still there. He felt better then. He touched his swollen face. Both eyes were nearly closed. But he could see, he reminded himself. He lay back, willing himself to rest. *Tonight,* his mind drummed, *tonight.*

He stirred to the murmur of voices. Willie was telling Horner and Kemp what had happened.

Jesse roused up in throbbing pain and climbed down with care.

"See they worked you over right smart," Horner said, peering at him.

"They did. Now let's talk."

"It's over. Why talk?"

"It's not over. It's time to put an end to this."

Horner drew back. "It's been tried before. We tried with some more boys."

"What happened?"

"They stood us off. We couldn't handle 'em."

"How many in the gang?"

"Seven here, most times. There's another gang in C Barracks. We had to fight them, too. If one gets wind they're threatened, the other bunch helps out."

"You mean they're free to move from barracks to barracks at night?"

Kemp spoke up. "No guards on patrol at night except at the gate and them in the towers. Taps sounds at nine o'clock, but nobody comes around to check. Most of us turn in anyway. The Copperheads stay up half the night playin' cards."

"Good." Jesse nodded. "That will give us some light. How did the other gang know to come in here?"

"Somebody snitched. I found out who it was. He was in such bad shape, the poor bastard, I couldn't take it out on him. Did it for a smidgin of bacon. He died a week later. I felt sorry for him."

"Is there any way we can block the door as a precaution?"

"Nope."

Jesse's mind was turning over fast, figuring, projecting. "You said seven Copperheads here. That means we'll need fourteen men."

"Fourteen?" Kemp questioned.

"They're well-fed and stronger than we are; therefore, I figure we need twice their strength. Can you and Lem fetch enough good men?"

"I think so. Trouble is, like before, somebody may let slip a word and the gang will get wind. There's a grapevine system here that's faster than the telegraph, believe me."

"Then don't say anything till a little while before taps. Have them drift over here. When taps blows, we'll ease down there and do our duty."

Reed's wasted face was screwed up in worried concentration. "You've all overlooked maybe the most important thing. Somethin' to fight with besides your fists. Remember, the gang's got clubs and knives."

"We can fix that," Horner said. "We'll bring in clubs with the firewood and issue the clubs here at our bunks."

The day seemed to plod by at half step. Jesse rested most of the time, while his friends played checkers and cards. The clubs were out of sight under the bunks at the wall end. The unbarred door worried him. As early darkness drew on, some men around them cooked the little that was left of morning's rations. Somebody had managed for some bacon. Traded some "contraband" maybe. The hungering smell made Jesse's mouth juices run. Lanterns cast cheerless tallow light, and the howling wind, which never seemed to cease, sent gusts knifing through the drafty building. Jesse shivered, but his purpose warmed him. *Tonight. Soon.*

About eight-thirty the north door opened and five men barged in. As they neared the bunks where the four friends sat, Kemp fixed Jesse a look of warning. "Some of the C Barracks Copperheads," he said after they had passed. "Now what in hell could bring 'em over here this time of night?"

"We can bide our time," Jesse assured him.

Time dragged. After a long while the five passed by, going out.

Jesse, rising, watched them leave the barracks. "There's no way they could be suspicious," he said, "but I want to make damn sure they go on to C Barracks." Rounding his bunk in the muddy lantern light, he almost bumped into Soggins crossing to the row of bunks on the other side of the barracks.

"Watch where yer goin', soldier boy," Soggins growled.

Jesse ignored him and strolled on to the door and opened it a bit. In the wintry light he could make out a small group of men heading for C Barracks, two buildings down. Satisfied, he idled back toward his bunk. Seeing Kemp watching him, he nodded and saw Kemp move away and speak to a man. Jesse paused at a stove, warming his hands, watching. Men began drifting toward the rendezvous. Jesse did likewise.

Soggins loomed before him, muttering, "What's goin' on?"

Jesse shrugged, but damning the man silently, and idled on to the bunks. There Horner was passing out clubs. Jesse hefted one, gripped it hard. The lonely notes of taps reached him, hanging in the cold air. Lanterns dimmed. Kemp said, "Let's go," and Jesse swung in beside him.

They set out quietly, guided by the sallow light at the end of the barracks where the Copperheads bunked. Jesse smelled food and coffee—good food and honest-to-God coffee—before he had gone far. His anger grew with each step, the unfairness of it all.

Suddenly he saw them, the seven, in the glow of a lantern. Some playing cards. Some lounging on bunks. A food-laden table between two bunks. Even had their own stove, even chairs. The burly leader was the first to sense danger, springing out of his lower bunk. "What th' hell!" The rest sprang up, shouting.

Jesse made for him, swinging the club. In his eagerness he missed and the man grabbed for a knife at his belt. Jesse struck him a savage blow across the pulpy face. Blood flew like mud. The man went down like a stuck hog. Jesse struck again, merciless, feeling the urge to finish this one. But when the man didn't get up, Jesse let him be, aware of the meaty crush of bodies around him. And yells and hacking grunts and the brittle crash of wood cracking skulls. Flung against a bunk, Jesse spun around in time to see Kemp wrest a knife away and drive the blade into the man's chest. At Jesse's feet a rotund Copperhead was choking a thin boy. Jesse kicked him off the boy and when the man flung around, Jesse split his skull like a melon. On Jesse's right two starved attackers backed a Copperhead against a bunk and methodically, with wild relish, beat him until he collapsed, his face a spongy mass of scarlet gore.

The tangle around Jesse was thinning out by now. Only two of the enemy were still on their feet fighting. The other gaunt attackers wheeled as one, Jesse with them, and charged, clubs swinging. It was all over in moments, no quarter given. All the Copperheads were down. The victors just stood there, spent, arms hanging, heaving, a kind of savage glow on their emaciated faces.

That was when Jesse heard the shouted warning. It came from the north end of the barracks, only seconds before he glimpsed men coming on the run. The C Barracks Copperheads. Not just five now, but more. With clubs and knives. In alarm he glanced at Kemp, and their eyes hung for a moment. Then, grimly, they turned to meet the attack.

Jesse clubbed the nearest onrushing foe, hearing a tattoo of thuds and grunts as the two forces collided. He took a swinging blow against his upper left arm that threw him reeling and down, flat on his back. He kicked with both feet as the man leaped to fall upon him. Jesse's shoes took him in the belly. The man gave an explosive grunt. Jesse rolled free and crashed his club at the cursing face. It changed bloodily and fell away.

Other individual fights were swirling around him. He struck out here and there, the well-fed foes easy to tell, taking about as many blows as he gave. Slowly, inevitably, the famished A Barracks men yielded ground. Some were down, too weak to rise. Others held up desperate clubs to ward off blows, others flailing out feebly.

It happened then. From somewhere, above the wild chorus of yelling and cursing, Jesse heard rallying shouts. Jerking that way, he spied Willie Reed in the walkway between the bunk rows. He was shouting and waving a cane like a sword. With him a gathering storm of angry men, clutching frying pans and chunks of firewood.

They charged, yelling, taking the C Barracks gang from the rear. That seemed to give the retreating A Barracks men heart, and they raised cries and closed again. The man facing Jesse whirled at the sound of the new threat. When he did, Jesse clubbed him to the floor.

Caught between two attacks, the C Barracks bunch broke. Jesse saw several get through. The rest, beaten down, crawled aside. Again it was over, Jesse saw, this time for certain.

"All right, men," Kemp called, holding up one hand. "Let's clean up this mess, then we're gonna eat high on the hog. What do you say?"

They cheered.

Three Copperheads lay dead, among them the A Barracks ringleader, another from A and one from C. These the victors dragged outside to the deadline and dumped there for Sergeant Vose to ponder next morning. The beaten C Barracks men were "paroled" to hobble and limp off to their quarters. The hated remaining A Barracks Copperheads were kicked to one side and told to stay there.

There followed a wild scramble for the Copperheads' supplies, much grabbing and pawing. Voices rose in dispute. Seeing this was about to lead to more fighting, Jesse called for order. Still the uproar went on. "Listen!" he shouted. "Listen! Let's set up a mess line so every man here will get an equal share. Who'll volunteer as cooks?"

The tumult died. Eager hands shot up.

"Now," Jesse said, "let's take stock of the commissary and see what we have. We'll divide what's left over."

More eager hands found two sides of bacon, a sack of potatoes, two sacks of flour, a sack of cornmeal, a small sack of dried fruit, a sack of coffee beans, and a coffee grinder. Yes, blessed coffee!

No man could help enough. They built roaring fires in the stoves, and hurried about duties, and before long Jesse smelled coffee boiling. The men lined up for that treat first. When biscuits and cornbread were ready, Jesse looked around for Willie Reed and didn't see him. But he knew where to find him. Taking a biscuit and a big piece of cornbread, some fried potatoes, and a strip of fat, mouthslavering bacon, he hurried to the bunk.

Willie lay there in his worn jacket like a small wraith, all hollow eyes in a field of grayish stubble, his sunken face creating the disjointed image of a man's head on a boy's wasted body. A touching, brave little man who did not complain.

"Here's your supper," Jesse said.

"Not hungry."

"You will be when you taste this." Jesse remembered his father saying that people dying of consumption often lost their appetite, which he feared had happened to poor Willie. Without another word, he raised Willie up, set the plate before him, found his tin cup and brought him coffee.

"This does taste pretty good," Willie said, smothering a cough.

"You're gonna eat that, then you're gonna eat some more."

But when Willie had finished most of the plate and coffee, he put both aside and steadfastly refused any more.

Jesse smiled down at him. "Guess you know you and the other boys saved the day. When the C Barracks gang jumped in, that was too much. They just about had us licked. I saw you lead the charge. I can still hear fryin' pans bangin' on heads."

Willie tried to shrug it off. "Just did what John Hunt Morgan learned us. When in doubt, charge."

Jesse had to smile again. "But how did the C bunch know? Just minutes before I'd looked out and seen 'em headed for their barracks. That's when I gave Abel the high sign. Remember?"

"I think I know what happened," Willie said. "I saw that Soggins feller go out when the fight started. Right after that, the C gang busted in."

It flashed through Jesse's mind then: seeing Soggins, surly as usual, when Jesse passed him going to the north door. On the way back, hearing Soggins ask, "What's goin' on?" Everything was clear now. He nodded. "It was Soggins, all right. We had trouble on the steamboat comin' up from Nashville. He hates me."

Willie's voice sounded weary. "Man that low ain't worth killin', if that's what you're thinkin', Jesse. Been enough killin' tonight."

Jesse had to agree, sickened of it.

4

At roll call next morning the bodies of the three Copperheads were gone. Curiously, Sergeant Vose said nothing. Jesse decided that he was playing a game. If someone inquired, Vose would arrest them. Yet three bodies meant three fewer mouths to feed. As snitches and bullies, the so-called Copperheads had served their purpose. There would be others to take their places.

Vose called again for volunteers. A tall, thin man, stooped and coughing, stepped out from Company B. Vose gestured and two guards took position on each side of the volunteer. At Vose's command they marched for the colonel's stone office. As they did, a hissing from the ranks followed them.

"Any reb who wears the bastard blue is a traitor to the South," muttered Kemp, beside Jesse.

While they sat around after breakfast, Jesse started to itch. Knowing the cause from previous experience, he stripped down and, searching, found graybacks—lice—in the seams of his trousers.

Horner laughed at him. "Are they drivin' in your pickets?"

"Worse than that," Jesse laughed with him, "they've got us on the run."

The others also were searching, smashing the flat-bodied vermin between thumbnails. "We have to do this about every other day," Kemp said. "Man needs to police himself."

"We had 'em in the Army of Tennessee, too. But seemed like we kept cleaner and healthier on the march than we did in camp. I know fewer men got sick. A little soap helps a lot."

"Which we happen to be plumb out of at this time."

"And have been plumb out of for some time," Horner mocked.

"And will be plumb out of for a long, long time," said Willie, mocking still more.

It was something, Jesse thought, that these men, prisoners since the summer of sixty-three, one of them dying, could still make light of prison conditions.

After the grayback hunt, they played a listless game of pinochle. Tiring of that, they sat around in moody silence, enduring, waiting. Waiting for the end, Jesse brooded, and the certainty was intolerable. He said, "I can't keep out of my head what Willie told me about the Alabama boys. How they had a tunnel goin' good when the Copperheads snitched. It keeps gnawin' on me. Now that we've taken care of the Copperheads, what's to keep us from diggin' one?"

"Takes right smart of work and sure as hell somebody would snitch to Vose, somebody in hopes of more smidgins," Kemp said, his voice discouraged.

"We could dig at night. Since I'm fresher than you boys, I'd be glad to do most of the heavy work."

"Dig with what?" Kemp asked.

Jesse hadn't come to that. "I see what you mean. A tin cup and spoon won't throw much dirt."

"I'm for it if Abel and Willie are," Horner said. "We'll have to scrounge a tool somewhere. Right now I don't know where."

"Remember that stove that got busted up the time we took on the Copperheads?" Willie said over a deep cough. "It's out behind the barracks. Maybe there's a piece or two we can use."

"I'll look this evening," Horner agreed.

Shortly before dark, after a supper on the last of the Copperhead booty, Horner slipped away. He was gone only a few minutes. He walked in with empty hands, and Jesse's hopes dived. Horner sat down on his bunk, leaned forward and, reaching inside his shirt, drew out a broken stove leg and a stove lid handle.

"This is the best I could do," he panted. "Had to break this leg off with a rock. Other busted leg was missing. The handle was under the stove."

"You did fine," Jesse said.

As a starting point, they chose the floor near the wall under a wooden crate they used as a table.

"Believe we forgot one little thing," Kemp said, folding his arms. "How to cut these boards across."

"Now don't expect me to go fetch a saw," Horner joked.

"Why, you boys have a saw right here," Willie put in. "Use the jagged end of that busted stove leg like a rasp. O' course, it'll take right smart of doin'."

"Willie's just chock-full of ideas," Kemp grumped. "Same as when he was sergeant."

The three able men worked without letup, taking turns while overruling Willie's offer to help. Taps was sounding when they quit and shoved the crate back over the site.

Jesse stretched out on his bunk, feeling a glow of purpose. At least they had taken the first step to get out of this house of the dead! He sniffed. Something smelled good. He leaned over the bunk. "Do you boys smell stew?"

"I do," Horner said. "Don't smell exactly like beef stew, though. Never been any beef in this barracks."

"Somebody's traded some contrabrand, I reckon," Kemp said. "But if it ain't beef, what in tarnation could it be?"

"It shore smells good," Horner said.

At morning roll call Jesse sensed that something was brewing by the rigid way Sergeant Vose stood at attention in the jail yard with his guards, his manner even more intimidating than usual, impatient for the companies to form.

After roll call Vose announced in an accusing voice, "Colonel Burnham's dog is missing. The colonel wants to know where the dog is or what happened to him."

No one moved.

Vose switched to an appeasing tone. "An extra day's rations will be issued to the man who comes forward with this information, now or later today, confidentially. Just pass the word to a guard. I'll tell you this: somebody had better say or the entire camp will be disciplined."

He swung away, and the companies formed to march to the commissary. A Company was moving off when Jesse heard a familiar voice from the rear rank drawl guardedly, "Well, I'll say this, Sarge. That shore was mighty good stew we-uns had last night."

To Jesse, the day seemed never to end, broken only by the endless card playing and checkers and the boredom of sitting in silence, of waiting, waiting. As soon as it was dark, the three started working on the rough wooden flooring with the broken stove leg, speaking in whispers.

It must have been around midnight when the last piece of raw lumber was cut, leaving an opening large enough for the passage of one man.

"Now for the easy part," Kemp grunted. "I figure fifty feet will take us just outside the stockade wall. If we run into much rock, we're whipped. I'll take the first shift."

"Hold on," Horner said. "What'll you bring the dirt up in?"

"A tin plate," Jesse suggested.

"And what do we put the dirt in to take it outside?" Horner asked.

"Ain't you boys never dug out of prison before?" Willie badgered them. "You put it in a haversack."

"After you take it outside in a haversack, where do you dump it?"

Willie was stumped, but only momentarily. "You scatter it in a latrine."

In the beginning the earth was loose and they made good progress, but when Jesse dug under the wooden wall, rocks barred the way. He came up to report. "It's not solid rock. But some rocks are as big as a man's head or bigger. I can't get by unless I break 'em up." He checked himself. "I know—I'll break rocks with rocks." With that, he crawled back into the tunnel.

When they quit for the night, covering the hole with the boards and shoving the crate over the boards, Jesse estimated they had dug a couple of feet beyond the wall of the barracks. "If we can average four feet a night, we can be out of here in two weeks," he whispered.

No one else spoke. In their weakened state, just one night had taken much out of them. Already their hands were blistered.

At roll call Vose let them stand at attention for fully five minutes before he spoke. "Since no man has come forward to say what happened to Colonel Burnham's dog, more discipline must be imposed. Starting this morning, rations will be cut in half for all companies until the guilty party or parties are made known to me."

A muttering swelled from the ranks. Kemp snarled, "What's half of a smidgin?"

Vose stationed himself where every prisoner entering the commissary had to pass him. He eyed each man, his gaze menacing. Jesse saw the venal eyes hook into him and follow him to the door.

Later that morning two guards entered A Barracks and halted at bunk eighteen. "Wilder," one said and motioned Jesse out. Jesse, wondering, glanced at his friends and ambled slowly out.

"Move, Secesh, move!"

Walking between them, he felt a rising surprise when he saw they were escorting him to the little stone office of Colonel Burnham. Inside, the colonel and Vose awaited him, both standing.

"At ease, Wilder," Burnham said, attempting another of his poorly portrayed pretensions of goodwill. "I notice that you did not salute. Why?"

"I'm a prisoner, not a Union soldier."

"There is such a thing as courtesy to another officer, Captain."

Jesse remained silent, still wondering what this was all about.

"This morning," Burnham continued, "dog bones were found buried out behind A Barracks. I want to know who's responsible. Do you know?"

"I do not."

"If you did know, would you say?"

"I would not. And your dog would be alive today, Colonel, if you fed us decently."

"We're short of supplies. Even so, I daresay we feed better than you rebs do at Andersonville."

"There is no excuse for that either. But this is not Andersonville, Colonel. This is Indiana. Fine farming country. A land of plenty."

"You still refuse to come forth with information about the dog?"

"It happens I don't know."

The bulldog features turned amused. "You only make it hard on yourself, Captain." Addressing him again by his rank, Jesse sensed, was just another playacting show of benevolence. "Tell me who did it and I promise you you will fare much better here. I might even find duties for you outside the stockade on a work detail. A bath and clean clothing and plenty to eat."

Food. . . . Bit by bit, Jesse crushed out his need, and when he knew that he had won, he answered, "I have nothing to say, Colonel."

Burnham spread his hands as if in amicable resignation. "It occurs to me, Captain, that you are in excellent physical condition compared to most of the prisoners, including the last batch, which was a sorrier lot than usual. As you know, a number of men have volunteered for the Army in the West—more than you might think,

Captain—but most have been below army physical standards. The army is in particular need of experienced officers—officers like yourself. Army of Tennessee, were you not?"

Jesse nodded.

"What campaigns?"

"Shiloh through Franklin, where I was wounded and captured."

Burnham's eyebrows shot up. He seemed to rise higher in his boots, a gleam of promise in his eyes. "Volunteer right now, Captain, and you can march out of here an honored soldier again. In two days you can be in Chicago. A good meal in your belly. In a clean uniform. You will sleep in a clean bed again. On leave, with a pretty woman. A bottle of good whiskey at hand. What do you say, Captain? Swallow your lofty Southern pride and volunteer for the U.S. Army in the West?"

Jesse could see it all before him just as the colonel described. All of it. Then he heard himself answering, his voice sounding strangely different from his own, "I can't do it, sir. I can't."

Shouting, Burnham made a casting-out motion with both hands. "Take this ungrateful reb out of here!"

Taking turns, they started digging as soon as taps sounded. Horner had traded a smidgin of dried fruit for two candles from an A Company man, and the mere presence of one sputtering, hoarded light was like a beacon of hope leading them on.

Jesse noticed that Willie wasn't his usual bantering self tonight. He lay flat on his back without complaint, breaking his silence only to cough. When Jesse mentioned this to Kemp, the Morgan man said, "Willie's fading fast. Runs high fever all the time. Just about quit eatin'. Afraid there's nothing we can do for him."

"There's no camp doctor?"

Kemp laughed scornfully. "All there is is a buryin' detail."

They went back to work. It was Jesse's turn to take a load of dirt in the haversack to a latrine. This part of their plan, they knew, also called for extreme caution. What would a man be doing carrying a haversack out of the barracks at night if a guard happened to stop him? There was no plausible reason.

One lantern burned at the north end of the barracks. The surviving Copperheads at the south end had kept quiet since the fight. No light shone there now. Shouldering the heavy haversack, he moved past the bunks of sleeping men. The hour was some time after midnight, Jesse figured, when he opened the door, stepping out into a blustering, biting wind. Head down, he set out for the latrine. As he did, he thought he heard a sound behind him. He glanced back, but saw no movement in the darkness. His long strides ate up the short distance to the latrine. He dumped the dirt evenly and hastened back, watchful. The only light was a lantern in the guard tower by the gate. The night air was crisp and clean. For an instant he allowed himself the indulgence of considering what lay beyond the tower: freedom.

He was striding past B Barracks when a figure stepped out from the deep shadows there. "What 'cha got in that haversack, soldier boy?"

Jesse knew the whining voice at once: Soggins.

His impulse was to ignore him and go on. Instead, fed up, he wheeled and rushed him, driving him against the barracks wall. "Let me be—or I'll kill you! Understand? I'll kill you!" Soggins seemed too surprised to reply. Jesse slammed him backward again and went on, taking with him a sound of alarm: They were being watched. Maybe had been all along. Maybe Soggins knew.

When Jesse reported what had happened, Kemp only shook his head. "What can we do, kill 'im? Others may know, too. Maybe he'll keep his mouth shut after you threatened him."

Worried, they returned to their dogged digging.

Soggins stayed clear of Jesse the following day and the next, and nothing happened. Meanwhile the feverish digging continued. Jesse decided his threat had worked. Soggins was a spineless bird.

Vose voiced his usual bid for volunteers at next roll call, but no man stepped out. Then, in a tone reeking of generosity, he announced, "As of today, full rations will be restored to all companies except A, which will draw full share only when the party or parties responsible for the disappearance of Colonel Burnham's dog are identified." He played his eyes back and forth over the line. "Colonel Burnham has generously instructed me to announce that any man who names the guilty will receive not only a week's extra rations, but will be issued new clothing and assigned duties outside the stockade." He let them consider that, then dismissed them.

"It's either snitch or volunteer to survive this god-awful hole,"

Kemp grumbled as they marched off for the commissary. "I reckon we'll all die here in due time."

"Like hell we will," Jesse said from the side of his mouth. "We're gettin' out of here before long. Don't you know?" If they could continue the progress made last night, they would be past the stockade wall in a few days. A wild excitement possessed him when he thought how close they were to freedom.

In anticipation of the night's work, they fixed their scant breakfast of cornbread, ate, and rested. Willie, who had barely managed to line up for roll call even with the help of his friends, took a few bites and lay back. Jesse studied him with gravity. His wasted face was flushed and so sunken, so down to cheekbones, his eyes like dark holes, his breathing so slow and labored. Now and then he wet his lips. He kept staring upward. Yet, when he caught Jesse's eyes on him, he grinned back and there was a flash of the bristly sergeant of Morgan's command.

Jesse sat down beside him and took the veined hand. "You've got to eat something. Come on."

"Can't. No taste to it."

"Try, anyway."

"He's as mule-headed now as he was when he ordered us around," Horner chimed in.

"Except we rode good horses—no mules," Willie chirruped back. "We always rode good horses, remember?"

"Need you remind me, Sergeant?" Kemp twitted him, assuming a pious expression. "It was uncanny how good horses just seemed to collect around us. Why, you'd look and there they'd be, like they begged us to ride 'em."

Willie's eyes had a looking back expression. "Sometimes . . . when the Yankees got to chasin' us . . . it was like a fox hunt . . . the way we soared over rail fences . . . in that beautiful bluegrass country. Remember, boys?" He coughed violently, held a piece of cloth to his mouth, and Jesse saw blood on it when Willie took it away. "Believe I'll have a little nap now," Willie said with a weary smile, and closed his eyes.

The three exchanged knowing looks. Sadly, eyes tight, Kemp shook his head. After that they sat down to wait for nightfall.

It was near noon, and Willie still slept, when Jesse heard a commotion at the north door. Glancing up, he saw Vose and a squad of guards virtually storm into the barracks. They rushed between the rows of bunks to eighteen and halted.

" 'Ten-shun!" Vose barked.

Startled, Jesse shot to his feet, Horner and Kemp with him. Jesse froze as Vose crossed to the crate, flung it aside, exposing the loose boards. He tore them apart and stared at the dark hole, nodding. He faced about. "Just as I thought—a tunnel. You're all going to solitary on bread and water." He turned to Willie, who hadn't moved. "Get up, Reed."

"He has nothing to do with this," Jesse said. "Besides, he's too weak."

"You're all in on this. You all go."

Willie still seemed asleep.

"Get him up," Vose ordered a guard, who went to the bunk and grabbed Willie's arm. Willie still didn't move. The guard stepped clear, eyes fixed on Willie. "Hell, Sarge, this man's dead."

The three friends crowded around Willie's bunk. Willie was indeed gone, Jesse saw, looking down at the still, emaciated face, at the open, lusterless blue eyes. Brave little Willie. He turned away, his emotions alternating between grief and rage at the cause of this.

Vose's voice jarred him out of his shock. "Move, you rebs."

Barely in time, Jesse remembered to grab his blanket from the upper bunk and to scoop up his utensils and fall in. Other prisoners stared as they went out, the guards behind them.

Soggins lounged on a bunk near the door. Seeing him smirk as they passed, Jesse felt a stab of blame. *I should have killed him that night. He knew then. I should've.*

The guards marched the prisoners to the far side of the stockade to a row of cells. Jesse was locked in a narrow, dirt-floor room with a bare bunk, a slop jar, and a barred window in the door. The cell smelled of dirt and old feces. From the banging sounds he gathered that Horner and Kemp were jailed on each side of him. He slumped on the dusty bunk, surrendering to a wave of frustration and accusing self-reproach. *I was weak. I should've killed him, but I didn't want to.*

He was still sitting there, beaten, when a key clicked in the door-lock and a guard brought in a pail of water. "You'll get your ration in the morning," he said. A jowly, rumpled, slothful man. Probably a home guard, Jesse judged, who preferred prison camp duty to serving in the army. He displayed a loose grin while he sized Jesse up and down. Eyes as corrupt as Vose's, with an added slyness. Jesse put that observation away for reference later. The guard wore a corporal's chevrons on his food-stained blouse.

"I'm Corporal Ellis," he said importantly, "in charge of all you rebs in solitary. I don't want no ruckus, y'understand."

Jesse gazed around in mock appreciation. "Why should I raise a ruckus? Got my own private room, and in the morning you'll serve me a nice breakfast in bed with tea and toast."

He knew he had taken the wrong tack the moment he said it. A humorless man, Ellis had an inflated opinion of himself and the importance of his jailer's duties. His grin faded abruptly. "I'll take no smart talk from you Secesh gents either. Nor any of your put-on, fancy Secesh manners." He went out and slammed and locked the door.

When it was quiet, Jesse went to the barred window and called softly, "Lem . . . Abel."

Both answered, "Yes," at once.

"It was Soggins that snitched," Jesse said. "I saw the look on his face when we left the barracks. I should've killed him."

"Don't blame yourself," Horner said. "Somebody else could have told as well."

Kemp said, "That's right, Jesse. Too late for that."

"I never told you boys, just Willie—didn't have time, I reckon. I've got a twenty-dollar goldpiece hid in my hair. I aim to use it to get us out of here. I believe this corporal can be bribed."

Horner's voice was discouraging. "I don't know, Jesse. Sounds mighty chancy to me."

"But if it's a chance, we'd better take it," Kemp said. "We'll all die here if we don't. Just like poor Willie, bless his soul."

Jesse let the matter rest.

Breakfast was a chunk of white bread the size of Jesse's fist, evidently torn from a loaf of bread. It was moldy.

Corporal Ellis lolled in the doorway, his foxy eyes busy while he observed Jesse's reaction. "Might eat better, Secesh, if you happen to have any contrabrand on you."

"Contrabrand," Jesse said, striking a musing pose. "I do believe Sergeant Vose mentioned that the day I came in. In more polite circles than this that would be called a shakedown or extortion."

"Hey, now, I don't like that kind of talk comin' from a Secesh."

Jesse, realizing that he was on the edge of bruising Ellis's touchy self-image, looked down at his hands and said, "If I had a ring, Corporal, believe me I'd be glad to swap it for food."

"After a few more days of this, Secesh, you might come across a nice piece of contraband you found you had forgot *all* about." Smiling greasily, he locked the door with pronounced emphasis.

Time was now Jesse's only companion, time, boredom, and the wolf of hunger. It seemed he could not remember a recent time when he wasn't hungry. Food and escape obsessed him. As the day passed in single file, he would get up and pace the cell; tiring, he would call to Horner and Kemp. There wasn't much to talk about. He would then go back to the bunk, ridden with misery and defeat.

"By the way," Ellis said next morning after the bread-and-water issue, a chortling tone to his voice, "guess you'd like to know what happened to a reb named Soggins over in A Barracks?"

"I hope whatever happened to him was fatal."

"Now that's no way to talk about a fellow Secesh. Wasn't he the one that told on you boys about the tunnel you's diggin' so you could escape back to Dixie?"

"He's the one."

"Well, just thought I'd pass on the good news that reb Soggins has been exchanged. He's on his way back to Dixie today. Fought the Yankees, he did. Got captured and now he'll go back home a hero. What do you think of that?"

Jesse said nothing.

"Say, Captain, I'm plumb sorry about moldy bread again. Might not be this way if there was any reason to make it a mite better. If there was, Corporal Ellis might be able to scare up some lean hog meat, some hot coffee, maybe even some flapjacks." He slammed the door and locked it, running the key back and forth, making it grate.

Jesse could only glare after him. *The son of a bitch. Well . . .*

Today was the time, Jesse decided when Ellis brought bread and water in the morning. Greed gleamed through the appraising eyes like grease. Behind them the subtle slyness that worried Jesse, yet a chance he would have to take.

"How much does the Union army pay you a month?" Jesse began.

"Damn little for all I do."

"How much? Tell me."

"Eight dollars."

"Not enough for a man with all your responsibilities, I'd say."

Ellis looked surprised and gratified. "Now that's somethin', comin' from a Secesh."

"How would you like a twenty-dollar goldpiece?"

Ellis's mouth fell. "That could get you some better vittles."

"I don't mean for vittles. I mean to get my friends and me out of here. Free."

Ellis's eyes got bigger. "Where would you keep a goldpiece?"

"Not where you could ever find it, if that's what's on your mind."

"I'd have to think about it, Secesh."

He did not return that day.

Come morning, Ellis brought the ration and left without speaking, but the look he gave Jesse contained the same studied avarice. Jesse said nothing in return. *He's thinking about it. I can see it in his eyes.*

Standing at the barred window, Jesse could see the stockade gate and by it the sentry box, occupied by only one guard. It was a wooden gate, across it a long wooden bar, which the sentry lifted when guards and officers passed in and out. Jesse watched throughout the day and noted the routine. About every four hours the sentry changed when his relief came through the gate. As darkness fell, the sentry left the box and no one relieved him. Guard towers stood at each side of the gate, and with nightfall Jesse saw lantern light in the towers.

So, he knew, the only guards at the gate during the night would be in the towers. None at the sentry box. That simplified matters greatly—if Ellis bit. Once Jesse and his friends were outside, the only danger would come from the towers. But wait! The gate would be locked, of course. His thoughts kept circling back to Ellis and his slyness. Wearied, he lay down to rest.

Ellis was later than usual next morning. He slopped down the pail of water, handed Jesse the hunk of old bread, closed the door behind him, and said, "I think I got it worked out, Secesh. But you'll have to give me the goldpiece first."

"Then have you back out on me? Oh, no, Corporal."

"You know I can't come back inside the stockade late at night and let you out."

"I thought you said you had it worked out."

"I have, maybe."

"Tell me."

"First, I'm takin' a big chance. You know that."

"And my friends and I could get shot if the break goes wrong."

Ellis spoke in a lower tone. "I'll make a late inspection about dark. I go off duty about then. On my rounds I'll leave your door unlocked and your friends'."

Jesse nodded. "All right." And almost against his better judgment, he said, "When you do that, I'll give you the goldpiece." What then? His misgivings rose. "What about the gate? It'll be locked."

"With lock and chain. A friend of mine, the last one on sentry duty at the box, will see that it's not. He owes me a big favor. I saved him from court-martial. All you'll have to do is lift the bar."

Everything sounded well-nigh too easy to Jesse. "What about you? How will you explain how we got out of solitary?"

"Easy. When I came by on inspection, you said you was sick. When I bent over you, you grabbed me, choked me till I passed out. You took my key and let your friends out."

"That still leaves the unlocked gate. How will your friend explain that?"

"Easy enough. It'll be dark. You and your friends tie him up, take his key, unlock, and skedaddle. He'll wait till you get there, since he's the last man on duty at the box."

"Don't tell me a rope is kept at the sentry box?" The plan was becoming more suspect the longer they talked.

Ellis showed the loose grin. "There will be tonight. Too, you rebs could have come up with a rope." He moved to the door and looked back. "It's up to you and your friends, Secesh. And remember I'll be takin' a big chance, too, just to help you out."

Jesse still had a question. "What this all boils down to is why do it for a reb?"

"I need the money." Ellis shrugged, leering. "I like women and women are expensive. And what if a few rebs escape?"

"Have any ever made it out of here?"

He held Jesse in his gaze for a tick of time before he replied, and

again that fugitive slyness appeared, fading even as Jesse saw it behind the corrupt eyes. "Been one or two, but never this many. But
there's always a first time for everything, Secesh." He left and closed
the door. Now, was it Jesse's nervousness or was Ellis deliberately
rattling the key longer than usual as a reminder of his imprisonment,
of his utter dependence on the guard?

Pacing the cell, he reviewed what Ellis had told him, taking it
step by step. Again, it seemed too easy. It was like a dark melodrama
being acted out on a stage, with Jesse waiting in the wings to play
his role. Again, why would Yankee guards do this? Money, Ellis had
said. Offhand, twenty dollars gold wasn't riches, yet it had seemed a
great deal to Jesse, and was, unpaid for months, when Pat had given
it to him. But it was the gold, Jesse reasoned, that Ellis really
wanted. The gold more than the dollars' worth. As Pat had said, the
color of gold could make a man greedy. *So now everything comes
down to one shiny goldpiece. On it hangs our only chance. We will
take it.*

With that firmly in mind, he went to the barred window and
called to Kemp and Horner. Afterward he ate what he could of the
moldy bread, drank some water, and lay down on the bunk. Sleep
wouldn't come. He was too tense, filled with second thoughts,
pulled this way and that as his feeling of distrust lingered. Time
seemed suspended. The morning slipped into afternoon. It was getting dark. Now minutes seemed endless. He forced himself to lie
still, to wait.

The rattle of a key in the lock cut short his thoughts. Still, he
waited, not moving until he heard the other cells being unlocked.
When that was done, he untied the piece of cloth in his long hair,
loosened the knot, and removed the goldpiece. Now he caught the
slow cadence of footsteps coming back to his cell. Now he waited at
the door, his breath coming faster.

The door opened and Corporal Ellis stood there, his eyes strip-
ping away his eagerness. He stepped in and held out his right hand.
Jesse placed the goldpiece in his palm.

Ellis fixed his eyes on the coin. "It's just like you said, Secesh."
Clutching the goldpiece, he slid it down deep in his pants pocket.
Saying, "I'd better make this look good," he opened his blouse and
ripped open his shirt. "Now you rebs get goin'. I'll have to give the

alarm in half an hour or so, when I come to," he added, giving a conspirator's wink.

The instant Jesse opened the door and stepped out into the early darkness and smelled the clean air, all his doubts vanished. Horner and Kemp joined him. For a pause they stared into the night, drawn together, then they sprinted into the jail yard for the sentry box by the gate, Horner and Kemp side by side. A luminous moon bathed the prison. Faces to the wind like wild horses, they ran past barracks after barracks, dimly lit in the still night.

Feet pounding, hacking hard for wind, they were within a few rods of the gate when the first shots cracked and Jesse saw the winking gun flashes. Shots from the sentry box and the guard towers. Minié balls snarled around him. Old battle instincts took over, and he dived for the gritty dirt and rolled to his right, at the same time hearing his friends cry out, hit, as they went down. He hugged the ground.

Suddenly the firing let up. Still sprawled, he whipped about, thinking of Horner and Kemp. They were writhing and jerking. Even as he watched, their movements became slower, and then they didn't move at all. And over him swept the awful realization that he had only led them into a trap. He wanted to go to them. But before he could, guards came rushing up and he knew it was over.

He staggered up. Rough hands seized him and hurried him back across the yard and to the cell and flung him in. Ellis wasn't there. Of course, he wasn't. *He was playing me all along.* When the door clanged shut, Jesse slumped down on the bunk. Head bowed, he put both hands to his face and wept, overwhelmed by grief and self-reproach. Again, he was the survivor. Why, why? And again the old guilt assailed him. He wished he had died out there with Lem and Abel. It seared his heart to think of them. He kept seeing their sweaty faces as they took turns digging the tunnel. For a time his mind bent under the strain. But gradually it seemed to right itself, and he fought the detested self-pity, because it was a weakness and he was weak enough. A long time later, the blessed anesthesia of sleep claimed him.

A different guard brought him bread and water in the morning. Sergeant Vose came next. "Wilder, you ought to know by now there's only two ways out of here: volunteer or go out feet first."

"You goddamned murderers!" Jesse raged.

"Depends on how you look at it. Your friends were shot while trying to escape. The same would happen to Yankees in a reb prison."

Vose left him.

That night his demons returned in all their fury. Took him back to the smoking, shrieking horror of Franklin. This time the faces haunted him. Wherever he fought, he saw the faces. When he clubbed muskets in the yard, he saw them. And then, like always, just when the Yankees were about to break and run, the crashing pain and utter darkness rolled over him.

He woke up in the usual cold sweat, but his head was clear and he was no longer terrified. His distress was relieved, in its place a kind of hard reality and peace of mind, an acceptance, a view of himself, Jesse Alden Wilder.

That day his soul-searching commenced.

He did not curse the guard, although he wanted to. He did not complain about the ration issue, if the decaying bread and brackish water could be called such. He accepted what there was, what little there was. He took stock of himself and what he believed, letting his mind course over the field of his convictions: his love of family and friends and native state, his pride as one of General Cheatham's boys. . . . He also loved his country, by God, as much as any damned Yankee did, more than any damned foreigner wearing the blue, the bastard blue, and there must be thousands of them, he thought. . . . Looking back, he saw that he had gone to war because his friends had, and they because he and others had. Because his state had. Because the South was being invaded. He had fought for states' rights, for his state's independence. Like his lighthearted friends, he had volunteered under the delusion of swift victory. . . . He had no liking for the institution of slavery. Slavery was one of the main causes of the war. Yet the North claimed it was only trying to save the Union. He'd wanted no black manservant with him to clean his boots and forage for rations and cook them for him. Some Southerners had a guilty conscience about slavery. He could understand why. It was wrong, dead wrong. . . . Yet why couldn't the North let the South go in peace? He guessed he knew why now. With the unbending abolitionists and the Southern fire-eaters there could be no peace. The war had to be fought. It was an emotional issue.

Before the war his father had spoken of "the materialistic, godless North," as if only the South worshiped God. He had not believed it then, and he did not believe it now. He had argued with his father about that. Too much Southern pride, which was another cause leading to the war. He could see that now.

So much for his beliefs. Harsh reality told him that he was going to die if he stayed a prisoner. He would die like poor, brave Willie, as Lem and Abel would have in time, both already extremely gaunt. He could still hear Abel Kemp's words: "If it's a chance, we'd better take it. We'll all die here if we don't." Some solace now, but not enough. Any prisoner, North or South, deserved decent treatment. His experience here had only deepened his feelings against the North, had only strengthened his determination to survive. He had that right as a human being. *But I will not serve against the South. I will not.*

So his searching went, back and forth. Time and suffering, he had discovered, had brought him maturity and clarity, and much bitterness.

On the third day he stepped to the barred window and called, "Guard, guard!"

After a wait a guard appeared. "What is it, reb?"

"Take me to Colonel Burnham."

"The Colonel? What fer? Won't do you no good to complain."

"Yes, the Colonel. Tell him I have decided to volunteer."

The astonished guard disappeared on the run.

In a very short time Sergeant Vose and two guards came to the cell and Vose unlocked the door. "Come out, Wilder. I see you've finally got some sense in that proud Southern head of yours."

"Not pride, Sergeant. Just the will to survive."

They escorted him to the stone office. Colonel Burnham eyed him at length before he spoke. "Captain, you understand that as a volunteer in the Army of the West you are required to take an oath of allegiance to the United States?"

"I reckon I do, sir. With the absolute understanding that I will not bear arms against the South. Nor will I be asked to."

"That is correct. Now raise your right hand and repeat after me."

Jesse had thought taking the oath would be like reciting by rote. But as he raised his hand he discovered that he hated himself, and his vision suddenly blurred, and the hard-marching years and the dim faces, forever young, forever gone, seemed to pass before him accusingly. Then, erect, eyes straight ahead, lips trembling, he repeated the self-diminishing words slowly and distinctly.

5

Beyond the window of the stagecoach, rocking on fore and aft leather thoroughbraces, the scorched land swept by endlessly, ever changing. Mesquite-dotted flats. Rolling hills studded with live oaks. A helmet-shaped lone butte. A copper-hued mesa. The sun a bloodied eye, glowering down, casting a veil of shimmering midday heat. In the distance roamed a band of pronghorn antelopes, bobbing rump patches a glittering white, as free as the wind, as illusory as a mirage in the glassy heat.

This vast Texas was truly merciless, Jesse thought, but it also suggested solitude and freedom. He felt completely at ease, content just to watch, filled with vague expectations, a relief from the cumulative tear and weariness of war.

His fellow travelers, like himself, had little to say, the rushing rumble of the coach and the hot wind and gritty dust discouraging any but shouted conversation. There was the booted cattleman next to him: erect, heavy, confident, a great hat shading his weathered features, set off by the curving white wings of a proud handlebar mustache. Across from him the derby-hatted drummer: paunchy and bored. Now and then he would draw a silver watch chained to his vest and glance at it, as if that might speed the passage of time. Boarding at Jacksboro with a clutter of sample cases, he had remarked that he would change to the San Antonio stage "down the line," and when that drew bare nods and no comment, he lapsed into jaded apathy thereafter, indifferent to the changing wild scenery.

Farther on, at Fort Belknap, a mild-looking little man carrying a carpetbag boarded at the last moment.

"Friend," said the drummer, eager for talk, "you almost missed it."

The newcomer shrugged without response and settled down in his seat. There was nothing striking about him. Just an unobtrusive man in a brown suit and vest and a pulled-down felt hat. He glanced at the cattleman, then at Jesse, noting the sheathed Spencer carbine against Jesse's leg. His bearded face was sunken, his eyes shadowed and puffy from lack of sleep. Yet there was a glint of constant guardedness about him, a harried look in the tired eyes, and he kept plucking at the buttons on his vest.

"Goin' far?" The drummer tried again.

"Anyplace is far out here, I'd say." The little man answered and said no more, looking out the window.

At the next station the driver called out, "Ten minutes—no more," and everybody got out to stretch while hostlers changed the mule teams. The brown-suited man stepped to the rear of the coach, where he watched the back trail for long moments before turning to take his seat in the stage.

Six fresh mules harnessed, the driver and guard climbed above, the driver yowled, and the teams, traces jingling, lurched away to the southwest. After a few miles the cattleman pointed and Jesse saw bunches of buffalo drifting into the wind, the first big shaggies he'd seen since leaving the northern Plains.

The dusty miles fell behind, and as far as Jesse could see, his eyes found buffalo, like dark chips floating on the undulating swells of the sea of short-grassed prairie. The stage slowed for a low, rocky rise, bouncing, swaying, and then, the driver yowling, the tough mules struck out across a long level stretch.

They were rushing along like that when Jesse heard the driver raise a warning shout and lay on more leather, the stage jerking as the teams ran faster. Instantly the guard's rifle cracked.

Looking out, Jesse saw a streak of dust boiling through mesquite, within the roiling dust coppery shapes on ponies coming fast. The cattleman, also seeing, drew a heavy revolver. Jesse pulled out the carbine. The drummer's face whitened. He held up empty hands. With a look of apology, the little man showed a squat-barreled derringer.

The dust streak was drawing closer now, the Indians racing at an angle to cut off the stage. Quite suddenly they were much nearer, a wedge of wild colors. Half-naked shapes on swift war-horses, on paints, bays, duns, blacks, claybanks. Bullets made frying sounds around the coach, and Jesse caught the distant popping of gunfire.

The cowman fired first, but the range was too far for a revolver and nothing changed. Jesse eared back the hammer of the carbine and sighted on the lead rider and fired. He fell sprawling. At that the others swung to the off side of their mounts, but still they came on, their hideous screeching carried on the wind, close enough for Jesse to see zigzag lightning stripes and hands and circles painted white on the war-horses.

With the range shortened now, the cattleman was calmly pressing off shots. Bitter powder smoke hung inside the coach. Overhead, the guard was firing. Deliberately Jesse picked his targets. A paint broke down, spilling its rider. A wounded Indian threw up his arms and fell, bouncing and flopping on the dusty grass. At once two others cut out of the charge. Spacing their horses like a trained team, racing head to head at full speed, they leaned down and swept him up, each grasping an arm. Jesse, intrigued, discovered that he had forgotten to fire. It was a brave and spectacular rescue.

As suddenly as the attack had developed, it slowed. The Indians drew off and circled out of range, still howling like wolves, and began another drumming run past the stage, hanging from the sides of their horses, firing under the horses' necks. Past, they seemed to melt into the smoky heat, gone like dust devils, and the prairie was as peaceful as before.

Jesse watched a while longer before he sat down. Removing the tubular magazine from the butt of the stock, he took tapered cartridges from a coat pocket and reloaded.

"That's one helluva carbine you've got there, mister," the cattleman said enviously. "I noticed you didn't reload after each shot. What make is it and what's its range?"

"It's a .56-50 Spencer. Holds seven rounds in the magazine. But you can insert a shell in the chamber and make it an eight-shot. You ear the hammer back for each shot. It can reach out up to four hundred yards."

"Some gun. Would you take a hundred dollars for it?"

Jesse grinned. "Believe not."

As evening drew on, a log stage station and the close huddle of several outer buildings took shape in the dimness. When the passengers piled out, the driver said, "We eat supper, then head on."

The stationmaster met them, a long-haired man, bony and lean and obliging, who reminded Jesse of some government scouts he'd

known up north. "Supper be ready in a few minutes. It's two-bits."
He smiled with self-mockery. "All you can eat, if you can stand my
cookin'. My Mexican cook ran off with a young cowboy yesterday.
Come in."

Jesse poured water into a tin basin on the back porch of the adobe
kitchen and dining room, washed up and dried with the well-used
roller towel, but passed up the community comb on a string. A
cracked mirror hung over the basin. When he glanced there, he saw
a face he hadn't seen in some time. An Alden face, it appeared. Fair
and even-featured, burned golden brown by sun and wind. A full
mouth, somewhat thoughtful. Wide-set gray eyes, wrinkled at the
corners. A passably straight nose. A close beard and long, fair hair,
bleached by the sun. The minié ball at Franklin had torn a path
along the right side of his head, and there would always be that strip
of naked scalp showing. He was twenty-seven years old, six of that
spent in war, and, he thought, *I look much older than that.* Though
appearance and age were of no matter at the moment. He felt good.
He was glad to be where he was, feeling the wind rising cool and
clean off the short grass.

He ducked inside the low-ceilinged, lantern-lit room and sat down
to a heaping supper of brown beans, thick sourdough biscuits, great
slabs of buffalo steak swimming in gravy, and coffee like quinine. He
ate ravenously. Glancing up over the heads of the hungry passengers, the driver and guard, wolfing food beneath swarms of circling
flies, he noticed the little man in the brown suit. He ate with a quick
hunger, without squeamishness or pause between bites, but his eyes
seldom strayed from the doorway opening on the yard where the
hostlers hitched fresh mules to the stage. While others conversed
sporadically, he spoke to no one. Nor was he spoken to. His concentration on the doorway repelled any talk. The first to finish, he rose,
paid the stationmaster, and walked out into the gathering night.

Afterward, drifting outside with the other diners, Jesse heard a
clatter of approaching hoofs. At the same instant he saw the little
man step back into the deeper shadows of the adobe.

The horse racket came from the west. A small body of horsemen.
A young second lieutenant rode into the out-thrown light, followed
by a detachment of cavalry, calling, "Hello, the station. Hello, the
station."

The stationmaster hurried out. "What is it?"

"We're 4th Cavalry, on scout out of Fort Griffin. There are war parties west of here along the trail. I suggest that you hold up all westbound stages till morning, when we'll furnish escort to the next station."

The driver shook his head. "Hate to be delayed like this. We had a runnin' fight east of here and got through. We're well-armed. Believe I'll go on."

"I wouldn't if I were you, sir. Everything's riled up west of here."

"What's caused the ruckus all of a sudden?" the stationmaster asked. "It's been quiet."

"More hide hunters moving in. Everything's riled up."

"That's warning enough." The stationmaster turned to the driver. "You'd better hold up till morning."

Before the driver could answer, the little man, who had moved out to the parley, spoke up. "I'll pay a hundred dollars if the driver will take the stage on tonight. It is of the utmost importance that I reach El Paso as originally scheduled by the stage line."

"Well," the stationmaster drawled, "I figure it's better to get there alive late than not a-tall. Bein' alive is more important than any damned schedule."

"Two hundred dollars!"

There was a startled pause, broken when the lieutenant, his voice terse and impatient, said, "I was going to report also that we found the bodies of two immigrant families along the trail. . . . Did what we could for them."

"Believe I will hold up till tomorrow," the driver said lamely.

"Isn't night travel safer than daytime?" the brown-suited man persisted.

The driver stabbed him with a level look. "I said we'd hold up." He walked away.

"Now, Lieutenant," the stationmaster called out, "you boys bivouac here with us. There's plenty of oats for your horses and hump meat for your supper." He directed them behind the station.

The others moseyed toward the saloon, an adobe extension of the dining room. Jesse tarried, assessing the little man's insistence on going on tonight. The cattleman's voice reached him. "I'll buy you a drink. Maybe I can talk you out of that carbine yet."

"Don't count on it. But I will take you up on the drink. Thanks."

The little man had posted himself at one end of the plank bar, a vantage point, Jesse thought, where he could watch the doorway for whatever it was he dreaded.

The small room was soon crowded and clouded with tobacco smoke. The elderly Mexican man behind the bar kept busy serving whiskey. Jesse sipped his and put it back down, shuddering. At best it could be judged as raw. A hostler came in, and the gregarious drummer soon had him cornered and engaged in conversation. At a table the driver and guard passed the time. As the evening wore on, Jesse, hearing horses, saw the little man tense and look up, then relax as two shaggy-haired buffalo hunters clomped in, smelling of sweat and hides. They downed two drinks before stopping. After a while the drummer's talk must have become boring, because the hostler got up and found an opening at the bar. The lieutenant, looking soldierly and sunburned, came in. He glanced over the mixed crowd with the interest of a young man to whom the world looked new and appealing. When he paused, the drummer went over at once and invited him to have a drink, which he accepted with impeccable manners.

Some time had passed, and Jesse was thinking of sleep, when he heard the rumble and rattle of a stage pulling up. Then voices, the stationmaster's cautioning tone mingling with another. The hostler left his glass and hastened out when the stationmaster called. The little man, still at the corner of the bar, seemed to relax when no one entered from outside, and he said something to a buffalo hunter.

He was still talking when a man in a white planter's hat came to the doorway and peered in, blinking against the light. His armless left sleeve was pinned against the breast of his heavy gray coat. His intense eyes, dark and gleaming, flicking here and there, contrasted with the ivory pallor of his face and his long raven hair. The eyes quit roving, they seemed to fix, and suddenly he moved, like an actor striding on stage. For a moment he was hidden behind the lieutenant turning to leave. Next he stepped past Jesse, so close Jesse caught the perfume of his hairdressing. He stepped toward the little man, still chatting with the buffalo hunter. The latecomer's voice rose dramatically. "Worship not the setting sun, brother," in the tone of a secret password.

The little man jerked around, fear clutching his face. His eyes bulged. He gasped.

"You betrayed us, sir!" the one-armed man shouted, and drew a pistol from within his coat.

On instinct Jesse grabbed the weapon and tore it free. Seeing that, the brown-suited man pawed his way clear through the crowd and dashed out the front door.

The gunman was furious. He raged at Jesse. "You let him get away. He's an informer—he betrayed us!" He reached for his gun.

Jesse held it away. "Betrayed who?" He could hear a horse going away fast to the west.

"There just went one of our horses," a hunter said dryly.

The gunman's dark eyes conveyed a fanatic's gleam. His face was quivering. "The Lost Cause, sir. The Lost Cause. Just when Southern sympathizers in the North were ready to rise up and overthrow Lincoln's nigger government, this man informed."

"You mean Copperheads, don't you?" Jesse said, showing disgust, thinking of his three lost friends from General Morgan's command and their failed mission in the North. "Copperheads never fired a shot. Never intended to. Never helped anybody but themselves. Helped themselves to Confederate gold—that was all. All talk and no fight. You know that."

"But I tell you—"

"The war's over," Jesse said, his bitterness spilling out. "Why can't you let it be?" He passed the man's pistol back to him and walked out into the chilling night. His mind was churning, his earlier ease gone. He hadn't yet put the past behind him. *It's even out here.*

Rolling into El Paso's plaza aboard the stage, Jesse hardly knew what he had expected to find in a Mexican border town. Not much. But this exceeded what he had reckoned on. The scattering of adobe houses and the few store buildings along the dusty streets, more village than town among the lofty cottonwoods, in the distance dormant grain fields, vineyards, and fruit trees, and the bright ribbon of the Rio Grande. After Indian attacks east and west of Horsehead Crossing, it meant rest, food, and drink.

His fellow travelers—two gamblers dressed in dusty black broadcloth suits, gaudy vests, and black hats, and a young miner of rugged build—hurried off first. The gamblers headed for the nearest saloon. The miner said he was going to take a stage to Piños Altos, in the

Gila region of southern New Mexico, where there was a gold and silver strike.

Stepping down with the cased Spencer, Jesse took his grip from the rear boot of the coach and set out for the lone hotel. A room? The Mexican clerk was most gracious. Indeed, *señor*. Fifty cents. In advance, please. Jesse smiled and paid, thinking the policy said something about the establishment's clientele. In the room he found a bowl and a pitcher of water, soap, and a thin towel, and blankets on the straw mattress, which he examined with care for bedbugs and, to his surprise, discovered none. Scrubbed clean for the first time in days, he lay down on the bed and closed his eyes, listening to the sedative hum of the settlement, still feeling the swaying motion of the coach.

When he woke up, evening shadows hazed the room and he knew an instant hunger. The obliging clerk directed him to a *bueno* restaurant across the street. The eye-watering meal was ample and satisfying, far more than army fare, simple though it might seem to the fastidious. From there he strolled over to a saloon. Games were going at two tables, holding forth at each one of the gamblers who had arrived by stage, dusty and worn, both now resplendent in ruffled white shirts, flowing black ties, black coats and hats brushed shining clean.

Jesse bought a drink of whiskey and leaned on the bar, letting his thoughts run free. Before long he would have to consider some kind of gainful employment. He had no hankering for mining or prospecting as eagerly described by the hopeful young man on the stage. For that, besides having an eye for color, a man had to be both an unfailing optimist and a gambler, and he was neither. Weary of stage travel and its limitations, he would look at some saddle horses in the morning.

His drink was still unfinished when angry voices broke the drone of low talk and the click of poker chips. Chairs scraped and crashed. Turning, Jesse saw two men standing at one of the tables.

"Sherman, a general!" A shaggy-browed man sniffed, pushing back his coat to rest his right hand on the butt of a gun. "In Georgia he wasn't nothin' but a low-down chicken thief and smokehouse burglar."

"Careful what you say, sir. I served under General Sherman all through the Georgia campaign as a major of cavalry." The speaker, a thin, beak-nosed man, drew himself up.

"Oh, the blue-bellied Yankee caval-ree. The privy-wreckers."

"By God, sir, you do rile me." He laid his left hand on the gun at his belt.

"Then let it rile you some more, Major Privy-Wrecker!" the first man shouted and dug for his gun.

The other was equally fast. Two shots clapped together as players dived under the table for cover. Powder smoke bloomed like river fog. More shots, fired rapidly. Both men reeled. Now both men were down, their cries agonizing as they grabbed at their wounds.

Jesse hadn't moved, astonished yet not astonished at the senselessness of the deadly argument.

The players crawled out from under the table. One was the gambler. Dusting himself off meticulously, he called to the bartender, "Send for a doctor."

"Doc's across the river at Paso del Norte. Won't be back till late tomorrow."

The gambler looked down at the gunfighters, whose movements had stilled. "Don't think he's needed after all. Just get the undertaker." He turned to the somewhat flustered players. "Now, gentlemen, where were we?" And they all pulled up chairs and sat down, looking for their cards.

The bartender shouted in Spanish, and a Mexican boy went bounding out the swinging doors like a deer. When Jesse looked in question at the barkeep, he replied wearily, "Before the war Southern men had a grip on the town. When the war came, most everybody pulled out. Now the Union men are comin' in to take over." He wiped an invisible spot on the shiny bar. "Hell, I thought the damned war was supposed to be over."

"Appears like it won't be for a long time," Jesse acknowledged. He finished the whiskey and pushed away from the bar, in his ears the resuming click of poker chips and the hum of voices. Outside, he paused. *The damn fools. Why won't they let it rest?* A sense of controlled detachment moved through him, sealing off his emotions, and he returned to the hotel, got paper and pen from the clerk, and began writing:

Dear Mr. Sawyer,

    I told you I would let you know my whereabouts. I am in El Paso, on the Mexican border. My plans are uncertain. But my health is good and I look forward to the future, whatever it may hold.

    I thank you once again, sir, for your most considerate attention to my family and our affairs.

Sincerely,
JESSE ALDEN WILDER

    Thinking of what he could not go back to, he had a sensation of immense loss, of aching homesickness, of infinite regret, and he realized the strain that had been upon him for so long. Yet, he asked himself, what had brought him here, this far? Quite simply, he knew, he had learned to endure, not in anticipation of any Elysian Fields. That was too visionary, too impractical. Not bloated Southern pride; however, he had pride as a man and, yes, as a Southerner. No, it was the plain force of will to survive—no matter what. That alone had carried him through thus far. He continued with these thoughts, coming to grips with himself. It wasn't good for a man to question himself too much. It was better to act, to move. Little by little his depression began to lift, which wakened an urgency within him.

    It was still with him next morning in the adobe corral behind the Acme Livery, where buyers looked at horses and mules. The mules not the big-boned, powerful animals his father had raised and sold. These were a wiry, smaller breed, like the ones that pulled the stages, more able, he judged, to withstand the punishing desert heat. He strolled around, looking for saddle horses.

    A hump-shouldered white man sidled over, his whiskered jaws working on a bulging wad of tobacco, his trader's eyes both deferring and sharp. "Guess you're lookin' for a saddle mount?"

    Jesse nodded.

    "Got a right nice mouse-dun gelding over here." He pointed to a bluish-gray animal tied alone. "He's six years old. Was the private mount of a local merchant who sold out."

    Jesse walked over to the horse and strolled around him. The animal was rangy, had sloping shoulders and stout hindquarters. He stepped to the gelding's head, opened the mouth, and looked in for several moments, reading the teeth. Unable to mask a grin, he turned to the trader and said, "I don't like to argue a point, but his lower nippers are round or just about so—as thick as they are broad." He smiled then. "Don't believe I'm interested. This fellow's about twelve years old."

The horse trader spread his hands and gazed at the sky, looking shocked. "Well, if that don't beat all. However, I have noticed my arm's not long enough when I start readin' a newspaper. Makes me wonder how many deals have slipped by me. On top of that, my memory's bad."

Jesse took that with amusement. "What else do you have?"

"There's a penful of saddle stock over yonder, but I won't hazard their ages," the trader said, quirking his mouth and rolling his eyes. "But you won't find any Morgans. They're all range stuff."

Standing at the gate, Jesse observed the bunch circling the pen, watching how they moved. A little blaze-faced, copper-colored bay caught his eye. "I'd like a closer look at that bay," he said.

The trader spoke to a young Mexican, who, taking a rope, went inside and dabbed a loop on the bay when the bunch whirled by. The bay reared and lunged, fighting the rope, forcing the Mexican to dig in. Shortening his hold, he gradually worked up the rope to the bay's head and led him out, nodding approval of his catch.

"I'll look at his mouth," Jesse said. But the bay would have none of that till the Mexican slipped on a halter and jerked his head down. Jesse looked. "He's a five-year-old."

"I'll have to take your word for it," said the trader, mustering a half smile.

Jesse, slowly circling the bay, noted that his legs were straight, his back short, his hindquarters well-developed, and he had a long barrel. He was on the small side, not more than eight hundred pounds. But he moved like a piece of silk, and his black tail almost touched the ground, and he had a proud way of holding his head, and there was a bold look in his eyes.

"He looks like he might be part mustang," Jesse said.

"Could be." The trader nodded. "He was in a bunch I bought off a rancher."

"How much do you want for him?"

"I'll make you a mighty fair price. Say, a hundred dollars."

Jesse had to whistle on that. Good horses were cheap on the Plains, and this likewise was fine horse country, maybe even more so, judging by the wild bands he'd seen from stage windows. He shook his head and had started to walk away when the trader said, "Make it seventy-five." Jesse kept on walking. "Fifty, friend, and not one cent less." Jesse didn't stop. "You're robbin' me. You can have the bay for thirty-five dollars, though I'll go broke at this rate."

Jesse halted and turned. Thirty-five was still a mite high, but he liked the bay. "Fair enough. But before we close the deal, I want to try him out. I don't aim to be left afoot where I might be in the next few days."

"Maybe you'd better let one of the boys ride him first," the trader suggested in a most solicitous voice, now that the sale was near. "He might be just a little bit snuffy."

"I'd better learn about the horse now—not down the trail."

"All right." The trader called, "Juan, put a hackamore on the bay and saddle 'im. Ramón, you'd better help. You'll have to snub 'im."

That required forcing the unwilling bay to the snubbing post, and when all was ready the snubbers looked at Jesse. Glancing around, he saw that he had drawn spectators. The mule buyers were watching. Particularly, one tall white man, who was smiling like an old friend.

Jesse approached the horse, seeing the quivering muscles, the eyes rolling, the nostrils flaring. The nearness of this waiting mass of violence seemed to make the coppery horse look much larger. A stab of doubt flicked Jesse.

"Ready, *señor?*"

Nodding, Jesse took the reins, stepped to the saddle, and settled himself, seeing Ramón grip the hackamore to hold the bay's head down while Juan jerked the rope free from around the horse's neck.

For what seemed like endless time nothing happened. Beneath him Jesse could feel the short back quivering. When he kicked with his boot heels, the little horse seemed to break apart, squealing and bucking, head down. Jesse's head and shoulders snapped back violently. Without warning, the bay switched ends, and suddenly there was nothing under Jesse, and he felt himself being hurled from the saddle. The dusty ground flew up to meet him. He landed on his side with a solid grunt, momentarily stunned, his wind knocked from him. He heard laughter. He felt his face grow hot as his temper flew. Sitting up, he saw the bay, motionless, watching him with evident disdain.

Rising and dusting himself off, he called to the snubbers, "Let's go again."

Juan's rope snaked out, caught. Together, he and Ramón snubbed the horse to the post.

Jesse mounted quickly. This time there was no hesitation. The instant the snubbers let go, the bay bogged his head, humped his back, and leaped, squealing and pitching, left and right, landing stiff-legged, which jarred Jesse's backbone. Jesse was beginning to catch the rhythm of the violent jumps, until, again without the slightest warning, the red horse swapped ends and Jesse went sailing off, his hat ahead of him. Somehow he managed a less jolting landing, though no less humiliating, when he heard the laughs. Rolling to his feet, he picked up his hat, dusted it off, and looked for the horse, which was standing as before, sweaty flanks heaving, head lowered, watching him alertly.

Seeing the snubbers eyeing him, as if in doubt, Jesse said, "Again. Let's go again."

Again Juan's rope snaked out and caught, and again, though on somewhat wobbly legs, Jesse marched up to the horse.

"Keep his head up this time," the trader shouted.

Jesse stepped to the saddle, and the little red horse flung away, pitching even before the snubbers were clear. Not waiting for the end-switching, Jesse wadded the reins in his left hand and yanked hard to hold up the tossing head, while his right hand jerked to each bone-jarring lunge. Off they tore, buck-jumping, here and there, left and right, scattering the mule buyers. Jesse thought he was ready when the bay tried to bog his head and change directions. Hauling one-handed on the reins, he yanked until his shoulder socket hurt. But still the horse twisted around. Jesse lost his balance, swayed, and felt the saddle seat slap his butt. He grabbed the saddle horn with both hands and held on, righting himself. Suddenly the horse quit pitching and broke running.

"Open the gate!" Jesse yelled.

There was a scramble among the spectators to swing back the corral gate. The horse, already headed that way, seemed to sense freedom and obligingly bolted for the opening. Along a dusty street of adobe houses they dashed, sending squawking chickens flying, pedestrians dodging, attracting an escort of barking dogs.

The town and dogs soon fell behind them, and they came to a

road that followed the shining river. Still the horse wanted to run. Jesse let him, and he ran for a long way, black mane flying in the wind. When he began to tire, Jesse punished him with the ends of the reins and made him run some more. After that, whenever his mount slowed, Jesse jabbed with his heels and used the reins as a quirt.

But enough was enough, he decided after a while. The little red horse who rode big had suffered enough. As to how much the gelding had learned in this short time, Jesse would soon know. A wry thought rose. *Or how much both of us have learned.* Circling, he brought the horse down from a run, ragged by now, to a slow gallop, to a lope, to a trot, then a cooling-down walk. They coursed on in that steady fashion for a way. Now Jesse reined left, and the horse hesitated, then obeyed. Jesse reined right and the horse followed through. Next Jesse reined him through a figure eight, and the responses were quicker. So far, good. Now the test as Jesse visioned himself alone in desert country, just a man and his horse, when a horse meant life.

He reined up and sat forward, hunched, tensed for mustang hell to break loose, if it was coming. It didn't—not yet. Cautiously, watching the horse's head, he lifted his right foot from the stirrup, expecting trouble any instant. It didn't come—not yet. Then he swung down from the saddle and drew the reins from under the horse's neck and held them up close.

"You're a hell of a horse," Jesse said. "Tough as an old boot. Now let's see how we'd get along, just the two of us."

Jesse put out a hand to touch the blazed face, murmuring nonsense as he did. Instantly the wide, dark eyes rolled, went wild, the nostrils flared, and the horse jerked back, giving a snuffling rattle. With both hands Jesse took up the slack in the reins and waited until the bay quieted down. Carefully, then, with this short hold, Jesse raised his hand and rubbed the blazed face and the lathered neck, yielding a little ground but not wanting to fight the horse while he tried to back away. Jesse dropped his hand and the horse quit backing.

Now could he mount the horse? He could try or he could lead the horse back to town, which was a long walk. He dwelled on his choices for a moment. Better to know now. But when he lifted the reins to bring them over the arched neck, the bay danced away in a circle. When that foolishness ended, Jesse led off walking down the road as a calming tactic, and the horse followed agreeably enough. A short way and Jesse stopped. Neither hurried nor hesitant, talking low, he slipped the reins around the neck before the horse moved away. Now, if ever, was the time! No chance for a stirrup. Without hesitating, he grabbed the saddle horn and half flung himself, half leaped to the saddle, there aware that the horse was still dancing sideways. Feet in the stirrups, he pulled the bay's head up, set for the buck-jumping to commence. Jesse could feel the short back trembling, but nothing changed. A tick of time passed. Another. Gently, Jesse shook the reins, and to his relief the red horse swung away into a steady trot.

When he rode into the corral, the trader stared at him in surprise. "Figured that horse would dump you and come in alone, if he came back at all."

Jesse pinned a mocking look on the man. "Thought you said this horse might be just a *little bit* snuffy?"

"So I did. Believe I told you too that my memory's gettin' bad." He scratched his head. "It just now comes to me that horse had never been rode."

The Mexican snubbers grinned knowingly, and the mule buyers chuckled.

"I'll take him for thirty-five dollars," Jesse said. "Although he pitched like a wild horse, he showed me a keen intelligence and he soon quieted down after a long run. Now I'll need a saddle, bridle, and a good horse blanket. Two saddlebags. And I'll want him shod before I take him out."

The transaction was completed for another thirty-five dollars, plus a dollar for shoeing and a dollar for each leather saddlebag. Jesse could get his horse that afternoon. "If I don't forget," the trader said in his droll way.

Jesse was walking toward the corral gate, feeling anew the punishment he had taken, when a voice behind him spoke hurriedly. "Hold up there, suh. I think it's time somebody bought you a drink."

It was the voice more than the offer of a drink that brought Jesse around. A voice that dripped of the Old South, so soft and lazy and genuinely courteous, so pleasing to the ear, so unexpected here.

It belonged to the tall mule buyer, who had smiled encouragement every time Jesse looked up after being thrown. He was smiling now, the smile like a fixture. He thrust out a quick hand. "Cullen Floyd, suh." A man spare and trim, a ginger beard framing a dark, carefree face composed of lively brown eyes that might seem to find amusement in an otherwise wearisome world, and a mobile mouth that could belong to an arm-waving backwoods preacher, and a long nose and a long jaw, in all that the glimmer of reckless devilment, perhaps even a hint of the devious if need be. A man about Jesse's age.

"Jesse Wilder, Mr. Floyd."

"God, Wilder, you are formal for out here."

Jesse smiled. "Not too much, I hope."

"Will you have some drinks with me? Don't tell me you don't need relief after what I saw you take."

"I need it and gladly take you up on it, *suh,*" Jesse said, stressing the last and finding it easy to laugh with Floyd.

Floyd turned in at the first saloon and led them to a table. When Jesse started to order whiskey, Floyd interrupted with a show of courtesy, "Let me suggest that you try tequila instead."

"Tequila?"

"Made from the century plant in Mexico. Beats the bad whiskey we get out here."

So they had tequila, then they had another. "It is smooth," Jesse agreed. "Kicks like a mule."

Leaning back, the smile never leaving his face, Floyd said, "When I heard you talkin' to that skinflint trader, I almost got homesick right there." He sized Jesse up and down. "From your accent I'm gonna say Kentucky or Tennessee."

"Tennessee. And you, I'll say Alabama or Mississippi, maybe Georgia. Deep South for sure."

"Mississippi. So far south in Mississippi that we used to think folks up north in Corinth were part Yankee."

"Never heard that one before," Jesse said, grinning.

A pause set in and Jesse sensed that the inevitable was coming, in a roundabout way, of course, for the observance of Southern manners. What was he doing here? Was he running from something? By the same token, what was a Mississippian doing here and why was he buying mules?

"It's not much easier out here for a white man than it is for a

Mexican." Floyd broke the silence. "But if you're on the lookout for employment, I might have a job for you."

"Such as . . ."

"Reckon you can handle a carbine or rifle?"

"I can," Jesse replied succinctly, and saw that Floyd waited for him to expand on that.

And when he did not, Floyd said, "That—uh—is the main qualification. A good man with a gun. A little guard duty. I will have a pack train of supplies leaving here tomorrow for a merchant in Chihuahua City."

"What's the pay?"

"Top money for out here. A hundred Mexican 'dobe dollars when we get to Chihuahua City. A dollar goes a long way in Mexico." He smiled roguishly. "Tequila, women, and song."

Still no question about my experience, Jesse thought, and, *Why would a Mississippian be taking supplies to Chihuahua City?* Each man was hiding something from the other. Jesse, his service in the U.S. Army, and Floyd, whatever he was really up to.

"Obviously, you need an armed escort," Jesse stated. "Why?"

"Bandits and Apaches. Apaches have devastated much of northern Chihuahua and Sonora. They like to attack at dawn, and they take no prisoners. Bandits are more of a nuisance, not so wily, but they will kill you for a two-bit piece if they get the chance." He smiled that infectious smile. "What do you say, suh?"

It neither appealed to Jesse nor turned him away, but he wasn't cut out for mining and there was little else, if anything, in El Paso for a man whose profession had become soldiering, it seemed, leaving out nearby Fort Bliss and his long-ago stint in that other world, that antebellum world of innocence, as a country schoolteacher. "I'll go," he said and stood.

"Good! Fine! I'll form the pack train about daylight tomorrow at the corral." Floyd pumped Jesse's hand hard, in seeming sincere appreciation, his eyes thoughtful, as if reflecting on things left untouched. "I'm mighty pleased you're going, Wilder. Be nice to have another Johnny Reb along."

Jesse let that go by without comment and took his leave.

So he knows. I figure him for the same. It will all come out on the trail.

6

In the stable behind the hotel, Jesse fed the blood-bay gelding grain and led him to a water trough. Then, saddling up without contest, he tied on two sleeping blankets rolled in a rubber poncho, a canvas shelter tent, a canteen, the two saddlebags jammed with cartridges, and looped over the saddle horn the strap of a leather-covered wood case with a hinged lid holding ten tin tubes of seven metallic cartridges each, which he could slip over his shoulder in a moment. A kind of forage bag contained extra clothing and personal items. Neither had he forgotten a small hatchet and a cavalryman's picket rope and pin. Floyd had said nothing about provisions, so a sack held a tin cup, tin plate, knife, fork, and spoon, a cooking can for making coffee or stew, a little wooden coffee grinder, and a small frying pan. Another sack held a slab of bacon, sacked dried fruit, coffee beans and flour, tins of sardines, and a supply of corn tortillas. Also a sack of shelled corn for the horse.

The mustang stood quietly enough during the packing, but when Jesse went to mount, early morning skittishness set in and the bay danced away with a snuffling rattle.

Jesse felt almost amused. "Whoa, now. I thought we'd settled our differences yesterday. Well, let's get it over with."

He led off to the adobe corral behind the barn, and when the horse repeated the dancing act and rolled his dark eyes something fierce, Jesse, taking the bit, forced the bay sideways to the corral wall. The instant his hindquarters touched the adobe, the horse flounced back fast and Jesse slipped a quick foot into the stirrup and swung to the saddle. At once the bronc bogged his head and switched ends. But Jesse, forewarned, was ready, and around the corral they stormed, bucking and squealing, Jesse flung forward and backward, from side to side, the sacks banging and flopping, which only made the mustang work harder to free himself of what was on his back. After a series of violent jumps, it was time for the usual run, only a brief run, however, because Jesse had closed the gate. Checked there, the bay cut away, running. Using the open reins like a quirt, Jesse whipped the horse to make him buck, and when he tired and wanted to run, Jesse quirted him again and again until all such foolishness ceased, then rode around the corral for some minutes.

Halting, Jesse stepped down and muttered, "Now, red hoss, let's get this mounting business settled once and for all."

As before, the bay danced away, but the dance was short and sweet, like the old woman's dance, Jesse remembered the saying went, and he achieved the saddle. He rode to the gate, leaned down and pulled it open. He rode through, grunting his relief. Fortunately, so there would be no runaway red horse on the trail, he had thought to buy leather hobbles, which he would buckle on the wild one's forelegs tonight. The thought lent him confidence, and he liked the travelin' way the tough little horse took to the dusty footing.

Outside the Acme corral a pack train of mules was lined up, with an escort of armed Mexicans in straw sombreros standing by. Cullen Floyd and the trader were talking.

"I'm a little late," Jesse said, riding up. "The red horse and I had another schooling session. But he didn't throw me."

Floyd nodded. Jesse saw his eyes go to the sheathed Spencer. "I see you've brought your own gun. I was going to give you an Enfield rifle to use."

"I'd rather use my Spencer carbine."

"Agreed. Well, let's go, suh." Floyd mounted a big dun gelding, Jesse reined in beside him, and they swung away. Above the town they crossed the river at a shallow ford and filed down through Paso del Norte to the thorny desert.

There Floyd sent flankers out to both sides, and the long day began under a glowing copper sun. "I don't expect any trouble before tomorrow," the Mississippian said as they rode along. "But in this country you soon learn to expect the unexpected."

"You do this often?" Jesse asked.

"Now and then. Depends what I have to do to make a living. Mexico is torn up now. Benito Juárez is president, but Maximilian still says he's emperor and still holds Mexico City. The French set him up. Guess you've heard about all that."

"Just enough to know that it happened."

"Well, Juárez is gaining strength, but the French still have some garrisons in the north. Some Mexicans fight with the French. There are even some native brigades." He was talking rapidly now, at ease with the subject. "I understand some Johnny Rebs joined up with Maximilian. I reckon he needs all the help he can get. The countryside is against him, but besides Mexico City he still holds Vera Cruz, Chihuahua City, and Saltillo." He paused, recalling. "And other strong points like Torreon, Querétaro, and maybe San Luis Potosí."

"I believe you are well-informed."

Floyd shrugged. "A man hears a lot of things. Rumors fly like buzzards in Mexico. You don't know what to believe sometimes."

"Do you think Juárez will win the war?"

"Eventually, because he's got most of the people behind him. One trouble is the Mexican government, his government, is broke. When he was elected, he suspended payments on all foreign loans. That brought in the French, and the Spanish and English for a time. Juárez will win by wearing the French down. He'll win because he's fighting for his country. But it hasn't been too long since he was holed up in Paso del Norte."

Jesse, further intrigued by Floyd's knowledge of Mexican affairs, tried a random shot. "Have you ever met Juárez?"

Floyd seemed put at a loss. "Why would I? But I'd like to. I understand he is one tough little Indian."

"An Indian?"

"A full-blooded Zapotec, they say. You see, Wilder, not everybody in Mexico is Spanish or part Spanish. There's a hell of a lot of straight Indians around. Indian slaves work the big haciendas for a handful of beans and tortillas. Them that are mixed with Spanish blood are called *mestizos*. And there are the Creoles, sons and daughters of Spanish immigrants born in Mexico."

Jesse nodded. "I see. That's interesting to know. I still say you are very well-informed."

"My ears are big and so is my mouth, which can get a man in a heap of trouble. I speak a little Spanish, enough to get by on. I've learned that Mexicans are brave people, proud of their heritage."

"You said Juárez will win because he's fighting for his country. That doesn't always hold true, as we know."

"The South lost the war because it ran out of cannon fodder. Not enough rebs left to make them damn-fool massed infantry charges the damn-fool generals ordered. We ran up against too many repeating rifles, same make as the carbine you're carryin'."

"Like at Hoover's Gap in Tennessee, for instance?"

Floyd's eyes showed a grim light. "Like at Hoover's Gap, which I've heard tell of, and some other places I've known firsthand and would like to forget about but can't."

That seemed to cast a pall over their conversation, and Jesse questioned why he had even brought up the dead past, yet a past that they could not ignore because it had shaped their being here.

The miles fell away without change, the desert shrubs appearing to float and sway as the gray-green land dipped and rose. When the pack train stopped at noon, the red horse seemed as fresh as he had been at the beginning of the day, and when it was time to mount and move on, his brief dancing away seemed more a proud reminder of his former feral state as a wild horse, lest Jesse forget it, than a hostile act. Then they were off, the bay striding eagerly, head high, at home in this arid wasteland. Flankers fanned out, right and left.

It happened suddenly as the train was halfway across a dry wash. Crashing rifle fire with blooms of white powdersmoke puffing along the wash's brushy bank froze every rider momentarily. A question flashed through Jesse's mind. The flankers? Where the hell were they?

Jerking his horse around, Jesse yanked the Spencer free and thumbed back the hammer. A guard shouted and fell from his mount, one foot caught in the stirrup as the horse flew wildly down the wash, dragging the rider. A pack mule was down, thrashing. Floyd was bellowing in Spanish, waving the guards to the near side of the wash. These bits Jesse glimpsed.

In his next breath he saw the Apaches, half-naked figures of sculpted bronze, bobbing out of the brush. They jumped down the bank, screeching as they charged in a wave. Jesse fired and a head-banded figure stumbled. Working the loading lever like a pump handle, he knocked down an Apache grabbing for the halter of the lead mule. Another Apache whipped around with astonished shock when a .50-caliber slug took him in the chest. Another Apache yelled and pointed in alarm at Jesse and broke down a split second later. Another ran screaming at Jesse, howling hate, utterly fearless, knife held high. Jesse fired when the man was scarcely a rod away. The bullet drove him backward and down on his haunches. He stayed down.

Suddenly the attack shifted from Jesse to his left, where Floyd was rallying the escort. As the Apaches swarmed with war cries, Jesse saw that he had them enfiladed. He began firing rapidly. He was on a third seven-shot magazine, the barrel now almost too hot to hold, when a piercing cry rose above the gunfire and the bronze shapes scattered like quail. They seemed to vanish all at once in the glassy heat beyond the brushy wash, gone like dust devils.

Not until then did Jesse think of his mount. The red horse had flinched and danced with each blast of the carbine, but he hadn't gone crazy and bolted like the one dragging the guard. Jesse was grateful to have found a horse with battlefield nerves.

Floyd was waiting when Jesse rode over. "By God, suh," the Mississippian said. "You changed the tide of battle damned fast with that repeater." He gestured at the scattered bronze shapes. "This bunch won't hit us again this trip. Be no daybreak attack. They're not used to these kinds of losses."

"What happened to our flankers?"

"I see the two on the left comin' in now. That means they got the others."

"I didn't hear any gunfire."

"Didn't have to. An Apache can bury himself in the sand with a reed to breathe through. When a man rides by on scout, he jumps up and knifes him. Silent and effective."

Floyd sent a guard down the wash to look for the runaway horse and rider. The first wounded mule was still kicking and another was hopping about, one leg dangling. Floyd put the cripple out of its misery. Dismounting to shoot the downed mule, Jesse noticed its canvas pack had come loose. Instead of supplies, he saw a bundle of rifles bound by strips of leather. Saying nothing, he did his duty by the poor animal and waited for Floyd to explain. Floyd said nothing, but spoke to a Mexican, who retied the pack and lashed it on another mule. He then switched the pack from the other dead mule.

"Let's move along," Floyd said. "There's a little water hole I want us to make before dark."

"You sent a man after the runaway horse and rider. He was wounded, I know. What about them?"

"They'll catch up."

Jesse was taken aback. "Catch up in Apache country? I think we'd better wait."

Floyd put on that carefree smile. "This is harsh country. Every man has to skin his own skunk. They knew it was risky when they hired on. I got just so much time to get this load to Chihuahua City. Besides, life's cheap out here."

"Not that cheap. You'll need every man if we get this pack train to its destination."

"Aw, hell, Wilder. Here they come now, just like I figured they would. But the man on the led horse won't make it far."

In that moment, Jesse saw, the mercurial face had changed from a veteran fighting man's hardened outlook to concern. Jesse guessed it was concern. Floyd was contradictory, difficult to understand at times, yet he was a likable man. As for the mystery of the so-called supplies, that would unfold before very long.

As Floyd had seen, the wounded man didn't last long. They buried him less than an hour later beside the stony trail while the guards crossed themselves.

Before evening they reached the water hole, and Floyd set out pickets. He distributed no rations; evidently it was every man for himself. Unsaddling, Jesse watered and hobbled his horse where there was a thin spread of grass. On second thought, he would sleep close to his horse tonight. A horse, with its keen senses, was always a good sentinel. Realizing further that a mount of this wild nature might still hobble off some distance, he also put the horse on picket rope and drove the pin in deep with the hatchet. After several attempts, he got a small mesquite fire going. One moment the desert sky was a cathedral dome shedding veiled light, in another there fell a cloak of purple darkness and a cool wind came sighing from the west. A rose-yellow sickle moon was on its high road. He made coffee in the can and cooked his simple supper of bacon, heating the tortillas in the frying pan, which beat hardtack anytime. The sardines and dried fruit he would reserve for the harder days to come.

He was sitting against his saddle, smoking his second pipeful, the campfire down to a bed of cherry-red coals, when Cullen Floyd loomed swaying out of the gloom, waving a bottle.

"Wilder, suh, I congratulate you on the—er—ah—deadliness of your—ah—field of fire today. It was superb, suh. You must have a drink with me, suh." He held out the bottle.

Jesse took a swallow of tequila and handed it back. "I would offer you a camp chair, suh, if I had one," he said with easy mimicry.

Floyd bowed from the waist. "Spoken like a true Southern gentleman, suh. A cavalier of the Old South." His blurred voice, a rich baritone, was mockingly correct. "And I hereby accept such courtesy, but you may have to get me up." He plopped down heavily and, pulling his knees up, carefully set the bottle between them. His jesting vanished. "The Southern gent I ain't no more an' maybe never was. It might as well come out now, Wilder, or later. Why we're both out here, and believe me we're not the first. I wore the Yankee blue out West, as much as it rankled me." Like a confession, Jesse thought, seeing the hurt in the now-bleary eyes. Floyd seemed to wait.

"I did the same," Jesse said, feeling a vague relief. "Although I felt like a traitor, I got used to it. I felt better when I found I was serving with other rebs. A whole regiment of us." His words flowed more easily now. "It was survival. I told myself we owed ourselves that much, as long as we'd fought for the South. Even so, I felt cheapened. I hated it, but I'd taken the oath of allegiance. I'd given my word. I—"

"Ah," Floyd said in a seizing voice, "the true Southern gentleman, suh. Your *word.*"

"A man had to hold to something."

"Did you desert?"

"I thought about it. You bet I did. I served mostly on the northern Plains, where you don't desert in the dead of winter if you want to live."

"More survival," Floyd said cynically.

"You damned right. I make no apologies. Those who went over the hill in the dead of winter didn't make it."

"What about springtime, when the flowers bloom tra-la and there's plenty of pony grass?" Floyd asked, growing more insulting. His mouth hung loosely.

"The Sioux got most of 'em. I guess a few made it to the Montana gold fields."

"How do y'know the Sioux got 'em?"

Jesse's tolerance tipped, then settled. Why argue with a drunk? "Because later we found their bodies along the trail. I suppose you conducted yourself very nobly all the time you wore the bastard blue? Saved the colonel's daughter from a fate worse than death when savage red men gave chase as she was out for a morning canter on her favorite Kentucky saddler with you her lone escort. Rode through a howling blizzard to take supplies to a remote outpost. Out on scout one day, your detail, undermanned as usual, ran into a big war party. When the chief rode out and made insulting gestures, you alone had the courage to engage him in mortal hand-to-hand combat. Upon your return to the fort, the colonel congratulated you and made you his personal aide for conduct becoming an officer and a gentleman."

Floyd was grinning slackly throughout the banter. "Aw, hell, Wilder, have another drink. I was just ribbin' you. Thing is, we made it. I served all my enlistment escortin' supply trains along the Santa Fe Trail. Did I desert? Hell, no, I was afraid to. Too many goddamned Cheyennes and Arapahoes lurkin' around." He carefully passed the bottle to Jesse as if it were precious beyond words.

"What camp did you volunteer from?" Jesse asked, after a long pull. The tequila was smooth and satisfying. It occurred to him that Floyd, shut off from his own world so long, was starved for talk and amusement.

"Rock Island. That was what the Yankees called it. We called it Hell on Earth."

"Mine was Camp Morton, out of Indianapolis. I won't bore you with the details. What got you there?"

Still full of self-mockery, Floyd staggered up and, swaying, struck a grandiose Napoleonic pose, right hand stuck inside his coat. "When the bugle sounded, I, Cullen Bradford Floyd, immediately offered my sword to my country, which immediately made me a private, which in turn wounded my feelings no end. Me, the son of a planter, a mere private? . . . 'Sorry, Mr. Floyd. What we need right now is somebody who can bite cartridges and aim a rifle. Your promotion will come on the field of battle.' . . . Joined the 35th Mississippi of Moore's brigade. Eventually we came under General Van Dorn. Had us a right smart of a battle there at Corinth. Street fightin'. Sometimes house-to-house. Got whupped, which just about ended Van Dorn too, but we did plumb good later when we caught the Yankees by surprise at Holly Springs and burned four million dollars' worth of stores. Shore made a purty fire, and Grant had to change his plans." He dropped the burlesque and sat down, reaching for the bottle. "How was I captured? I'd like to say it was in a big battle. But it wasn't that way a-tall, Wilder. It was in west Tennessee. I didn't think there was a Yankee within fifty miles, so I rode out to see a country girl I knew. Oh, we had a time. Her folks invited me to dinner. An' before I left I told her how purty she was, an' she told me how brave I was, an' I kissed her, an' she kissed me, an' it was sorta agreed that after the war . . . Well, on the way back to camp damned if some Yankee foragers didn't capture me. I wasn't even on the lookout. I still had my mind on that girl." He shook off the memory. "Now, suh, mind tellin' me yours?"

Jesse told of Franklin and his capture and recovery from wounds and the trip on the steamboat, but gave few details on Camp Morton. Floyd listened attentively, nodding often, and then they had a drink of tequila.

"We're just outcasts," Floyd mused. "No homes to go back to."

"I don't want to go back the way it is," Jesse said. "I did right after I was mustered out. All I could think of was home and family. It was a big mistake. It won't change back there for a long, long time."

"I know. I went back, an' my father, bless his fire-eatin', Yankee-hatin' soul, didn't even invite me into the house. He came out on the veranda, looked me straight in the eye, an' told me never to come back. Said he never wanted to see me again. Called me a traitor to the Confederacy. A Judas, I remember he said." Floyd took a long breath, then a long swallow of tequila. "I just stood there. I couldn't say a word. In his eyes I saw that he despised me. Not one little hint of understanding. I'd disgraced him, y'see. . . . I just shook my head an' walked away. Never looked back. But it hurt. It tore my heart out."

"Is your mother living?"

"No, God rest her sweet soul, an' if she had been that day, she sure as hell would've invited me into the house where I was born. By God, she would've!"

"Sorry, Cullen. I reckon we're both a little homesick tonight."

"I'm not afraid to admit it, Wilder."

Jesse's lips curved into a small smile of reproach. "I think it's time you called me by my given name."

"I was fixin' to do that." Floyd's blurred voice had drawn down to a mumble. By now the bottle was empty. He tossed it aside. "Speakin' o' names, I've run across a few rebs like us here an' there. Some'd changed their names. I'd never do that. I'm not ashamed of m' name." He was mocking again, his voice growing thicker. "Me, th' son of a Mississippi planter? Me, from Mississippi, th' hallowed home of th' immortal Jeff Davis, ol' Flint Face, who led us down that long road of no return. I mus' carry on th' name of Floyd, suh. As for wearin' th' blue-bellied uniform, I remain unbowed." He smiled a crooked smile. "But I won't brag about it either, Jesse, m' Tennessee frien'."

"There's a little matter I want to ask you about," Jesse said. "I saw those rifles when that mule's pack broke open. I thought you said the packs contained supplies for a merchant in Chihuahua City."

Floyd waved a scoffing hand. "Ain't rifles supplies? Sho' they are. I'll tell you all about it when we get there. Never mind."

"But . . ."

With a flippant wave, Floyd turned away and lay down, his back to Jesse. In seconds he was snoring.

Jesse studied him a moment in sympathy, equally amused and skeptical. But as much as Floyd had exaggerated, what he had said was all too true. *Any man who wore the blue is an outcast. Most of all we've lost family. I can never reconcile myself to that. But life goes on.* Quietly, then, he unfolded a blanket and spread it over Floyd. He picked up his carbine and started to stroll the perimeter of the camp. Floyd had organized the defense well. The sentries were posted at regular intervals. The mules were inside, on short picket ropes. A few campfires still glowed like tired eyes. The now-and-then undertone of voices reached him. He smelled tobacco smoke, pleasant on the desert wind, mingled with mule sweat. This was a good camp. Strolling back, he realized that he had been so much a part of war for so long that all this—the sentries, the guarded stock, the night sky, the keen smells, the threat of what morning might bring —fit a familiar pattern, one in which he felt comfortable and competent. *Like a mercenary.* And disliked the thought.

Floyd was still snoring. Jesse gouged hollows in the sand for his

right shoulder and hip, then rolled in the other blanket and lay back
with his hat on, in his ears the steady cropping sounds of the red
horse grazing the sparse desert grass. Hoofs stamped as he hobbled
about on the picket rope. The hustling sounds of a good keeper.
Sounds to sleep on.

Deep into the night a strange sniffing presence stirred Jesse
awake. A cold chill gripped him. On instinct he reached for the
carbine, only to draw his hand back. A long, moon-lit face loomed
over him, still sniffing, so close Jesse could smell the warm, grassy
breath. It was the red horse. Jesse didn't move, filled with surprise
and a kindling curiosity. The horse smelled of the blanket and on to
Jesse's hat brim, where, as if satisfied that all was well, he drew away,
moving awkwardly on the hobbles, and resumed his busy grazing. A
twinge of guilt came over Jesse. *Those damned hobbles; they're hard
on a horse. Maybe I can leave 'em off tomorrow night if he behaves
himself.* Smiling, pleased, he went back to sleep.

When he opened his eyes, Floyd had gone. The sky was a covey
of drifting murky clouds. Daylight was about an hour or less away.
He sat up, taking in the early morning freshness, his mind moving
into familiar channels of concern. What Floyd had said about
Apaches' favorite tactic of attacking at dawn. Yesterday's war party
had suffered heavy losses. Even so, why not think like an Apache?
The pack train would not be expecting another attack so soon. And
there was revenge for the dead warriors. In turn, think like a Mexican or a Johnny Reb pack train commander. Expect the unexpected.

He got up on those likely assumptions. The Spencer in hand and
the cartridge case slung over his left shoulder, he crossed to the
center of camp, sensing more than seeing the vague movements of
the Mexicans, hearing the restless jangle of mule halters. Pausing, he
jerked toward a soft voice at his ear. "Mornin', friend Jesse." A reb
voice that wasn't blurred.

"Where'd you come from?" Jesse whispered.

"Been right here for some time. My eyes are used to the dark.
Couldn't sleep. Got an uneasy feeling. I figure they'll come out of
the east with the sun at their backs. They'll come a-hellin' to make
up for the warriors they lost."

"What can I do?"

"Stay right here. We're on a little rise. Gives us a field of fire,
which we didn't have at Corinth when we tried to take Fort Robi-

nette. I'll be back in a bit." He slipped away, a tall shape dissolving in the shifting murk.

Jesse faced the east. The camp was quieter now. Time always dragged when you waited, not knowing. Time stood locked. He shifted the case and, looking at the sky, saw the first trace of light. *Not yet. Not yet.*

Floyd slipped back, his voice a whisper. "Won't be long now."

The sky was turning the color of a pink rose. Jesse eared back the Spencer's hammer. *Now. Now.*

They charged in a screeching rush out of the desert brush, timed just as the sun blazed through into the eyes of the defenders. Half-naked shapes. Avenging faces streaked with white. Black hair streaming back from headbands. Breechclouts flapping. High leather leggings on flashing feet.

There was a quick splatter of rifle fire along the perimeter. Powdersmoke drifted like down. An Apache dropped. The others rushed on with hellish yells. Jesse fired at the lead Apaches. They raced through the clumps of brush, incredibly fast. Sometimes he glimpsed only heads and shoulders. Beside him Floyd was firing and reloading a muzzle-loader with veteran swiftness, eyeing the line.

"Over there, Jesse—quick!" Floyd yelled, pointing.

A knot of Apaches had appeared suddenly on the right. Jesse emptied the carbine there, and the flanking attempt stalled, drawing the guards' fire as well while the attackers fell back. But as he drew the empty magazine from the buttstock and slid in cartridges from a tube, jabbed the tube back in its case and reinserted the magazine and locked it, he saw the flanking move was only a feint.

A big bunch of Apaches, until now not firing, seemed to leap up from the desert floor like jumping jacks near the center of the line. He switched his fire there. But he was too late. The Apaches had reached the perimeter. Guards' yells mixed with Apache screeches. Jesse could see hand-to-hand fighting. Knives flashing. Rifle butts swinging. Other guards had to hold their fire. He moved to his left, looking for an open shot. It did not come. He started forward, but Floyd's shout checked him. "Wait—wait!" Floyd dropped the muzzle-loader for a handgun. "Get ready—here they come!"

Nothing changed for moments. Just a snarl of struggling bodies a few rods from Jesse. He ventured two shots.

Then they broke through the guards, a wedge of bronze hate, painted faces screaming death, knives high.

Side by side, Jesse and Floyd met the charge. The Spencer snapped empty. No time to reload. Swinging the carbine like a club, Jesse smashed a shrieking face. Metal on bone *thunked*. A knife flashed. Jesse felt a hot ripping down his upper left arm. Whirling, he crashed the Spencer's short barrel across a dodging head of wild black hair and saw the hating obsidian eyes spring wider in shock from the blow and the face with white stripes across the broad nose and flat cheeks fall away. Before he could free himself from the melee, someone tore the Spencer away, an infuriating, intolerable turn. He grabbed for it with both hands, caught, and the two of them tugged and heaved and wrestled. A stalemate. No end to the Apache's strength. A blur of faces and bodies around them until he heard running feet, and, he thought, guards' voices and Floyd's voice. A gunblast bellowed in his ear, and the furious, sweating face before him suddenly dropped back, and the brawny arms loosened, and Jesse found the Spencer his again. He jerked around. It was Floyd, gripping a smoking handgun, and Floyd said, "Reload—be quick. There's still some inside."

He flung away, searching, Jesse reloading as he moved with Floyd. A guard ran up to Floyd, shouting in Spanish, gesturing, exclaiming. Floyd swept his gaze around, hacking for wind, as if uncertain of something. He nodded. "They're finished," he said. "The few we didn't kill when they broke through, either the guards on the other side did or they cut their way clear. Better have a look around, though."

Jesse hadn't seen such devastation in such a short time in years. Two guards were motionless. Survivors were assisting three others. Some eight or ten Apaches lay scattered around the perimeter. Inside lay five more, the high tide of the charge. He and Floyd drew up in the center of the camp, still looking about.

"I'll have to eat crow for when I said back there they wouldn't hit us again," Floyd drawled, sounding worn down, but in high humor that they had survived the attack. "But I can guarantee you for certain this war party has shot its bolt. I'm sho' obliged for your one Spencer. What we couldn't do with ten more, even five! Ever hear such screeching? Like fiends, puts fear in a man. Can paralyze him. Reminds me of our ol' rebel yell, except it's higher, more savage."

Jesse added nothing. He was beginning to feel weak. He touched his upper left arm and his hand came away bloody.

Floyd was saying, "Now the Yank yell was different. It was more like a shout or a hurrah. Deeper—" He stopped and looked at Jesse. "Hell, man, you've been hit!"

"Knife. But I can move my arm." He walked over to his pack, took off his ripped shirt, and sat down, feeling woozy. After pouring tequila on the slash, Floyd handed the bottle to Jesse. "Take a stiff slug." He waved an old Mexican over. They spoke briefly in Spanish. Nodding his understanding, the old man disappeared into the desert and came hurrying back in minutes, grinning broadly, holding several flat, round greenish pieces of something that looked wet.

"Prickly pear," Floyd said. "Makes a good poultice when you cut out the stickers. Keeps the wound clean and pulls it together so it heals. Mexicans learned it from the Apaches. Better than anything we had in the army. This is Pedro. I call 'im Doc."

Pedro cut off the bloody sleeve of Jesse's shirt and used that to bind and tie the pieces of pear into a long poultice.

Leaving the bottle with Jesse, of which he seemed to have an endless supply, Floyd took further stock of the pack train and escort, now down to ten men, Jesse saw, counting the wounded. One man started making a fire. "We've got to have some coffee before we break camp," Floyd said, coming back.

Afterward, their dead buried, their wounded cared for, the Mexicans gathered curiously around Jesse while he cleaned the Spencer. He showed them how it worked, and filled the empty tubes while they watched, and let them handle the gun. Soon Floyd shouted the train into motion. Looking back, Jesse could see buzzards already circling the camp.

Short of sundown they bivouacked around a desert well.

"Suh, would you feel like standing a little sentry duty tonight?" Floyd asked him after supper. "Wouldn't ask, but we're short-handed."

"I'm all right. Sure."

"Would another bottle of tequila help?"

"I've still got most of the bottle you gave me this morning."

Floyd pretended to reproach him. "You're not drinkin' enough. In this country tequila is medicine for a white man. Good for colds and fever. Like the old fellow back home used to say about his daily

shots of bourbon, medicine's no good if you don't take it regular.
. . . You take the first watch then with two others. That way you
can get some sleep. I'll stand with the last detail. Tomorrow Pedro
will fix you another poultice. I'll bunk alongside you tonight. I feel
more comfortable close to that Spencer."

Jesse laughed. "No more than I do." When darkness fell, he took
his turn. The desert night had turned cold. Huddled in his coat, he
strolled back and forth, the carbine cradled in his arms, listening,
watching, seeing little in the filmy gloom beyond the camp's perimeter. What moonlight there was seemed like a spectral mist. . . . A
wounded man groaned. . . . A mule shook its halter. . . . The
red horse, off the hobbles and on picket rope and pin, grazed busily
behind him. He preferred to think that the mustang, with its feral
senses of the wild, filled the role of another sentinel. Its cropping
and occasional stamping and sniffing meant all was well. A loud
snort could mean something wrong. As Jesse paced on, an impression of utter strangeness crept over him, a sort of dull disbelief, that
he should find himself here, still fighting. A desert war this time,
which, he now decided, he should have been wise enough to stay out
of, knowing there was more behind Floyd's offer than mere escort
duty.

He ceased his slow pacing, haunted by an aching loneliness, an
absolute detachment from all that was familiar. In fancy, he could
see his family again. He could hear their happy voices. He could see
the house on the hill. It all seemed like only yesterday. . . . He
made a jerking-away motion. He was thinking too much again, he
was brooding. The low moment passed. He paced on, glad when the
relief sentry came on.

Going back, he approached the red horse, saw him lift his alert
head and become motionless, watching, assessing, trusting nothing,
sniffing the wind, testing it for friend or enemy. *Good.* Jesse drew
closer, murmuring, "Easy . . . easy," and slowly held out his right
hand for the horse to smell. The horse sniffed, yet did not pull away.
Good. You know who I am. We know each other. Still murmuring,
Jesse stroked the blazed face, now the neck, then walked over to his
pack.

Floyd was snoring, rolled in a blanket. Jesse lay down and pulled
up a blanket. Sleep came almost at once, lingering in his ears a
chorus of wailing coyotes singing, high-pitched and drawn-out, the

wild falsetto notes seeming to rise up to the stars, and, finally, the steady meshing of the red horse cropping grass.

He had no inkling they were coming. For sometime now he had been free of them. The long, grueling day had passed without alarm: the monotonous crunch of hooves on sand and rock, before his eyes a never-ending wasteland of mesquite and creosote brush, the sun a great copper plate afire, the undulating desert a sea lapping the distant mountains, everyone watching for what might strike from behind a spiny hummock or when they crossed the stony bed of a deep arroyo. Perhaps they returned because he was weary and his stiff arm, painful at times, made him restless and somewhat feverish.

The night was old when the bad dreams burst upon him, tearing and clawing. Fragments of scenes: In the Shiloh woods wet with dew, birds singing of spring. Everybody aching to fight, to drive the Yankee invaders from Southern soil. The gray lines coming like an avenging tide out of the rose-pink dawn, driving hundreds of rabbits and a few deer before them into the somnolent Yankee camps. John Hanover, Jesse's boyhood friend, going down soon after. . . . Now Franklin. Always fateful Franklin. Franklin at its worst, the bloody fighting around the Carter House. The shouts and yells, the powder-smoke like fog, the constant crack of rifles, the muzzle flashes like angry red eyes. Seeing Jim Lacey and Todd Drake fall, unable to help them. And, as always, the rebs unable to drive the Federal soldiers to the river. And then, as always, the pain and darkness enveloping him. . . . At the sharp angle in the line at Kennesaw Mountain. Firing from beneath head logs at the charging blue waves. The woods catching fire, burning the wounded. The broiling Georgia sun. Confederate dead and wounded stacked in the trench. Jesse wet with blood and sweat. Parched tongue cracked for water. His face black with powder and smoke. . . . Still, the brave young Yankees came on, like wooden men, it seemed, until Jesse sickened of killing them. Like shooting stock in a pen. A boy's face stood out before him, so young, so cool in the face of certain death. A boy hardly younger than Jesse himself. His slim face coming nearer and nearer. Jesse lowered his rifle, raised it, lowered it again. He could fire no more. Still, the boy marched on, miraculously unhurt while others dropped around him, bayoneted rifle at the ready. He seemed to lean against the hail of lead. His blue eyes wide and staring. A wooden boy soldier.

Faster than thought, Jesse sprang to the top log and yelled, "Go back—go back!"

He remembered no more; he saw the face no more.

A distant voice broke in. "You all right, Jesse?"

Why, that was little Willie Reed calling to him in the dead of night. Poor, brave Willie Reed. Calling from the lower bunk in the prison barracks. Jesse knew it was the barracks because he could smell the stale blankets and sweat and woodsmoke.

"Jesse, you all right?"

Jesse struggled up, sweating and cold. His head cleared. A hand touched him, and Cullen Floyd's voice said, "What's the matter? You were yelling."

"Bad dreams is all."

"Go back to sleep. I was just gettin' ready to stand guard."

Jesse lay back, exhausted in mind and body, thankful for clarity and his red horse nearby and the star-decked sky above. After a while he fell into deep sleep.

7

The night must have glided by swiftly, Jesse thought, because when he opened his eyes the early light was strong and the camp was stirring, and although he had slept as if drugged after the nightmares, he still felt wrung and drained, low in spirit. Floyd stood over him, grinning like a mischievous boy. "You slept like a log. Reckon you needed it after yesterday. You have them bad dreams often?"

"Not often, thank God." Jesse put on a wan smile. "Guess it's my conscience after me."

Floyd's carefree face sobered. "It's the war, ol' Flint Face's war. It'll haunt us all our lives. It's marked us forever. We can't forget it, yet we can't go home." He flung up a dismissing hand, and his easy nature took over. "Let's have breakfast together. I insist that you dine with me, suh, as my honored guest." He bowed mockingly from the waist. "Mistuh Jesse Wilder, late of Tennessee, the man with the seven-shot Spencer, and who knows how to use it."

Jesse pushed up, feeling the usual stiffness from sleeping on the ground. Floyd gave him a hand to his feet. "In turn, I am honored to accept your gracious invitation, Mistuh Floyd, suh," Jesse said, going along with the jesting. As if his lighthearted nature could not be suppressed for long, Floyd could swing from the painful past to nonsense in a moment, a relieving quality in a camp undergoing the stress of fighting. It was an infectious thing, Jesse had found. He forced a grin. "Perhaps I should inform you that my middle monicker is Alden, of the South Carolina Aldens, no less, who conducted themselves so nobly, leaving behind a string of brokenhearted girls, a good many disgraced with child, and mounds of debts from betting on horses that ran faster in the morning than they did in the afternoon."

Floyd assumed an abject expression. "A thousand thanks, suh. A most unfortunate breach of etiquette it would be to overlook the noble name of Alden." He made a sweeping gesture. "Now for the tempting viands of the incomparable Doc Pedro, who also serves as my cook. His main forte is chilis hot enough to clean out a gun barrel. Now go with God to the festive board, Jesse Alden Wilder, and keep your canteen handy."

As a prelude to breakfast, Floyd brought out the inevitable tequila. It helped this morning. After a breakfast of chilis with red beans and tortillas, Pedro cut more prickly pear and changed the poultice, nodding as he did so, and talking to Floyd.

"He says your arm looks good," Floyd explained.

"Tell him I'm grateful, but I guess he can see that in my face."

As the pack train strung out, Jesse observed that the escort had lost about one-third of its original force. Closing up the column, Floyd sent out the usual flankers. "You can never afford to be lax at anyplace, anytime in Chihuahua," he told Jesse. "We should be beyond the reach of Apache war parties by now, but as we go on we get into *bandido* country. Trade one for the other."

"How can you tell?"

"Bandits hang around the villages. That way they can see what's passin' through. Sometimes they keep a lookout posted in the villages to tip off an outfit in the desert."

"Were you attacked on the way up?"

"No, because they could see we carried nothing of value and were well-armed. Why fight for nothing of value?"

"Mules are valuable."

"Most of the mules I bought in El Paso."

Jesse reflected in silence for a time. "Seems to me the people wouldn't want bandits making their village a base for preying on pack trains and travelers."

"Money buys anything in Mexico. Guess it does most places, for that matter. Bandits spend money in the villages. In the stores, in the cantinas. They give to the poor, and believe me there's a passel of poor people in Mexico. Local officials also share. It's called *la mordida*—the bite, or bribe. If some high government officer from Chihuahua City rides in on the prod, questions the local *alcalde* about complaints received of bandits operating in the area, the *alcalde* just shrugs." He struck a beseeching pose. " 'My village is very poor, Your Excellency, as you well know and can see with your eyes of compassion. There are few men who can fight. We would catch these bad hombres if we could. We would crush them! But life is hard. Sometimes the people go hungry. The heathen Apaches kill us and take from us. Always they come. You understand, of course. We are honored by your presence in our poor village, Your Excellency.' "

He bowed, low in the saddle.

"I believe you've summed it up," Jesse said, smiling.

"It's a way of life," Floyd added thoughtfully. "A way of existence in a hard land. It's never easy."

Trotting along at a good cavalry gait of about four miles an hour, the wiry pack mules covered the arid stretches with unwavering steadiness. By noon the out-scatter of a little sunbaked village came in sight. From a distance nothing seemed to move there. But as the train entered the outskirts, the place seemed to come alive. Curious faces appeared at windows. Dogs ran out barking. Barefoot children watched shyly from doorways, their dark eyes like smoking coals. When Jesse smiled at them, they smiled back. A man came to the door of a cantina, his eyes settling on the loaded mules.

While the train stopped at a well in the plaza, Floyd said to Jesse, "Come with me to the police station. See what the *jefe* can tell us about *bandidos.*" He pulled a bottle of gold-colored tequila from a pack. *"La mordida,"* he grinned.

"You know the chief?" Jesse asked as they headed up a dusty side street.

"Enough to bring him a bottle now and then. So far he's been reliable. Never had any trouble around here. On the other hand, there's always a first time—our packs look heavy."

They entered a one-story adobe building and Floyd spoke to a young Mexican behind a desk. A jail cell held two dejected prisoners. Nodding courteously in reply, the Mexican went to a room, came out after a moment, and waved them in.

The *jefe* rose at once from a desk. *"Señor* Floyd." He shook hands, then with Jesse when Floyd introduced him. He bowed them to chairs. A man of considerable bulk dressed in a high-collared dark green jacket, the *jefe* beamed cordiality and dignity. Black mustaches drooped over full lips. Bold black eyes looked out from a high-boned face. "What . . . brings you . . . to my humble station?" he asked, his speech slow and carefully chosen.

"Salud, Señor Jefe," Floyd began, his liquid Southern voice perfectly courteous. "We are only too happy to reach the refuge of your

well-protected village, safe from the heathen Apaches." At the same time, his graciousness devoid of the slightest pretension, he placed the bottle of tequila on the desk to the right of the chief.

The *jefe* acknowledged the gift with a decorous nod. "You have been attacked. I regret to hear that."

"Not once, but twice after leaving Paso del Norte. Our pack train lost some men, but we managed to fight them off. There'll be much wailing when what's left of that war party staggers into the home *rancheria.*"

The *jefe* smiled from the teeth. "I have not heard such good news in months." He spoke with less preciseness now, as if, Jesse thought, assured that this *Yanqui* would make no burdensome request. "Unfortunately, Apaches are like fleas on a dog. There are always more. Mexico is a resource for them. We furnish part of their living. They do not kill us all or take everything. That way there is always something to take the next time." He spread his hands in resignation. "Perhaps when Juárez regains what is rightfully his, there will be adequate protection for all the northern villages. Not just from the heathen Apaches, but from the marauding *bandidos* as well. . . . Is there news of our courageous *presidente* in Paso del Norte?"

"Just rumors," Floyd said. "But good rumors. That the *presidente* is gaining strength and before long the French will be driven out of the country."

The *jefe* smiled forlornly. "Rumor or dream. There is little difference. But we all know Maximilian still holds Mexico City, and his garrisons still hold strong points north of there." He seemed to remember his official position suddenly and straightened, speaking in a conferring tone. "You are welcome to rest your pack train in our village. Our people are poor, but hospitable."

"*Gracias, Señor Jefe.* We're all right. But we must go on today. I came here to ask you about bandits. Have you been bothered? Is there a band operating along the trail south? We've seen none to the north." He made a wry face. "Only the heathen Apaches."

The *jefe* balled his right fist and shook it. "Vah! Those slinking coyotes know better than to come around here. We are poor and not many, but we are brave. We shoot straight. We would drive them back into the desert. Their bones would bleach in the sun." Smiling inwardly, yet understanding, Jesse thought of Floyd's impersonation of the imaginary *alcalde*. Either the *jefe* was a very good actor or tough as nails; maybe both, for this was a harsh land and a poor village such as this would need leadership. "So there is little I can tell you, *Señor* Floyd," the *jefe* continued. "No attacks have been reported to me. I would say that is good news. Few riders have come through lately. Yours is the first pack train in weeks." He looked down sadly. "Our country is torn up. Commerce is at a standstill. Will be until the *presidente* kicks out that son of a goat Maximilian, hiding in Mexico City. That is all I can tell you, except to be on guard as usual." He smiled then, his teeth like piano keys. The interview was over.

Nodding thanks, Floyd rose and Jesse trailed him outside. Going down the narrow street, Floyd murmured aside, "In Mexico style is more important than results, sometimes. Even so, style gives people hope. Makes the present seem better than it is."

"You've become a philosopher," Jesse said.

"More like a sho' 'nough cynic or a realist. Mexico has been a good teacher to me. If there's one thing a Mexican peasant has learned, it's to appreciate damned little. A slave back on the Mississippi Delta had more than some of these Indians or mixed-blood *mestizos* have on the haciendas. They're slaves, too, in a way. If they revolt, they get shot. The big haciendas have their own little armies, you know. If they don't get shot, they can end up in Yucatán labor gangs . . . and they don't come back."

"Can Juárez change that?"

"Will if he has time. He's already separated church and state. Before he was elected, I understand the church owned one-third of all the land. He broke that up. When he did, hell popped."

"What about land for the peasants?"

"If an Indian owns a little piece, the haciendas are after that, too. It's unfair as hell."

"Now you've become my teacher, Cullen."

Floyd waved the pack train forward and set out at a fast trot. After a few miles, beyond sight of the village, he led off into scattered mesquite and ordered camp. When Jesse looked at him in surprise, he said, "From here on we lay up durin' the day and travel at night. Post guards, of course."

Desert sunlight struck with a dazzling glare, piercing the eyes. Jesse unsaddled, picketed the red horse, fed him corn in a nose bag, and got under a mesquite, its scant shade offering some relief. Head propped on the seat of his saddle, idly watching his horse, he let his thoughts roam. As much as he liked the man, Cullen had not been entirely honest with him, shrugging off the question of the "supplies." Meanwhile, the attacks and the strain of being on constant alert had put off further talk. Too, Jesse had let the matter drift. He decided he would force the issue before they reached Chihuahua City. Beyond that, if he did not, he might find himself in a Mexican jail.

As the sun marched on past late afternoon, little supper fires began licking the fading light. Jesse cooked his lean rations, smoked, saddled up, and waited. Shadows purpled the desert floor when Floyd assembled the train and the mules struck out for the trail, behind them the winking eyes of the cooking fires.

"Think that will fool some wily bandit band?" Floyd said, looking back.

"If anybody's watching us, it should hold 'em till daylight," Jesse said. "And night travel will be easier on the stock. Question is, will it fool 'em twice running when they find an empty camp in the morning? What about the next day?"

"You would bring that up, suh. One reason why I never made general. I did get up to second lieutenant, though. Twice. Each time I got busted for nippin' on duty."

"A damn poor reason, when General Beauregard wasn't demoted after Shiloh for h'istin' the jug, I've heard said. Another Southern excuse for not pushin' Grant into the Tennessee River. And if Albert Sidney Johnston hadn't got himself killed early in the battle, the South would've won for certain. Another *if*. We rebs are famous for our *ifs*."

"You're makin' me feel better all the time, Jesse. At least I avoided what happened to General Van Dorn. I only got captured when I went callin'."

"How's that?"

"It happened after the big bonfire at Holly Springs I told you about. The general wanted to celebrate the victory, they say, so he visited a pretty lady at Spring Hill. I figure it was around midnight or so. And what happens but the lady's husband, a plumb inconsiderate cuss, comes home unexpected and blows the general's brains out."

"In the bedroom?"

"Oh, suh, us Southerners couldn't possibly stoop to such an assumption. Unthinkable even to discuss it. It wouldn't be honorable, suh. A lady's name is involved. A general's reputation as an officer and a gentleman, suh. And think of our pride as Southerners, Mistuh Jesse Alden Wilder. Think of our pride."

"Honor and pride," Jesse said, in a dry voice of amusement. "Together they've killed more Southerners than anything. Poor General Van Dorn. We could've used him later in the Army of Tennessee, before Hood played hell at Franklin."

"Another *if*, Jesse, if the lady's husband hadn't come home just then."

Jesse dropped back to take the rear guard. Glancing now and then at the starry sky and the dark shapes of the pack train bobbing ahead of him, he had the obscure feeling of traveling through an unreal world. The centuries-old road before him sugar-white in the half light. The brush on both sides like crouching forms. In his ears the squeal of saddle leather and the constant beat of the red horse's hooves on the hard-packed earth like a pulse. A land of sharp contrasts. Scorching daytime heat. At night, like now, a chilling wind rising off the desert floor, bringing little flecks of sand. He raised his coat collar.

The miles fell away. The night seemed to loiter. He caught himself dozing and jerked upright. He had fallen behind the pack train, which he could no longer see, but it could not be far. Going on, he was fully awake now. The hours slipped by. He felt a growling hunger.

The night was old, the first hint of coming light in the flawless sky, like a faint brush stroke, when he noticed a change in the way the red horse, so steady all night, was traveling. A little farther on, the difference was more pronounced. Hell, his horse was limping. In alarm, he pulled rein and dismounted at once. "Huh . . . huh," he said as the horse danced sideward, then stopped. Jesse led him on a short way, staring hard. It was the left foreleg.

He pulled up the foot by the fetlock and felt inside and around the shoe, finding nothing wrong. Again, more slowly and carefully. This time his fingers touched a rough edge. There it was—a sliver of rock under the front end of the shoe. With thumb and forefinger he tried to pull it out; it wouldn't budge. He tried again; no luck. He could see faintly better now. Taking a pocketknife, he dug at the rock as the horse grew restive. It came loose with a *snick.*

He swung to mount and the horse, eager to go, was moving when Jesse reached the saddle. As he did, an intrusion clawed at his senses, a wrongness. It came from behind him, back down the road. A faint shuffling, growing louder by the second. Horses. Many horses or mules. He looked and saw only the chalky stretch of the road at first, but way back there he could see a dark mass, and it was moving.

He hesitated no longer and heeled the horse off the road, into the thick brush, and reined about, head cocked, listening. The steady shuffling swelled to a drumming. Very close now. His horse stirred nervously. At that Jesse dismounted and held his left hand over the wide nostrils, ready to shut off a nicker.

Mixed with the sound of hoofbeats, the squeak of leather, and the jingle of spurs, he heard voices approaching. Spanish voices. Just a few words. Nothing distinct. He waited, afraid his horse might make a racket in the brush.

They loomed before him then, a body of horsemen kicking up gray dust. He could make out a face or two now. Dingy light shone on gun barrels. Twenty riders or more. Maybe thirty. No pack train. Just riders on the prod.

When they had passed, he led the horse back until he couldn't hear the others, mounted and kicked out in a run parallel to the road. The horse dodged a mesquite, nearly throwing Jesse, who grabbed the saddle horn and hung on. The little horse straightened out, running hard. They tore through a stand of low-growing catclaw that tore at them, the horse getting the worst of it. They came to a narrow wash, a discernible white in the dim light. The horse jumped it without breaking stride, dodging hummocks, mesquite, and stately yuccas. Jesse let him go on his own so long as he stayed on course, because the horse could see better than he could.

He started figuring distances. Another stretch, a hundred yards or so, and they could cut back to the road. They covered that in a rush. Angling, he headed them back, still at a run. Suddenly the road opened before him. At its edge he pulled up hard, the horse still eager to run, fighting the bit, and looked up and down the road before he rode out on it. Nothing moved back there yet. But they had to be close and the light was coming stronger. He eased the horse forward and gradually let him out into a run for the pack train.

He found the mules trotting along placidly, guards trailing on each side. Floyd was up ahead. He turned with a yawn as Jesse raced up. "Just about time for breakfast, suh."

"Breakfast, hell, Cullen! There's riders a few hundred yards down the road, and they're comin' fast. Take cover!"

"Riders?" Floyd sounded incredulous.

"A big bunch. All armed for bear. No pack animals. Come on!"

"Bandits?" Floyd's sleepy tone was still a little skeptical.

"For certain we'll find out soon enough. Better get a move on!"

Floyd gave an order and led off into the brush. Within a minute or two the mules were bunched and tied, the red horse with them, and the guards posted along both sides of the road in ambush.

"I've passed word for the boys not to fire till I do," Floyd said, and added with mocking concern, "Don't want to shoot any pilgrims on the way to church."

"Don't think we'll have to worry about that with this bunch."

Time seemed to hang. Off in the brush hooves stamped. There was the *tink* of halter metal. The light was breaking faster now, yet the road was still empty. It occurred to Jesse that more ground must have been covered than he'd figured on that circling run. Tonight that punishing dash by a damn good horse had given the pack train vital time.

Watching, Jesse saw the formless murk down the road change just as the sky shifted from dark gray to a pinkish rose. A black wedge materialized, raising little puffs of dust. Riders coming at a cautious but steady trot, slower than when Jesse had watched them pass. He could see heads turning, eyeing the brush on both sides of the road. In this light more riders than Jesse had guessed earlier from the brush. Mounted on good horses, too. Rifles at the ready. All big sombreros. Not a single uniform in the bunch that Jesse could see. A rider moved ahead like an advance scout. Jesse checked the Spencer. Trouble was coming.

They came on boldly, the scuffing sound of their horses a rising beat. The lead rider flung a nervous glance at the changing sky and reined slower, eyes digging at the brush. But the guards were hunkered down, well-hidden.

Floyd, beside Jesse, raised his Enfield and eared back the hammer, holding. At that very instant, as if timed, a mule brayed, a hoarse honking as shattering in the stillness as a bugle call. Jesse winced and lifted the carbine.

Startled, the lead rider wheeled in the direction of the braying and fired his rifle.

Floyd blasted away a fraction of time later. The rider reeled sideways as if from a heavy blow and fell from the saddle. His horse bolted straight ahead.

The mass of riders charged to their right, toward the sound of the unbroken braying. Unwittingly, they gave the pack train guards on their left a flanking fire. Rifles crashed and smoke puffed. Riders and horses went down in a tangle, but the charge didn't pause.

Jesse, firing into the pack, saw the bandits break through the train's thin line, leaping their horses over the guards, shooting as they went. They tore for the mules. Jesse and Floyd ran across the road, with them the guards on that side. Muzzle-loaders roared. Saddles emptied. Jesse could see riders tugging and cutting at the mules' halter ropes. In the smoky confusion there, he couldn't spot his horse. His Spencer was empty.

He'd just reloaded when Floyd yelled and pointed, "Quick—Jesse—they're gettin' away!"

Jerking that way, Jesse saw two riders leading balky mules. The range was almost point blank. His carbine banged twice, Jesse feeling the solid jump of the recoil. The riders swayed, let go the ropes, slumping over their saddles, and the mules ran away.

By now Floyd and the guards had reloaded. They poured a volley into the riders. Big gaps appeared. Jesse kept firing while the others reloaded. It was too much. All of a sudden the riders broke, singly, in pairs, scattering, tearing off through the brush.

It was over. Globs of dirty white powdersmoke drifted like cotton balls.

Jesse slid in more cartridges, tasting the bitter smoke, his ears ringing. For a bit nobody around him moved. In the distance he could hear horses going off, circling, it sounded like, back toward the road. It was almost full daylight now. He was beginning to feel a familiar after-battle letdown. Floyd's voice, dry and hollowed-out, reached him. "Guess we'd better look about, Jesse."

Together they walked over to the pack train. Some of the mules had been cut loose, Jesse remembered. They'd have to hunt for them.

He started looking for his horse, concerned that he wouldn't find him, that he might never see him again. Scouting beyond the mules, he noticed movement behind a mesquite. A mule? Before that answer came, he caught a glimpse of blood-red hide. Circling, to come in behind, he saw his horse turned watching him, head up, with that wild alertness he would always have because it was bred in him, the dark eyes warily judging. The knotted reins dragged, still wrapped around the branch of mesquite he'd been tied to when he broke away during the wild shooting. Jesse frowned when he saw the dash through the catclaw had left long slashes on the forequarters.

"Huh . . ." Jesse said softly. "Huh . . ." thinking, *You had your chance. You could have run away and been free again forever, but you didn't. Why, red hoss? Why?* But the horse was not quite his yet. Slowly, he approached the vigilant face, the keen eyes taking in every move of Jesse's body. An arm's length away, Jesse paused. "Huh . . . huh." He stood motionless for a suspended moment. Another long breath and he held out his hand. The horse snuffled, but did not shy away. Whereupon, Jesse took hold of the reins. As he did, the horse danced sideward, then stopped. Jesse smiled. *You've got to get in that reminder of what used to be, haven't you?* On that, the reins in hand, Jesse removed the branch and stepped to his pack, took shelled corn from a sack, and held out a cupped handful. The red horse ate greedily. When every grain was gone, Jesse led him back to the mules.

Floyd and Doc Pedro were waiting. "Want you to see something," Floyd said, and touched a bandit body with the toe of one boot. Black leather britches and jacket trimmed in silver. Drooping black mustaches. The eyes still bold.

"The *jefe*," Floyd said. "Reckon I sho' wasted a bottle of good tequila." He still had time for a touch of morning mockery. Shrugging, he spread his hands. "So it goes."

The cries of the wounded made Jesse think of other fields. Doc Pedro got busy with the few of his own. For a change, there would be no burials. The wounded bandits he left for the wolves. A half hour's search produced the missing mules, after which Floyd formed the pack train at once.

"One more attack like this," he told Jesse as they moved out on the road, "and we won't have enough whole men left to get in on. I've pretty much guessed wrong all along on this trip." His expression turned scoffing. "I wonder if this is catchin'? If I got it from certain Confederate generals who never guessed right even once in four years? I said the Apaches wouldn't hit us a second time and they did."

"But you were ready when they did," Jesse said.

"A lucky late hunch. And I thought night travel would keep us out of other trouble. It didn't. This morning we got lucky again. If they'd hit just at breakfast, we'd've been wiped out."

"But they didn't," Jesse emphasized.

"Because we had a rear guard on a fast horse, and this rear guard totes a Spencer carbine. What do you think, Jesse?" Floyd was dead serious now. "How should we proceed here-on?"

"I'd prefer daytime marching. Early bivouac. Night sentries. Early departure. On the trail by daybreak."

"Sounds good. We'll do that."

It was Jesse's turn for ridicule. "Which is how we started out from Paso del Norte."

Floyd threw up his hands. "Leastwise, I ain't ordered any damn-fool massed infantry charges across an open field against entrenched Yankees with repeatin' rifles."

"Amen, Cullen."

Late in the morning they passed through a dusty little town and that evening spread an early bivouac near a brackish lagoon. Soon after supper Floyd ambled over with the usual bottle of tequila. "Well, suh," he said expansively, seating himself, "in a couple of days we'll be in Chihuahua City, the queen city of all Chihuahua. Where the women are noted for their beauty and . . . uh . . . for their hospitality to . . . uh . . . weary *gringos.*"

"Now that's interesting to know," Jesse said dubiously.

They talked for a while about the reduced strength of the escort and the condition of the mules, where they would find water tomorrow, and passed the bottle, and then Jesse came to the point. "Look, Cullen, we're good friends, but I want you to know now that I have no hankerin' to get involved in another war. Don't have to remind you that we've just been through one. Two attacks by fanatic Apaches and that cavalry charge by the *bandidos* would be classed as more than a skirmish. And you call this escort duty?"

Floyd, taking another tipple, cleared his throat. "That's escort duty in Chihuahua, my friend. You can't say I promised you a ride through the countryside, pickin' daisies on the way."

"Didn't expect that. But when you pay me off, I'll head right back for El Paso. I mean if we get to Chihuahua City alive."

"I understand, but I wish you wouldn't. We could have some times, believe me."

Jesse had another pull on the bottle. "Why are you in this, Cullen? Runnin' guns and riskin' your life for your so-called merchant friend?"

"A true Southerner, suh, who no longer has a passel o' lovin' darkies around to wait on 'im hand an' foot, obeyin' ever' little bitty whim—fetch me this an' fetch me that—is faced at last with how to make a little ol' livin' for his own self. Y'know, the need for corn fritters an' fatback an' such. Ah, I can taste 'em now. A feast for th' gods. All fixed by my dear ol' mammy." His self-belittlement was truly flowing tonight, Jesse saw.

"I had in mind something more favorable to your health," Jesse said. "Maybe work on a ranch. Or something in El Paso."

"Like enlist at Fort Bliss an' wear th' blue-bellied uniform again?"

"You know I don't mean that."

"What do you mean exactly?" Floyd's voice had lost its bantering tone.

"Something more long-lasting. This is war all over again."

"It's a livin'."

"A damned precarious one."

Suddenly a wall of tension seemed to spring up between them. Jesse curbed himself, mentally backing away.

"Don't preach at me, Jesse." Floyd stood, weaving a little, clutching the bottle like a torch.

"I'm not. I just want you to stay alive—that's all."

Floyd took a drink and ran a sleeve across his mouth. "The ol' survival thing, eh? Like gittin' out o' Yankee prison camp? Like servin' out West? Gawd, how I hate the word! Makes me sick in my guts." He stared unseeingly at the ground, then whipped about with a canny look. "You said find somethin' in El Paso. Did *you*, Mistuh Jesse Alden Wilder?"

"I didn't. I didn't have to look. A Mississippi gent offered me a job ridin' escort." He attempted to shrug it off with a lame grin, but could see that Floyd wasn't going to let it end there.

"Hell, no, you didn't look! You snapped up my offer like that." Awkwardly, Floyd tried to snap his fingers, but misfired. "You did because there was nothin' else in a border town for an ex-Johnny Reb. All we know is shootin' an' killin'. We're goddamned good at it, too. Best in th' world. Look at th' practice we've had. . . . You can play a tune with that Spencer . . . like an angel plays a harp." He appeared to find wry amusement in the comparison, but the expression faded almost as it formed. He helped himself to the bottle again, bungled the drink, and tequila ran down his beard. "Tell you somethin' else, Mr. Preacher Man, Mr. High an' Mighty. These guns are bound for the Juáristas. The Johnny Rebs of Mexico. My kind o' folks, the Juáristas. The only folks I've got anymore." He faced away from Jesse, and in that one moment Jesse saw that he was crying. Holding the bottle high in mock celebration, Floyd staggered off into the night.

Jesse watched until the darkness swallowed Floyd, watched with a sad understanding, and without anger. *He's got his demons and I've got mine. . . . I had no right to lecture him, but I want him out of this bloody dead end.*

He waited till the last coals burned out before he went to his blankets. There he watched the stars glitter for a long time, his only comfort the contented sound of his picketed horse grazing. Later Jesse heard the horse come quietly over and smell of the blankets and then of him and then leave as quietly, the ritual ended. Much later, Jesse heard the horse lie down, his sentry work done for the night. After that Jesse slept.

The pack train was slow getting started in the morning. Floyd never glanced Jesse's way once during breakfast and saddling up. After the mules were formed and single flankers sent out, the outfit down to that now, Floyd rode to the head of the column and at last they were moving. Jesse joined Floyd as usual.

They had gone but a short way when Floyd turned to him and said, "I owe you a big apology, Jesse, and I do so now."

"Forget it. No apology is expected or necessary."

"I'm sorry as hell. I said things I didn't mean."

"I did preach at you a little. I'm sorry, too, Cullen."

"You're like a brother to me, Jesse."

"I understand that sometimes brothers disagree," Jesse said, and punched him playfully on the shoulder. He wanted to say more, but he didn't quite know how, so he said nothing.

They shook hands and rode on.

A light rain began to fall, freshening the stock. Jesse unrolled his rubber poncho and donned it, slipping his head through the slit in the middle. When the shower passed after half an hour or so, and the sun came out like a great golden ornament, stirring a wave of sweet scents, the pack train seemed to travel through a jeweled land of dazzling light. To Jesse it was a wonderful day in more ways than one.

Well into the afternoon Jesse saw a group of horsemen drawn across the road several hundred yards ahead. Thinking of bandits, he told Floyd, "Looks like trouble, though I wouldn't think they'd be so open about it with that small a force. Unless they're bait."

After a careful look, Floyd said, "It's all right. I see our flankers. There's a parley goin' on. Now you'll get to meet my Juárista friend. I reckon plans have been changed, else they wouldn't come out to intercept us this far north of Chihuahua City. Come on!" He broke his mount into a gallop.

8

The riders were dressed in peasant white. A few carried rifles, the rest machetes. In their center sat a bearded man of slight build on a brown mule. Instead of a huge straw sombrero, like the others wore, he favored a small gray hat. Floyd shook hands with him, their greetings manifestly warm.

"Father Alberto," Floyd then said, "this is my good friend and compatriot, Captain Jesse Wilder, late of the Southern Confederacy's Army of Tennessee. For certain he helped us get here. Two Apache attacks, one by bandits."

Alberto put out a quick hand, and Jesse, looking into the dark brown face of finely chiseled bones, found a mixture of friendliness and a keen appraisal.

"I am honored and happy indeed to meet you, Captain." He had a beautiful speaking voice, genteel and musical in tone. A man of hidden years, Jesse judged. Forty, fifty?

For an instant Jesse was unsure how to respond. "Pleased to meet you . . . Father."

"I see surprise in your eyes, Captain. Perhaps you expected to meet a fierce guerrilla chieftain with a proud mustache, two bandoliers across his broad chest, two huge pistols, and riding a prancing Arabian stallion purloined from some wealthy *hacendado?*"

Jesse had to smile at the descripton, which wasn't far off. "Maybe something like that."

Now Alberto smiled, a truly magnificent, perfect flash of white. "This is no time for false impressions. Instead, the person you see is one humble Alberto Garza, an unfrocked priest who still loves his church, but loves his poor country as much, sometimes more."

A horse was coming from the south at a pounding run. Everybody swung around. The horse shot into view, running all-out, the rider quirting and glancing over his shoulder. He was shouting in Spanish as he rushed up.

"A French scouting company of mercenary Hussars," Garza said quickly for Jesse's benefit. "We barely beat them at that." To Cullen, "We can't let them take what you all no doubt paid dearly to bring to us. You know where to go into the sierra. The old camp. We'll serve as your rear guard." He turned his mule to the west.

The trotting mule train was still at least two hundred yards distant. Swinging his hat, Floyd pointed the lead riders westward. A brief pause, and the guards cut away, waving those behind to come on.

Looking south down the road, Jesse caught the solid movement of cavalry. Sunlight on steel. He nodded to Floyd, and they reined back into the brush. But shouts told them they had been discovered. A bugle sounded. Around them Garza's men spread out like a fan as they retreated. To their right, the pack train was angling in, loads flapping, the escort lashing the mules. On the road Jesse could hear horses running. Very close now. He pulled the Spencer from the leather sheath and brought the red horse around.

Clattering, the Hussars bulged suddenly on the road, appeared to reform, and at a command came charging into the brush. Helmeted men in brilliant uniforms, on big stout horses. Floyd's Enfield blasted just as they wheeled together, maintaining a perfect front, four abreast, sabers out. Jesse fired and kept firing, hearing Garza's few riflemen joining in. Floyd held a handgun at arm's length, composedly picking targets. The leading four of the Hussars broke down, now the next oncoming four, either swept from saddles or, sorely wounded, vainly trying to hang on. Loose horses bolted.

All at once the charge checked abruptly. It became a confusion of onrushing cavalrymen from the rear colliding with the smashed front fours. Shouted commands rose. There was a pulling back to the road and along the road. Watching, sensing, Jesse reloaded. *With sabers. They didn't expect a bunch of poor Indians to stop and fight. They thought they'd cut 'em down. Just like the tactics book says.* An unexpected elation surged through him.

Several of the machete-armed Mexicans ran forward, picking up sabers, snatching side arms and sheathed carbines. One wounded Hussar resisted. A merciless machete chopped down.

But it was no time to linger. Jesse turned with the others, riding fast. Before long they came upon the pack train.

The afternoon was fading into early twilight when Father Garza, in the lead, rode to the mouth of a wooded canyon, halted, and raised his voice, calling. Nothing stirred for a minute or so, until two riflemen suddenly appeared as if dropped from the sky. They waved, everybody waved, and the Father led away into the narrow canyon, which swallowed the column in moments.

They followed a well-beaten trail, Jesse saw, that twisted and rose. Only a few riflemen posted at the mouth of the canyon could stand off a large force. In a while he began to smell junipers and piñons. Climbing, always climbing, he felt a rush of cool air. On the singing wind, he smelled ponderosa pines. By and by they entered a parklike area that rolled gently away under the tall pines. Over there the indolent voice of a rushing stream. Pungent woodsmoke flavored the keen high-country air.

Jesse turned in surprise at an approaching swell of voices. Men, women, and children streaming in greeting from the forest. Dogs barking. This an armed camp? They reached for the Father's hand, beaming, exclaiming, touching, some beseeching, it seemed, and he touched their hands and spoke to them.

Jesse stepped down from the saddle at the stream and let the red horse wade in and drink, himself beside his horse on hands and knees, mouth buried in the cold water. Filled, he scrubbed face and hands and hair, removed coat and shirt, and scrubbed some more. Freshened, he found Floyd close by, saying, "What say, suh, we bivouac together tonight? We can rest easy for a change. The *padre*'s got this place guarded tighter'n the cob stopper on a planter's jug of Kentucky sour mash. And supper, too?"

"Good. And I'll bring what I've got. But tell Doc Pedro to go easy on the chilis. I've got a cast-iron stomach, but it can take just so much fire."

"Why, I'm surprised at you, Jesse. In time, you'll get to where you cry for chilis the way a little kid begs for candy."

Jesse unsaddled and fed the red horse shelled corn, now in short supply, and picketed him. Afterward he and Floyd sampled the latter's apparently exhaustless supply of tequila, ate a fiery supper, and sat around a leaping piny fire.

"What do you think of Father Alberto?" Floyd asked.

"He's a leader. I like him. I'm impressed. I saw everybody come out to greet him. It was moving . . . their voices . . . their faces."

"Guess you kinda sensed what they were saying?"

"Some seemed to be pleading for something."

"Yeah. They were saying, 'Father . . . help . . . us. Father . . . save . . . us.' "

"And what did he tell them?"

"He gave them his blessings and said, 'The Lord will provide in his own time. . . . Be patient. . . . Meanwhile, be brave and fight for your country against the invaders. Remember your rightful president, Benito Juárez.' "

"I can see he's a gentle man."

"True. But behind that gentleness . . . which I know is sincere . . . there's the white heat of a genuine patriot. He's tough. By the way, I know you were surprised when he spoke such perfect English."

"I was. Speaks like an educated man."

"He joined the priesthood to get an education. The only way a poor Indian or *mestizo* or creole can. He's a Zapotec Indian, same as Juárez, though he grew up in Sonora. Not a drop of Spanish blood in him. Attended the Colegio de San Nicolas, one of the oldest in the Americas. Was an honor student, hungry for knowledge. Learned to speak five languages, and I mean fluently. Imagine!" He marveled. "There's more I can tell you."

"Then tell me. He is a man."

Floyd passed the bottle. "When Juárez busted up the Church, took over its holdin's, as we say back in Mississippi . . . booted out the archbishop an' the bishops, Alberto joined the cause. He was in the north with Juárez till about a year ago. As a poor parish priest, he'd seen enough fat bishops while people went hungry and tithed. So the Church defrocked him. But he's still a priest. They love him." Pausing as if to collect his thoughts, he seemed to smile at some recollection.

"I'm still listening," Jesse said.

"Well, when Alberto took up arms with Juárez . . . You see, there was a civil war goin' on as different factions, the Church included, tried to seize control of the government. This was before Napoleon the Third brought Maximilian in. . . . Alberto's people wanted to call him General Garza. But he'd have none of that. Said they's too many self-promoted generals and not enough fightin' men. For instance, some guerrilla leader would gather fifty men around 'im and call himself general. Like I told you, they like style in Mexico. So it's plain Father Alberto, my son, my daughter, my child. No fancy uniforms or titles. He's still a humble priest at heart, still a teacher. Hates what he calls the 'Darkness of Ignorance,' which he says leads to poverty. So he teaches the young ones."

"A warrior priest," Jesse suggested.

"But not a violent man at heart. Only in the name of freedom, and when he has to be."

"What's his strength here?"

"Around two-fifty or three hundred, Indians and *mestizos*. Varies. They go home when they choose. Not like when our rebs had to slip off home to put in or take in a crop, else their families'd go hungry. Some men have their families along. Makes for happier *soldados*, you bet. . . . When I say that many men, I don't mean they're all armed. There's not fifty good rifles in camp; half them ancient and some need fixin'. Every man carries a machete, and, believe me, a machete can be mean at close quarters and quicker than a bayonet."

"So Alberto needs arms badly?"

"Anything that will shoot. We'll unpack in the morning. As usual, not enough. Not all good enough. You'll see."

"Where is Juárez?"

"I have no idea. I don't think the *padre* knows. The main thing is to fight the French garrisons, wherever they are. But he can't do much till he gets more to fight with. It's just hit-and-run now."

Jesse yawned, the heavy supper and strong tequila like a drug. "Believe I'll turn in, Cullen."

"Same here. Thanks for helpin' make certain we got here."

"Guess we'd all better thank each other. Good night." He hadn't yet set up the canvas shelter tent, and he didn't tonight. In his blankets, just before he drifted off to sleep, he remembered that he hadn't asked about his pay. And, with some wryness, he recalled further that Floyd hadn't mentioned it. At the moment it seemed of little importance. Tomorrow . . .

He woke up to a mélange of camp sounds: cheerful voices, braying donkeys, the *thunk* of wood being chopped, and the light chirp of children already at play. Somebody was even singing. It was broad daylight, the morning air cool and bracing, sweetened with juniper smoke. He sat up. The obliging Doc Pedro was building a fire. Beyond, women made tortilla dough on stone metates. A happy encampment, even at this hour. Floyd was not in sight.

Rising, Jesse led the red horse to water, drank, and washed his face, led the horse back for morning feed and picketed him on grass. From his provisions sack, he took the little boxlike wooden coffee grinder, in it ground some beans; estimating again, sparingly, he ground some more, enough for three men, filled the cooking can at the stream, set the can on Doc Pedro's fire, and when the water was boiling, poured in the ground coffee, while the Mexican smiled and nodded approval.

Floyd joined them just as breakfast was ready. "I have a keen sense of smell and timing," he said.

"I plan to head back this morning after you unpack the guns," Jesse said, expecting Floyd to bring up the pay. He waited, but nothing was said.

"Just wish you'd wait awhile," Floyd said, and meant it.

"I mean after I get paid," Jesse said, with a crooked grin.

"I'll talk to Father Alberto."

They finished breakfast, drank another cooking can of coffee made from the same grounds, quite weakened by now, but still tasting like coffee, after which Floyd sought out Garza and they started opening the canvas packs before an expectant crowd.

Jesse frowned when he saw more Enfield muzzle-loaders, some old carbines, ranging from Sharps and Burnsides to Ballards, even a few shotguns. *Not enough. Not all good enough.*

With a show of great ceremony, the Father passed out the weapons with supplies of paper cartridges and percussion caps. In turn, the peasants' dark faces glowed with pride and near-reverence as they accepted the old weapons. The issue soon ran out, in all about fifty assorted weapons.

"It was the best I could do with the little money Alberto could wrangle," Floyd said aside to Jesse.

"Wrangle?"

The ghost of a smile played across Floyd's ginger-bearded face. "The *padre* says the Lord always provides some way. Sometimes well-heeled *hacendados* see fit to contribute." His mouth twisted scornfully. "But seldom more than a few grudging 'dobe dollars now and then, some grudging beans and corn, a few stringy beeves, when they have thousands on the range." A glimmer of a smile returned. "Therefore, it is sometimes necessary for the Lord to see that the contribution is added to. . . . We've got to do better than this. Father Alberto saw you handle the Spencer in action and was much impressed, he told me this morning. I said you would be glad to show him all about the gun. How it works."

"Sure."

"I'll get him now."

Father Alberto came in a flurry of loose white, his sandals flapping lightly, right hand extended, smiling warmly. Without his small gray hat, his black hair hanging to his shoulders, his fine, dark features seemed more pronounced, in a way that reminded Jesse of a traveling gypsy he'd seen as a boy.

"*Señor* Jesse, I am much deficient in prompt manners, but not in humble appreciation. I thank you now with all my heart for your brave fight with us against the heathen Apaches and the robber band and the mercenary Hussars. Before long, when the Lord so grants, your pay you will receive, I promise, which I pray will be soon. Now, your repeater gun I should like to see, if you please."

Removing the tubular magazine from the buttstock of the Spencer, Jesse said, "This holds seven rounds. Another cartridge inserted in the chamber, like this, makes it an eight-shot repeater. The trigger guard levered downward opens the breech and ejects the empty cartridge. When raised back, closed, like this, a new cartridge is carried up into the breech. The hammer has to be eared back for each shot. This is a carbine called the Indian Model. Came out in '65. Here, handle it."

He passed it to Garza, who had followed intently each move and explanation Jesse made. The *padre* lifted the weapon up and down, then handed it back quickly, as if wishing to distance himself from its dormant destruction. "It feels strange in my hands. What . . . is its caliber, *Señor* Jesse?"

"This is a .56-50, which means the shell case is .56 with a .50-caliber bullet inside it. The earlier rifles and carbines were .52 caliber. A spring in the magazine keeps the cartridges pushed forward."

The *padre* scowled and chewed his lower lip, visibly projecting in his mind the weapon's use. "You say the magazine holds seven shots. In the heat of battle, a peasant might be inclined to shoot up many rounds, too many. I keep thinking of our short supplies. We are always short of cartridges."

"Men can be trained not to waste ammunition." Next Jesse showed him the cartridge case and the tin refills and, removing the magazine from the buttstock and holding it against the barrel with his left hand, how to slide in the cartridges. "However, Father, I should point out that cartridge cases aren't as common on the frontier as the Spencer rifles and carbines. I bought this one in Fort Leavenworth, Kansas. It's called a Blakeslee Quickloader. Repeaters can change the course of a fight in a short time. Even without the refill tubes, a man can still outshoot a muzzle-loader, though an Enfield muzzle-loader like the ones you have here will outrange a carbine, which is accurate up to around five hundred yards. On the other hand, one Spencer carbine or rifle is the equivalent of five muzzle-loaders in firepower."

"At least," Floyd put in.

"The main purpose," Jesse continued, "is to keep up a sustained rate of fire. Spencers can stop a massed infantry charge. Cullen and I saw that happen more than once in the War Between the States. At Hoover's Gap, Tennessee, an Indiana regiment had Spencer rifles. They slaughtered us. It's been my experience that a soldier's rate of fire with a muzzle-loader is two or three shots per minute— three at the most. A good man with a Spencer can fire fourteen times per minute. He could also fire all seven shots in ten seconds or less, but then the barrel would get too hot to hold. I'm talking about fourteen aimed shots. Do you know what guns the French and their mercenaries use?"

"Muzzle-loaders, but I don't know what you call . . . the make."

"The few carbines the boys picked up off the Hussars were a Belgian make," Floyd said.

The *padre* stood in silence, arms crossed, in an attitude of careful reflection. He dropped his arms and turned a questioning gaze back and forth from Jesse to Floyd. "These carbines or rifles—the Spencer, you call them—how much do they cost? And could they be purchased in El Paso?"

"About thirty dollars apiece," Floyd said, and looked at Jesse, who said, "Maybe as high as forty."

Garza shook his head in dejection. "A fortune in Mexico."

"I asked a *Yanqui* gun dealer in El Paso about Spencers," Floyd said. "He laughed when I offered him ten dollars apiece for twenty-five. Said I'd have to come up with a heap more'n that. So I bought what we could afford."

"So he had Spencers at hand?" Jesse asked.

"Just indicated he could get 'em fast if he saw the shine of good money. He's a slippery cuss. Calls himself Sam Dodd, which strikes me as phony. Probably wanted back in the States. I checked every weapon he showed me. Some I threw back as worthless. I figure he's got connections at Fort Bliss, if you get what I mean."

"I get 'cha."

"You did well with the few dollars the sweet Lord could provide at that time," Garza assured Floyd and fell to reflecting again. "A hundred Spencers would be the equivalent of five hundred muzzle-loaders . . . only much faster. My ragged ones would be a force to be reckoned with then. Ah . . . but I am dreaming." He cast the impossibility aside with a wave of one hand and turned to Jesse, hands now clasped, dark head bent, his manner appealing. "*Señor* Jesse, we now have enough arms for a review of my boys, my Juáristas, my volunteers. Proper, perhaps, I can now refer to them as troops. You and *Señor* Cullen must stand with me when they march by." He left them on that high note.

"Ever see anything like him?" Floyd marveled. "Nothing stumps him for long. Nothing. Makes do with what he has. Is thankful. If something fails to work out, he finds another way. I tell you . . ."

"I think it's called faith," Jesse said thoughtfully, his eyes following the receding white figure. "I'd almost forgotten."

Shortly, a bugle blared and they walked over to an opening in the pines, beyond the tents and brush huts and the corraled stock, where Garza awaited them, stringing out on each side of him the chattering women and the coltish children still gathering. In the distance the *soldados* were forming, if you could call it that, Jesse observed. From here it looked like a rabble. An armed mob milling about in confusion.

A strange sound, faint at first, a pulse rising above the murmur of the voices. A drum? It was, so unexpected here. A different drum sound, Jesse thought. A lower, deeper sound. A savage beat. That pulse. He strained to see, but the drummer wasn't in sight. Just the milling peasants, some holding their weapons like sticks.

The bugle sounded again, a call that Jesse didn't recognize, if it was a call, and at last they formed and moved this way, out of step, nobody calling the cadence. Nobody leading. No officer. No file-closers. A formless mass. Now he saw the drummer. A mere boy—weren't all drummers mere boys?—on the far flank, slapping a wooden drum with his hands. Just his hands. No drumsticks. An Indian drum, Jesse thought, nodding to himself. And now it was providing a cadence to the column of marchers. They were marching in unision, an uneven column, true, in the first line four men, six in the next, behind them six or more, but on they came together, their faces like stone images turned toward the Father. Marching. Marching. Some armed only with machetes. All with fire in their eyes. These simple people would die for their country and *presidente*. Jesse sensed that and was moved. In instinctive recognition he found himself saluting. Floyd was doing the same. Garza made the sign of the cross as the marchers passed, then held his arms high in blessing.

It was soon over. Garza, jubilant, turned to Floyd and Jesse. "Thank you for honoring my people. My ragged ones, my mule drivers, my *campesinos*—my boys. Now that we have more arms, we can come out in the open and fight the French."

Jesse disliked what he was going to say, but it had to be said. "Father Alberto," he began gently, "I have to tell you the truth. Your boys are not ready to fight the French in open battle. In time, yes. But now it would be murder. I doubt that some of them have ever fired a muzzle-loader or a handgun. They are willing to fight, and I can see that, but first they need organization and training."

Garza's spirited face clouded. "Organization?"

"Yes. They need to be broken down into squads, platoons, and companies. In good order. That's eight men to a squad. About fifty or seventy-five to a company. You have enough men here for four to six companies. Enough to make up a battalion. Maybe a small regiment if you stretched it. . . . You need noncommissioned officers —corporals, sergeants. Some lieutenants and captains and so on."

The *padre* brightened. "And training, you say?"

"Without training, your men would be slaughtered. Like an armed mob fighting veterans."

"Jesse's right, Father," Floyd said.

"*Señor* Jesse, my friend, I understand only the general meaning of the word. The details of training a soldier escape me. I have the spirit, but not the instruction. Please enlighten my poor brain."

Jesse paid him a broad grin. "You have the spirit, all right, Father, and that is good. In training a soldier learns how to fight as a unit. Your boys need drilling. How to march together and maneuver. They need to learn the manual of arms. How to handle a weapon, how to load and fire their arms. How to deploy in battle. They need discipline. . . . Looking at them, I'd say they are accustomed to hardships, so they'll make good soldiers." A late thought struck. "Another thing. You need somebody to look after the wounded. The women could help."

A budding realization seemed to come over the *padre*. He clasped his hands and inclined his head in that imploring, undeniable way he had. *"Señor* Jesse . . . would you . . . be so kind as to help train my people? *Señor* Cullen has spoken of this dire need in the past, but he has been away on missions for us. And then we engaged only in guerrilla attacks. You understand? A little raid here. One there."

Inwardly, Jesse backed off. He should have stayed out of this. Should not have spoken out, but could he not when the need was so obvious? Still, he held back. "I have to leave, *Padre*. I would like to help, but I'm weary of war. I've had all I can take. I've carried a rifle or carbine since '61. Then from bloody Shiloh through the Battle of Franklin south of Nashville. Then on the Plains, fighting Indians. I'm literally sick of fighting."

"I understand." Impulsively, Garza touched Jesse's arm. "I don't mean for you to take part in our war. No. I mean . . . just to help us better prepare ourselves, which you have stated well: to organize and train, giving us the good order we need." He played that engaging smile upon Jesse. "Just for a little while."

"I'll help if you will," Floyd said, and put on a pious look of promise. "We'll leave out any escort duty."

Jesse kept silent. Father Alberto was so warm and sincere, so unassuming and open, so likable and honest. Yet also so naive about the horrors of war. Jesse would hate to turn him down. So ran his thoughts. With Cullen's Spanish, the two of them could give instruction in the basics while Jesse waited for his pay. No time would be lost. Against his better judgment, he heard himself saying in a dull monotone, "All right, I'll help with Cullen. Why not start first thing this afternoon?"

"*Gracias!*" Garza exclaimed. "*Un abrazo, amigo.*" He hugged Jesse hard and went hurrying off, as jubilant as ever.

"I didn't think you'd do it," Floyd said.

"I had no intention to at first. It just came out of me in a weak moment, I guess. It's hard to say no to that little man."

In an opening under the tall pines, the peasant soldiers gathered at the urging of Father Garza, carrying their hybrid arms, even to machetes.

Floyd looked at Jesse, who, after a moment's indecision, said, "Let's count them off into companies of fifty men each, in two ranks, then see what we have."

With the *padre*'s help that was accomplished, and when the men were lined up, Jesse said, "Five companies. Guess we can call ourselves a battalion."

Floyd scratched his chin. "Reckon we'll need company captains. Some lieutenants and sergeants and a batch of corporals for the squads. Alberto knows these men, we don't. Why can't he select 'em?"

"I agree. And when it comes time to pick the *comandante* or major for the battalion, he's right over there. The *padre* himself. A natural-born leader if I ever saw one."

"Since we've agreed to help, he oughta agree to lead. Trouble is, he's so damned humble and modest, he might refuse the promotion."

"On second thought, Cullen, let's put off pickin' the officers till after they've all learned the manual of arms, how to march down the field and back again, and how to load and fire."

"It's all right with me. Man could get his ass shot off by some Indian wonderin' what a firin' piece is all about. Like, 'What's that little thing there these *gringos* call a trigger? Let's see. Believe I'll pull it.' Bang! 'Oh, I just shot me a *gringo*. But what's one less *gringo?*' "

Standing in front of the battalion, Jesse executed the manual of arms from order arms to inspection arms, to present arms, to right shoulder arms and left shoulder arms and at ease, leaving out parade rest, while Floyd called out each command in Spanish. They went through that time after time, until Jesse noted a semblance of uni-

son. Then, moving to what they called Company A, they repeated
the manual, and on down the line through the last company.

"Now let's try it all together," Jesse said and took a central position before the battalion. "Ten-shun." When Floyd repeated the
command, there was a stiffening along the ranks with the weapons
at order arms. "Right shoulder—arms" started out all right, except
some men did left shoulder arms.

Father Garza spoke, explaining the difference between left and
right. Before long the companies, except for a few offenders, had the
manual down reasonably well. Venturing further, Jesse and Floyd
showed them right face and left face. Again, reasonably executed.
But when Jesse yelled, "Right face!" for the whole battalion, some
men turned left, which stirred a ripple of laughter in the ranks, and
again the Father explained.

And so the afternoon passed.

"I realize now we should've had the men with machetes take
turns handling guns during the manual of arms," Jesse said to Floyd
and Garza. "We'll do that in the morning."

"Then let's do some marching in column of squads, left and
right," Floyd said, "and some comin' into line as companies. I think
we need that before we show 'em how to load and fire. There has to
be order first."

"Spoken like a true citizen soldier, Mr. Floyd," Jesse said.

Garza was all enthusiasm. He thanked Floyd and Jesse over and
over. "My boys, they learn fast what you call the basics, eh?"

"No worse than some Johnny Rebs I've seen," Jesse assured him.
"Some didn't know hay foot from straw foot."

"What do you really think, suh?" Floyd said later.

"They're tough people. They'll make damned good infantrymen.
I'd hate to face 'em at close quarters."

"The main problem is still lack of firepower."

Come morning they worked through the manual of arms again,
after which the machete-armed men handled the rifles and carbines
and the shotguns. Every bronze face struck Jesse as dead serious
about learning. Again the two patiently schooled each company
while Garza watched, at times adding a word when needed, always
encouraging.

"I can see progress," Jesse told Floyd after the battalion had executed the manual of arms. "Why don't you take over the marching?"

Floyd readily agreed. Working with the peasants, he seemed to have lost his habitual mockery, Jesse thought. *He's getting outside himself.* First, Floyd explained the commands to the companies. Now, with the companies formed in line, came the moment for movement by battalion. Arms were brought to shoulder, and at Floyd's command, the battalion swung right into a column of fours, or rather that was the intention. Instead, there followed a period of much stumbling and men running into each other, as some turned left—the old bugaboo. It ended in chaotic milling. Floyd shouted halt.

"Worst mess I've seen since Corinth," he said to Jesse, shaking his head. "We'll start over."

The second time, with Garza helping, the battalion swung right, marched to the end of the clearing, turned column left at Floyd's command, turned left again, and marched back in cadenced step to the steady thump of the Indian drummer.

"Try'n beat that, Mr. Johnny Reb," Floyd chortled as they passed Jesse. "In step, too. Hut-two-three-four. Hut-hut. Hut-two-three-four."

"I trust this is all accordin' to Casey's *Infantry Tactics?*" Jesse guyed him.

"Casey, hell, suh. He was a damned Yankee. I go by General Hardee's *Tactics.* Wasn't he in your famous Army of Tennessee?"

"He was, suh. I regret the omission and offer my sword in apology."

Garza was beside himself with approval, rushing about in a most unmilitary manner, exclaiming, "Review! This is a true review! *Gracias, Señores* Cullen and Jesse. *Gracias.* We are ready now."

"Not quite, Father," Jesse cautioned. "This is just the beginning. This afternoon we instruct them how to load and fire. Since we're short of weapons, the men will have to take turns."

"I know. We are still woefully short." His enthusiasm faded, only to lift irrepressibly. "But we are far better prepared than we were."

"True, Father." The man's spirit was catching.

"Jesse, I cannot fully express to you and Cullen the extent of my appreciation for what you are doing."

Jesse shrugged it off.

Loading was done in nine steps, Jesse, with Floyd interpreting, explained to the patriots standing at ease that afternoon. Borrowing an Enfield muzzle-loader, he began.

"At the command 'Load,' the musket is brought from the side and placed in front of the body. At 'Handle Cartridge,' a paper cartridge is placed between the teeth. At 'Tear Cartridge,' the paper is torn open, exposing the powder, like this."

Step four, "Charge Cartridge," he went on, called for pouring the powder into the barrel, then unwrapping the bullet and placing it in the muzzle.

Next, at the command "Draw Rammer," he instructed the intent men to pull the ramrod from under the barrel and place the big end on top of the bullet. At "Ram Cartridge," to push the ramrod down the barrel, forcing the bullet down on top of the powder at the bottom of the barrel. At "Return Rammer," to withdraw the ramrod and replace it in its groove under the barrel.

Finally, at the command of "Prime," Jesse told them to place the hammer on half cock, take a percussion cap and place it on the nipple. The rifle would be ready to fire when the hammer was pulled back to full cock, but not now. In frustration, he turned to Floyd. "That's too many cussed commands for such a simple thing as loading. Just tell 'em at the command 'Load,' to tear the cartridge, pour the powder, place the bullet, ram it down, and for God's sake remember to take out the ramrod before they put the percussion cap on the nipple, cock and fire. But not to fire until ordered."

Floyd did so. Afterward, using the abbreviated instructions, he and Jesse went from company to company, demonstrating and explaining.

"Now," Jesse said as they walked back to the center position before the battalion, "I reckon we've got enough cartridges and caps to fire a practice round or two. You better take it from here, suh."

"This time," Floyd said, "I think we'd better stick to the manual: ready, aim, fire. At 'Ready,' I'll remind 'em to pull the hammer back to full cock. At 'Aim,' to aim high."

He called the battalion to attention and shouted the first command. Eager hands, some fumbling, Jesse saw, brought weapons forward and, still fumbling, pulled hammers to full cock. At "Aim," barrels tilted up, some slowly. Just before Floyd ordered "Fire," a man dropped his rifle. It went off like a cannon, the ball making a screeching. Then the battalion was firing and bullets seemed to be flying and whirring everywhere. Jesse and Floyd hit the ground. Father Garza, off to one side, watched in admiration, maybe thinking it was part of the drill, Jesse thought, looking up through the smoke.

Floyd got up and felt of his slouch hat. He took it off, examined it, and stuck a forefinger though a ragged hole. Ruefully he said, "Like I told you, Jesse, a man could get his ass shot off around here, if not his head. From now on we practice firin' one company at a time."

"And the instructor will stand at a flank instead of in front of the company like a Dumbjohn," Jesse said, unable to cover his amusement.

"Hey, you're laughin' at me. Hell, I coulda been fatally shot."

"I'm glad you weren't . . . but you look so mighty insulted, as if nobody is supposed to shoot at a Floyd of the Mississippi Floyds."

A shouting boy ran up, breathing excitement, black eyes bulging concern. He kept pointing toward the camp.

Floyd listened, waved him back, and said, "The casualty report—one dead donkey, two cookin' pots. Next time we move the firin' range beyond camp. What say we dismiss the battalion and retire to the comfort of our quarters for some rounds of needed libation?"

Assembling for drill next morning, Jesse didn't see Father Garza, and he asked Floyd, "Wonder where the *padre* is?"

"Doc Pedro just told me. Seems our good father is off foragin'. Left before sunup. Took twenty-five men on horseback and mules, the cream of our mounted command, if you please." He seemed to frown and puzzle over the number. "More than he usually takes. However, the camp is short of beef. Could be he plans a little roundup in the Lord's name on the range of some neighboring *hacendado*."

They drilled the willing Juáristas in companies, manual of arms and forming double file and fours, and finished the morning with another battalion "review," Floyd marching by in erect command.

"I believe you're actually enjoying this," Jesse badgered him after the dismissal.

"An overdue honor, reb Jesse. The officer's commission so unfairly denied me when I enlisted." Putting on again, he exhibited a face of lugubrious hurt. "But it's only brevet till the *padre* comes back."

Midmorning of the fourth day of Father Garza's absence, Jesse heard shouts and barking dogs heralding an incoming party. A column of men on horses and mules rode into camp, Garza in the lead, looking bent and weary, but, as always, cheerful of demeanor. He waved and smiled. The camp waved as one and raised greetings. Behind him surged a bunch of wild-eyed, horned cattle in a cloud of dust, closely herded, and a string of big, strong mules bearing packs, some of which, Jesse noted, had bloodstains. Behind them followed two men humped over in saddles, obviously wounded.

Watching, Floyd said, "Looks like the *padre* ran into unexpected trouble and had to call on the Lord for some none-too-gentle persuasion."

"I guess we can forget about any drills today," Jesse said.

"There'll be a homecoming fiesta—barbecue, music, dancing. Much happiness. Always is when Alberto and his boys return, even when the pickin's—er—uh, I mean the contributions—are lean. Good for morale. In a few minutes you'll see beeves butchered and fires goin'. Nobody has more fun with less than a poor Mexican."

Jesse and Floyd were cleaning weapons when the *padre* came over, worn down but gracious. Without preliminary, he took gold coins from a sagging leather saddlebag of apparent weight and paid each man. "Our good Lord has provided again, although at some cost as you observed when we rode in," he said. "We have food for a month or two and the people will rejoice tonight, which I insist upon, because life is meant to be enjoyed. There will even be wine, once again provided."

As Jesse thanked him, he sensed hesitation in the *padre*'s words, something left unsaid. And then Garza clasped his hands and inclined his head and said in his soft voice, "Also at cost, the Lord has provided means to purchase the Spencer guns, which you call repeaters. Without them I realize we cannot win." His voice trailed off a moment. "Will you two good friends, in the generosity of your hearts, please journey to El Paso and buy the Spencers, rifles or carbines, and much ammunition from the Anglo gun traders?"

A thoughtful pause and Floyd nodded. Jesse, taken by surprise, didn't answer.

"Just one more favor for the poor people of Mexico, *amigo* Jesse.

You would not have to fight with us. Just go with Cullen and others and bring back the guns. I know I am asking much of you, a man weary and sick of war. Could you do that, please? This once?" He was regarding Jesse with the most hopeful and appealing of expressions.

Jesse looked down, then slowly up. A flash of thought occurred to him that these poor people, like his own South, were fighting invaders. Yet with far less than the South had. He could do this much, this little. Almost before he knew it, he found himself saying, "I'll go with Cullen, and we'll bring back the guns."

9

They assembled at dawn, some thirty Juáristas in poor-Indian white and peaked hats, all mounted on good horses, each man carrying a muzzle-loader.

"Our best men," Floyd said. "Note the fifteen pack mules this time. The big mules Father Alberto and the boys brought back with the gold and silver. Doc Pedro assures me no mules in all of Chihuahua are faster or stronger than these long-stridin' critters of the devil. Perfect for totin' you know what."

"A *hacendado's* most generous contribution," Jesse said, bowing his head with exaggerated solemnity.

"Indeed, suh, and greatly appreciated."

The Father blessed them all and they swung away.

Traveling fast, flankers out, alert for trouble and making a show of their strength, stopping in the villages only for water, they reached Paso del Norte late the third day without being attacked, forded the Rio Grande at the crossing, and camped along the river. After idling around camp next morning until ten o'clock, Floyd saddled up and asked Jesse to accompany him.

"I hate to waste time," the Mississippian drawled, "but Sam Dodd is not an early riser. We'll start with the nearest saloon."

Although Dodd was not there, nor in the second saloon, Floyd was not discouraged. "Man like him would starve to death if he had to get up early to make an honest livin'. He'll show up by noon along saloon row. Meantime, let's enjoy ourselves a little and have another leisurely drink."

They were doing just that when a round-bodied man in a rumpled suit and a low-crowned hat entered the saloon.

"Here he is," Floyd said and waved.

Dodd saw them and moved easily through the mixed crowd of Anglos and Mexicans, nodding casually here and there. An inconspicuous man, Jesse thought, a desired impersonation for his shadowy profession.

"Have a mornin' phlegm-cutter with us, suh," Floyd offered genially, and made the introductions.

After perfunctory handshakes, Dodd drew up a chair and ordered tequila. His face was flabby under the mosslike brown beard, and a mane of greasy-looking grayish hair fell to his neck. His mouth was loosely relaxed. He appeared to loll, indifferent to his rough surroundings. In contradiction, the sharp black eyes under the bushy brows seemed to miss nothing.

He sipped tequila. "You're back soon, Mr. Floyd." Dodd's voice was low-pitched and formal.

"I am."

"Did you get the goods delivered?"

"We did."

"*We?*"

"Captain Wilder was along with the boys. It was tough going. We lost men. Four fights before we reached camp."

"My, my." Dodd looked shocked.

"It's every dog for himself across the river. Bandits as bad as Apaches. Will be till President Juárez regains control and there's some kind of order."

Dodd folded his arms. "I have the highest regard for President Juárez. A noble man. A true patriot. Speaking of causes, what can I do for you this time, Mr. Floyd?" He cracked a broad smile, revealing teeth as yellow as maize. He kept turning his glass.

"Where can we talk?"

"Here's as good as any."

Floyd looked around before he spoke, keeping his voice low. "I want a hundred Spencer rifles or carbines. A minimum of a hundred rounds for each weapon, and a hundred cartridge cases containing five or ten refill tubes for each weapon."

Dodd spun the glass faster. His eyes widened. His ropy lips formed a tuneless whistle. "Cartridge cases? You are speaking of the celebrated Blakeslee Quickloader, sir."

"Reckon I am."

"Might as well ask for the moon."

"We'll take that if we can get it."

Dodd broke into the yellow smile again. "You are definitely a man of needs, Mr. Floyd. To start with, the Quickloaders are out of the question. I doubt there's one this side of Fort Richardson."

"Quickloaders are last on the list. What about the rest?"

Dodd finished his tequila neatly, wiped his mouth with the back of his left hand, and said, "You understand, of course, we are speaking of surplus ordnance?"

"The Yankees oughta have plenty," Floyd replied, some of his bitterness seeping out. "They always did."

Dodd bit off the end of a cheroot, struck a match on the underside of the table, lit up, inhaled, and spoke through an exhaled cloud of odorous smoke. "That will take some doing, Mr. Floyd."

"No surprise. But can you and when?"

"You are in a hurry, as usual, which is understandable. But an arrangement of this delicate nature cannot be hurried. First, I'll have to ascertain whether the articles in question are obtainable." In his matter-of-fact voice, he reminded Jesse of a storekeeper taking an order for sundry items.

"How much per rifle or carbine?"

"Depends."

"On what?"

Dodd shrugged and studied his cheroot. "What my connection has to do. How difficult it will be to bring about this transaction. Certain steps must be taken, you know, certain parties must be figured in on the matter, and certain safeguards taken." His roundabout manner seemed to recede by degrees. "Which, in turn, brings up the logical question. What would the remuneration be in, gold or 'dobe silver dollars?"

"Both," Floyd snapped. "You've always been paid, remember?"

"True. Quite true, Mr. Floyd. I do not question your integrity. Not for one instant." He smiled that unsightly yellowish smile. "However, 'dobe dollars don't carry the worth they used to."

Floyd's impatience hit. "But they still happen to be the coin of the realm, and I notice they spend right good here on the border. Just bought our drinks with a couple."

Dodd lifted plump hands in tactful retreat. "I just mention that in passing, Mr. Floyd. What's good is good. There would be no disagreement there. Anything but paper money." He stood abruptly. "Meet me here tonight after dark. Good day, gentlemen." He left as he had entered, his presence hardly noticed.

"Well, what do you make of him?" Floyd asked Jesse.

"As slippery as a greased pig. But I guess there's no choice."

"There's not. I've tried several men who claimed to be dealers, and Dodd was the only one who could deliver. But, like I've said, you have to watch him."

On the way back to camp they stopped for supplies. Jesse bought some personal items and a sack of shelled corn and a little barley.

"You take good care of that red horse," Floyd observed. "I can understand why."

"Can't pack much. But just a handful of feed now and then lets him know I'm looking out for him."

In camp they had a fiery Doc Pedro dinner, cooled this time with beer, and as Jesse lay down for a siesta, his eyes followed his grazing horse, and a vivid conclusion sprang to his mind: *He's got the eye of an eagle and the step of a deer. He has.* Jesse mulled that over, liking it more and more.

When darkness fell, Floyd and Jesse saddled back to the saloon, the latter taking the carbine this time.

Sam Dodd was waiting and in evident good humor. "I suggest that we open preliminaries with a goodwill drink, then we'll take a little ride to meet my business partner."

"Why not meet him here?" Floyd asked after the drinks were brought.

"He prefers that we meet there . . . for certain precautionary reasons. You will understand when you see him."

"Can you get the guns?"

"That—and price—we'll take up when we get there." The drinks soon finished, he started to rise, then stopped, eyeing Jesse's carbine. "I noticed the Spencer first thing when you came in. You always pack that baby Gatling gun?"

"I fetch it along like most men do handguns."

"Guns close up make me nervous," Dodd said, quirking his mouth. "I prefer to have 'em on paper, where I can handle 'em." His attempt at humor was more like a grunt. "Well, let's go."

Mounted, he led off at a fast trot and the little ride turned out to be a circuitous route to the lower part of town, peopled sparsely at this hour with Mexicans. Behind an adobe house at the end of a narrow street, Dodd tied his horse, motioned for the two to follow, and went inside. A lantern hanging from the wall cast shallow light.

At a table sat a slim-faced man with a close-cropped beard shot with gray. He wore a forage cap, a dark blue jacket bearing sergeant's chevrons on both sleeves, and light blue pants stuffed into black cavalry boots.

Jesse slowed step, thinking, *So that's how they work it.*

The sergeant stood, and Dodd said, "Mr. Floyd, you and your friend have a chair. This is Sarge."

Floyd came to the point at once. "Can you get us a hundred Spencer rifles or carbines with ammunition?"

"Believe I can," the sergeant answered, his tone precise. "Which do you prefer?"

"Rifles."

"A hundred you say?"

"Yes. And a minimum of a hundred cartridges for each weapon. More, if you can get 'em."

"All this is going to cost you a good deal, considering the size of the order . . . and the risk."

"How much per rifle?"

"Fifty dollars."

"Whoa, now!"

"I'm making you a fair price."

"Like hell!" Floyd said, glaring. "You aim to rob us."

"Gentlemen, gentlemen," Dodd's moderating voice broke in. "Guess robbery is involved, in effect, when we keep in mind where the guns have to come from." He gave the grunting laugh again. "Pray tell, what do you consider a fair price, Mr. Floyd?"

"A damned sight less than fifty dollars."

"Then name it," the sergeant said amicably.

"Twenty dollars," Floyd answered, and Jesse knew that he didn't expect to deal on that.

"You're not even close," the sergeant said, amused. "But I'll horse trade with you. I'll come down to forty-five."

"Now you're not even close," Floyd said, amused in turn.

"How does forty sound to you?"

"I thought this was surplus ordnance," Floyd said, smirking. "I will come up to twenty-five."

The sergeant ran a considering hand over his beard. "I'll come down another notch to thirty-five, but no more."

Floyd looked hard at him. "I'll go up to thirty, but no more."

No one spoke for an interval until Dodd said, "Gentlemen, we are deadlocked over a mere five dollars. What do you say we flip for it?"

The sergeant nodded. Floyd did not.

Seeing that, Dodd said, "Mr. Floyd, you can call it, if Sarge agrees?"

The sergeant dipped his head in agreement.

"Fair enough," Floyd said, "but I want to see the coin first."

Feigning insult, Dodd laid a U.S. dollar in his left palm and Floyd, after examining both sides, nodded and said, "All right."

As Dodd flipped the coin upward, Floyd called, "Heads," and as the coin fell, Dodd caught it deftly. Holding it out for all to see, he said, "Heads it is, Mr. Floyd. You get the rifles for thirty dollars each." He pursed his lips. "Which comes to three thousand dollars."

A fair price for Yankee repeaters, Jesse thought to himself. Now for the getting. It seemed almost too easy.

Floyd, nodding, said, "What about the ammunition?"

"Comes in wooden thousand-round boxes," the sergeant said, and went to stroking his beard again, ". . . at thirty dollars a box."

"That's high," Floyd said.

"Repeaters are no good without cartridges. I won't come down on the boxes."

"What if I don't have that much money?"

The sergeant only shrugged.

"We'll pay you twenty-five dollars a box."

"I told you I won't come down."

He meant it, Jesse saw, and now had the deal in hand. Floyd could take it or go empty-handed. The tone of Floyd's voice was resigned as he said, "How many boxes can you get us?"

"Between ten and fifteen."

"We'll take what you can get at thirty dollars a box."

"It's agreed then."

"When can you deliver?"

"Tomorrow night—here."

"What time?"

"Ten o'clock—say."

"We're camped near the river crossing. Why can't you deliver there?"

"This is safer."

"Don't see why. That's away from town."

"Shorter distance to travel, and Mexicans don't ask questions. Too, less risk of running into a detail from the post out to pick up drunks along saloon row."

"We'll be waiting," Floyd said tersely, twice balked now.

Dodd spoke at once. "Fine, gentlemen, fine. And may I add . . . in delicate negotiations of this kind . . . to clear up any doubts . . . it is appropriate to put some money down in advance."

Floyd bristled. "There'll be no money in advance. You deliver the rifles and ammunition here, you get your money then—hard money."

Dodd glanced in question at the sergeant, who said, "We'll deliver everything as agreed." He stood up, and Floyd and Jesse left the house. Riding off, Floyd said, "They give the impression it's all cut and dried, easy pickin's as a bird nest on the ground. If I was stealin' arms from the Yankee government, believe I'd say I'd get it if I could. That sergeant sounds like all he's got to do is go get it."

"Where did Dodd deliver before?"

"Always had a cache out in the country. He'd lead us out there."

In camp next morning, spreading the gold coins and the 'dobe silver dollars on a blanket, they counted some $4,500, far more than enough for the rifles and ammunition. Inspecting the wooden pack saddles and the accompanying rawhide bags, the *alforjas,* they decided more ropes and canvas were needed for wrapping the rifles and tying the boxes, which thus necessitated a trip to town.

The rest of the day seemed to drag, yet a good time to rest the stock for the hard travel to come. After the evening meal the camp was cleared and the packs readied. It was after nine o'clock when Floyd collected the pack train. Skirting the main part of town, he circled around toward the lower section, posting the train down the road not far from the house. A last-quarter moon gave filmy light.

A few minutes before ten Floyd and Jesse rode up to the adobe house and tied their horses beside two others. A dull light shone in the house. Floyd went in first, carrying the coins in a canvas bag.

The sergeant was standing by the table, Dodd at his left with arms crossed near the open door into the kitchen.

Jesse paused when he saw no boxes or stacked rifles. Floyd halted at the same time.

"There's been a change in plans," the sergeant said, his voice coming clipped across the dim, lantern-lit room, dimmer than last time, Jesse thought.

"What the hell do you mean?" Floyd said, his suspicion rank.

"Couldn't get the stuff tonight. My helpers are in the guard-house. Maybe we can make it in a day or two." The sergeant pointed to a bottle on a table. "Let's have a drink and talk."

Jesse had a growing thrust of wrongness. Somehow everything was too set, too stiff, Dodd standing like a post, contrary to his usual indolent manner. On that wariness, Jesse cocked the Spencer's hammer and heard the faint click. Floyd also seemed to stiffen.

"Well, if you won't have a drink," the sergeant said, talking faster now, "there's a pack of brand-new .52-caliber Spencers over there by the wall for you to take back to camp tonight."

Floyd and Jesse turned to look. As they did, the sergeant bawled, "Put up your hands! You're covered! Don't move!" Jerking toward him, and hearing boots scrape at the kitchen doorway, Jesse saw two armed shapes bulging there.

He shot the first man, levered in another shell, and the next bang sent the second one crashing against the wall just as the man's rifle boomed late, the rounds making a great din in the tight little room. Dodd was jumping around like a giant hoptoad in a dirty fog, wildly firing a handgun that made bright stabbings in the dimness. Jesse heard Floyd's handgun blast and saw Dodd flop across the table. The sergeant made for the back door. On instinct alone, Jesse dived for him and knocked him to the floor.

"Hold the Yankee son of a bitch!" Floyd yelled, rushing over, coughing on the acrid powdersmoke, grabbing for the noncom.

For an instant they froze like that, hands clamped on the man, wrapped in stunning stillness, broken when Dodd rolled off the table, screaming. A rifleman was groaning.

"Nothin' but a goddamned phony deal all along," Floyd hacked between coughs. "Should've known. Too easy, too easy."

The back door opened and a tentative Spanish voice called, *"Se-ñores—señores."* It was Doc Pedro and a rush of others.

"Tie this two-bit bastard up," Floyd ordered. Other pack train men filled the room. "Now what?" Floyd said inconclusively. "Where are the guns?"

Jesse, in a voice that sounded like any but his own in his ears, said, "They have to be in an ordnance warehouse at the post."

"So . . ."

"The sergeant knows where."

"My God, Jesse. You know what that means? Crackin' a U.S. fort?"

"And more. But what choice do we have?"

For the length of a held breath there was silence between them. Then Floyd said, "What the hell, we've come this far. Let's go."

"Don't forget the money bag."

"God, no. And get the lantern, Pedro. May need it."

"Damned if I'll help," the sergeant swore while his hands were being tied behind him.

Jesse dragged him to his feet. "You're gonna take us to the warehouse or these Juáristas will use a machete on you. And when they get through whittlin', you won't be a man anymore. Savvy?"

"You're bluffing."

"Doc Pedro, show 'im your machete."

He did so with a display of overdone pleasure, grimacing fiercely as he ran a relishing forefinger along the edge, then jabbed the noncom's belly until he cried out, "No—stop! I'll help. But I can't do much. There's a sentinel on duty at the post's entrance. You have to pass him to get to the warehouse."

"You'll help us get by him too," Jesse promised. He then gagged him with a bandanna, shoved him outside, and mounted him between Floyd and himself, with Doc Pedro, machete handy, close behind.

Taps sounded from the fort as the pack train started out under a last-quarter moon. The post, not far away, Jesse recalled, was mainly a cluster of adobes. The bunched column reached the main service road to the post and went on. Floyd halted when a muddy beam of light marked the location of the sentinel box. He loosened the noncom's gag and said, "What's the sentry's name and rank?"

"Don't know," came the stubborn refusal.

"Hell you don't. In a dinky little four-company post like this you know 'most everybody's name. Why, you can run around at night when you please. Refresh his memory, Doc Pedro."

When Doc Pedro obligingly jabbed the sergeant's buttocks, he flinched, grumbling, "It's Hull—Corporal Tom Hull."

"And what's your handle?"

"Mitch Quinn."

"All this had better be right or Doc Pedro will sho' make you one sorry *gringo*. Understand?"

"Guess so."

"No guessin' about it." Taking the sergeant's forage cap, Floyd donned it. He walked his horse up to the sentinel box and called in a low, conspiring tone, "Hey, Hull . . . got a little somethin' special here for you." Dismounting, leading his mount, he sauntered toward the box, waving a bottle of tequila.

A head peeked out. "That you, Quinn? You're in early."

Floyd waved the bottle, keeping it high before his face. "Yeah. Have a drink."

"Ah. . . . Believe I will."

Hull stepped out eagerly. He was reaching for the bottle when Jesse saw Floyd ram a revolver into the corporal's middle. His mouth flew open and he stepped back, hands lifted. In another moment Floyd marched him back to the pack train, where guards tied his hands and gagged him to be brought along.

"Now," Floyd told Quinn, "lead us to the warehouse."

There was no argument this time. The warehouse lay some seventy-five yards to the right, Quinn said. But after the pack train had gone a short distance past the sentinel box, a building with a lighted lantern out front barred the way. Floyd halted.

Jesse grabbed Quinn by his jacket front. "You didn't tell us we'd come to that. What is it, the guardhouse?"

He didn't have to answer—Jesse knew.

"You sneaky bastard!" Jesse gagged him and they angled wide around the guardhouse and moved on faster. The post, its quarters dark since taps had signaled lights out, now cast in the moon's skimpy light, appeared no more than a scattering of buildings and sheds tossed carelessly on the broad floor of the gray desert.

On the way Quinn mumbled behind his gag and pointed with his head: the warehouse. It was a low adobe, black with shadows.

"There it is," Jesse told Floyd, who pulled the pack train in close to the warehouse. He and Jesse ran up to the door, Floyd there first. He swung around in dismay. "It's chained. But what would a man expect?" He shook his head, at a loss.

"It's adobe," Jesse said. "Maybe we can break in."

"But the door's wood. It'd make a helluva racket."

"Not the door. Maybe we can—"

The arrival of Doc Pedro and another man cut him off.

Floyd broke into rapid-fire Spanish, whereupon the two Juáristas started hacking at the adobe wall next to the door with machetes. It seemed like a long time to Jesse, but shortly they had chopped and gouged a hole big enough for a man to crawl through. Obviously it wasn't large enough yet. They kept working without letup. Choking clay and straw dust rose. Crumbling bricks fell. Now . . .

Doc Pedro handed Floyd the lantern and they all followed him inside. Striking a match, Floyd lit the lantern.

Jesse's elation sagged when he saw only stacks of Springfield rifles and boxes stenciled .45 CAL U.S. SPRINGFIELD (.45-70). Not that they couldn't use Springfields! Then, facing the other wall, he spied a line of rifles—Spencers, by God, and of boxes of 'em, and cartridge boxes marked .52 CAL U.S. SPENCER (.52-46), some opened. He whipped around to Floyd, but Floyd had seen too. Talking fast to Doc Pedro, he started a chain of men passing loose rifles and boxes through the gap, where quick hands tied them on the pack-saddled mules.

After a while Jesse sensed that time was beginning to press. He glanced with warning at Floyd: *It's time to go. Don't overplay our luck.*

Floyd nodded the same and hurried out and back. "This is all we can take," he said, and waved everybody out. As an afterthought, he carefully blew out the lantern and set it by the door.

They mounted and swung off, trotting, Jesse again making certain Quinn was gagged and between Floyd and himself. They were about halfway to the sentinel box now, the guardhouse off to their right.

It burst just then, shocking in the quiet, a high voice shouting, "Guard, guard!" With that, the sound of boots crunching gravel.

Jesse knew before he jerked a look and glimpsed the fleeing figure. In the confusion of getting the pack train started, Hull had slipped to the tail end of the column, somehow loosened his gag, and dashed free.

The pack train broke into a faster trot. A man ran out of the guardhouse, swiveling his head all about. Apparently he caught the trotting sounds, because he ran back in, shouting. Floyd spurred into a gallop, and the pack train, packs and boxes flopping, followed hard after him. Passing the silent sentinel box, they came out on the service road. Soon Jesse could see the town's sprinkling of lights.

The shortest distance to the river ford was straight through town, and Floyd, therefore, turned into the main street. At that moment a bugle at the post blared assembly, which sent a quickening through the laboring column. Jesse did a fast reckoning, in his mind's eye visualizing the troopers tumbling out of the barracks, and the call to stables, and the barked commands forming the pursuit. With good luck, the pack train had five or eight minutes to reach the river, less if somebody at the post cut the formalities. Too, the pursuing detachment would be coming on the run, while the burdened mules at best continued at a heavy, tiring gallop.

In a few minutes the town slipped behind and the pack train, slowing somewhat, seemed to be feeling its way while it lumbered through the humid darkness, guided by the pallid light of the moon marking the greasy band of the river. They were getting close to the ford now, Jesse knew, but unease caused him to pull out of the column and halt. Facing the rear, he waited while the mules passed in a dusty cloud.

Head bent, he detected no threatening clatter. Relieved, he reined to go. But what was that sudden noise? He turned back and leaned forward, straining to pick it up. It was the drum of horses in a hard run; the drumming kept building. He heeled the red horse away, running for the mules. He found them already crossing, already in a line, Floyd by the water's edge urging everybody on, while the insistent voice of the river seemed to say, "Hurry, hurry."

"They're comin'!" Jesse yelled.

Floyd tore the bandanna from around Quinn's mouth and untied his hands. "If you want to live, ride back and yell at 'em to hold their fire—that it's you. Now go!" Quinn hesitated, but Floyd slapped Quinn's mount across the rump, and the startled horse took off.

For a tight interval all Jesse could hear was the horse running. The last mule was plunging into the water, one man yanking on its halter, another lashing its hindquarters, when Quinn began shouting. Jesse and Floyd jumped their horses into the river. The red horse sank to his chest, rose, and thrashed for footing against the current, found it and started making for the far bank.

Across, they rode on a way in silence before pulling up. There wasn't a sound on the other side of the river. They looked at each other, and Floyd, in a slumping voice, said, "By God, we made it. I think this calls for a drink."

"I agree."

Floyd dug into his pack for a bottle, uncorked and passed it to Jesse, who took a long pull and handed it back.

"Another generous contribution, Mr. Floyd, of the Mississippi Floyds," Jesse said, expelling a deep-drawn breath. "In fact, I would call it a noble contribution to the cause."

There was a lengthy gurgling before Floyd replied. "Indeed, suh, and appreciated more than ever when you consider the complete good-heartedness with which it was given."

10

Their watchful journey in the next few days proved uneventful, though somewhat to the regret of the Juáristas, each armed with a repeater and eager to use the new arms. Their laden return to camp set off a celebration. Father Garza could not thank them enough, embracing the two expatriates again and again. "And no loss of life," he said. "It was a blessed trip."

"And here is your treasury," Floyd said, ceremoniously handing him the heavy canvas sack, "except for some 'dobe dollars spent for supplies and, I must confess, Father, for some tequila."

Garza looked puzzled. "I don't comprehend."

"The guns and ammunition are free," Floyd said, tongue-in-cheek, "a contribution from the United States Army."

Garza frowned even more. "The supplies and tequila I understand and approve for subsistence. But this . . . this arsenal. You purchased it from an arms dealer, did you not?"

Floyd told him in a few words, skipping the gory details, as if not wishing to offend the Father, only saying there was a shootout in the house.

"So there was killing?" Garza asked.

Floyd nodded. "They were going to murder us for the money."

"A miracle you were not." Garza brightened. "Now show me what all you and the boys brought back."

The rifles were unpacked and counted, a tally of 117.

"All brand-new," Floyd said.

The *padre* looked intently at the rifles, engrossed, but did not pick one up or touch it, and Jesse saw again his conflict of need and abhorrence.

"At last," Garza said, "we can fight the French on even terms, or, better, to our advantage."

Jesse felt the impulse to speak, but held up for Floyd. "Not yet,

Father," Floyd said patiently. "Your boys still need more training. Now we'll have to show them how to handle the repeaters."

"I know I'm impatient," Garza said. "But we've waited so long for adequate arms. How long will the additional training take?"

"Hard to say exactly. A few weeks. Without more training they wouldn't stand a chance against the French veterans and their Hussar mercenaries. We's just gettin' started good when we went to El Paso."

Garza said no more, but his disappointment was evident.

The training began next morning. Two companies of Spencer riflemen were formed. In explaining the loading, Jesse, through Floyd's Spanish, stressed the one dangerous feature of the repeater. How, with seven rimfire cartridges lined up nose to tail in the magazine, the whole works might go off with disastrous results if the butt was banged hard on the ground. By the same token, he said, rough jolting might set it off when the rifle was carried on horseback. Therefore, when a column was on the march, on horseback or by mules, only one cartridge should be carried in the magazine. Going into battle, a man could load fast enough from a cartridge sack or bandolier.

"I've been lucky this carbine hasn't gone off," Jesse remarked to Floyd. "Believe me, I make certain mine swings easy. Otherwise, a man could get a leg blown off."

Confusion marked the remainder of the day as the two men repeated much of the earlier training. After supper, resting in camp, Jesse said, "I don't like to bring it up again, Cullen, but when we think the boys are ready for battle, I'm going back to El Paso."

Floyd was about to take a drink of tequila. He put the bottle down and didn't move for a long count, his eyes resting on Jesse. "I was hopin' you'd put that off a while longer. Father Alberto will be sad to hear it. He's mighty fond of you, Jesse. And I will lose a good friend. Our tracks probably won't cross again."

"Don't say that."

Floyd took the drink and said, "Out here it's a long way to water, and so damned many things can happen to a man. Most of 'em fatal."

"Why don't you come with me? Maybe we can start a ranch together. We'll find something. El Paso is growing. There's talk of a railroad from East to West someday."

"Someday is a long way off out here. Like never."

"Well, think about it. The two of us as partners. We'd make it."

"Can't now. I have an obligation here."

Jesse couldn't refrain from a little mockery of his own. "The ol' Suthin' honor code, eh?"

"I threw that up to you once, didn't I? Maybe it's part that, maybe not. I just feel like my place is here right now. Kinda hard to explain." He seemed almost embarrassed by the thought.

"I hope you understand why I'm leaving?"

"Oh, sho', Johnny Reb," Floyd said, trying to shrug it off. "Sho'." He passed the bottle.

In the days after, progress seemed to ebb and flow, working with raw recruits more accustomed to machetes than modern rifles. The two instructors showed them how to use the adjustable leaf sight on the Spencers, with an accurate range up to about five hundred yards. Forty-six grains of black powder couldn't do more than that. No matter. In battle the fighting was usually much closer, a few hundred yards or less. He and Floyd marched the willing Juáristas to what passed for a firing range and directed them to shoot at selected targets of trees at various distances. As well, there was more schooling in muzzle-loaders, which fired the conical minié ball, supposed to give the Enfield rifle a range of one thousand yards. But if that meant you could hit anything at that distance, Floyd said, it was but to laugh.

To make more efficient use of the old, hard-hitting rifles, the former rebs taught the infantrymen to fire from two ranks. The front rank fired and dropped back to reload, then the second rank stepped up and fired, doubling the rate of fire to six rounds a minute.

Intensive drilling and marching and maneuvering by companies and in battalion strength followed, mixed with more instruction in weaponry, until the day came when Floyd said, "I think they're about as ready as we can get 'em. What do you think, Jesse?"

"They're eager to fight, all right. But one thing still bothers me. I've noticed it all along."

"What's that?" Floyd looked surprised.

"Lack of officer leadership and discipline. If something happened to you or Father Alberto, this bunch would fall apart."

"The *padre* picked the men he thought best suited as captains and lieutenants. We can't change that."

"I don't mean change 'em. I mean impress on all the men respect for command. Other day, when a boy fell behind on the march and a lieutenant told him to close up, the boy, who was a little tired by then, just shrugged and ignored him. Maybe they came from the same village."

"Did you say anything?"

"I hollered at him and pointed for him to close up. He did, but he still gave the lieutenant a go-to-hell look. That won't work. They have to respect their own people first."

"Guess some are gettin' a little cocky. A good sign in one way, bad in another. I'll talk to the Father. Work through him. Have him impress that on the whole battalion. They'll listen. You bet they will."

Every night and morning now they made big campfires, for winter was coming, though the afternoons were still crisp and sunny. Jesse had lost all but a vague grasp of time. It was early December, he guessed; maybe later. Not that time mattered. Days, weeks, and months were mere small coins, which he spent prodigally because he had so many. He had felt a sense of purpose here with Floyd and the Juáristas. Now he was about to set off drifting again, and he had mixed feelings about leaving, which he would in a few days, after the training was completed. But where? Other than El Paso, he had no idea. Maybe California, maybe not. Maybe Arizona. He reminded himself it was wise not to muse too far ahead about the future. Nor did he care. Nor did time bring relief from the troubled past; it only blurred it. The old woman was wrong.

His sleep was broken that night, yet this time, thankfully, he escaped the hellfire of the haunting nightmares. He woke up to find snow on his blankets and his red horse standing nearby, head down, watching him, looking a bit forlorn and hungry.

The sight touched Jesse, erased his early morning gloom, and he got up and fed his horse precious shelled corn before he fed himself.

Floyd broke the news after breakfast. Because of the weather, Father Alberto had decided it was time to move the encampment to lower country, out of the sierra and into a district friendly to the Juáristas. That reported, Floyd's expression altered to a hesitant question, wordless because he didn't want to ask it: You're not leaving, are you? Not because we're moving?

"I'll go when the training's finished," Jesse said. "There's the problem we spoke about. Father Alberto hasn't talked to the command yet. There'll be hell to pay if orders are disobeyed in the heat of battle."

Floyd's cheerless face broke out into a broad smile of relief. "Just what I had in mind, ol' reb. First thing I'll bring up when we bivouac."

Moving the camp, Jesse saw, was like a migration. A noisy strung-out procession of families, of barking dogs and laden donkeys and mules and the walking commissary: the long-horned cattle, "contributed" by the unnamed *hacendado,* herded mostly by boys on ponies and worn-out horses.

"Good thing we're not tryin' to sneak up on anybody," Floyd said, shaking his head.

"But no noisier than when we were marching up from Corinth to Shiloh, with recruits firing their rifles now and then to see if they worked good," Jesse said, smiling. That was something, if he could smile back at the then pending three-day horror in the woods.

The move required two days under sunlit skies, ending by a wooded stream that ran through the rolling hills like a vein of silver.

Father Garza joined Jesse and Floyd at their evening campfire. In striking fine spirits, he greeted them with a dazzling smile and gave each man the *abrazo;* then, his amiable features sobering, he said, "Half a day's ride from here is the little town of San Juan de Río. There is a French Foreign Legion garrison there commanded by a Colonel Dubray, a veritable offspring of the devil incarnate. There is a company of Hussars there as well. For some months now, ever since Dubray took command, the invaders have terrorized the countryside for miles around. Any captured guerrillas are executed in the plaza and their bodies left there for some days as a public example to the citizens. Peasants are shot if they protest when their produce and few cattle and mules are taken." He paused and his soft voice hardened. "Sometimes young girls are taken from their families. Most do not return to their homes. The few who do are broken in body and mind, disgraced forever. It is very bad, my good friends of the Lost Cause." He played his gaze from Floyd to Jesse and back.

"Now that we are ready to fight, I want us to attack the garrison and destroy it."

Jesse bit his lip and remained silent, looking down.

Floyd rested his chin on his left hand before he spoke. "That is easy to understand, Father. The need, the right. But there is still one matter with your boys that needs fixin' before they fire a shot."

"Oh . . ." The *padre* was startled. "I thought our boys were ready. The training with the repeaters, the hard marches, the maneuvers. You have worked them like mules, which they needed." In the vestments of his innocence, Jesse thought, he was not unlike a small boy suddenly puzzled by something beyond his maturity.

"They are ready, Father, except for one thing lacking. Respect for discipline. Jesse and I have talked about this."

"Respect?"

"Some not only are slow to obey commands, they ignore their officers. Maybe it's because many are near the same age, or they knew each other before they became Juáristas. Like the old sayin', 'Familiarity breeds contempt.'"

The *padre* frowned. "What do you think should be done?"

"Have a general review and tell them to obey their officers. If they don't, tell them they'll be sent home. In other words, kicked out of the army. You'll have to be tough. A dishonorable discharge, you could call it."

"I will do that. Yes. After that, we will attack the garrison. Yes?"

Floyd nodded. On that approval, Garza looked at Jesse, and although he did not make the appealing hand gesture, Jesse saw it in the warm dark eyes and heard it in the genteel voice. "*Amigo* Jesse, I respect your wish not to engage in war again. You have been through so much. Yet I have yet another request. Will you join the fight against the garrison as an adviser with Cullen?"

Jesse hung back, feeling the old sensation of being pulled both ways at once. He heard the *padre*'s voice like a chanted prayer, both sad and sweet and compelling:

"For the poor ones of Mexico, wrapped in their sorrows? To cut the strangling rope of the invaders choking off their lives?"

The *padre* stopped and the silence hung heavy. Jesse, finding his voice, said, "Floyd has had much experience in war. I could add nothing to what he knows."

Garza listened genially, with all his warm courtesy. "Cullen is a

fine soldier and friend," he said, speaking gently, "and so are you,
Jesse. Both of you bear the marks of war . . . the bitterness, the
tear and weariness, which is cumulative. I see it in your eyes, I hear
it in your voices. You are young in years, but war has aged you in its
terrible crucible. You've seen too much of death and the suffering
that goes before. But you are not afraid to die, because we all have
to die someday in the arms of our Lord. What you fear is the terror
and the physical and mental pain . . . all the horror . . . that pre-
cedes death in battle. But you are brave, and still you go on." He
touched his forehead and bowed his head. "How many times have
you and Cullen faced death together just to help some poor Mexicans fighting for their country? . . . Twice against the heathen
Apaches . . . then the ruthless *bandidos* . . . then the mercenary
Hussars . . . and last the El Paso cutthroats who tried to rob and
murder you." He shook his head in wonderment. "You didn't have
to do these brave and generous deeds, but you did because you
wanted to help others not so experienced as yourselves."

Jesse hadn't moved. He discovered that his eyes were wet. It was
all true, what Father Alberto said about war. It was.

The gentle voice went on. "Why are you both here, in faraway
Mexico, where a man's life isn't worth that of a 'dobe dollar or a
bony mule, or sometimes even a string of chilis or a sack of beans?
Why? Because you have no homes anymore. You're like leaves before the wind. Just drifting here and there. But somehow God has
sent you here where you're needed, just as there is a direction in the
lives of all good men . . . a purpose which good men sense but
cannot quite understand. That is why you're here, Cullen and
Jesse."

He bowed his head in silence and when he spoke again, his gentle
voice was almost inaudible, scarcely more than a whisper. "I have no
army. My boys are just a band of peasants. They know little about
the intricacies of war. They're like little children at the mercy of
men while attempting to play men's games; meantime they cry and
pray for land and enough water to raise their simple chili and corn
patches. . . . If they are defeated when they attack the French
garrison, as they must, they will scatter like desert dust whipped up
by the wind, and it will all be over. If they send the invaders fleeing,
word will go out all over Chihuahua and Sonora, and others will rise

up and before long our country will be ours again, thanks to the good exiles God sent us in time."

He lifted his hands in blessing, murmuring to himself in a tongue which Jesse recognized as Latin, and then, touching each man's head, he left them.

The fire was low, down to dull-glowing eyes. A wind came shouting through the pines. Jesse didn't know how long Cullen and he had sat there without stirring, but presently he looked up and he said distinctly, "When you saddle up for San Juan tomorrow, I'll ride with you."

Awake before daylight, he got up feeling a strange malaise. Breakfast, usually enjoyable, was tasteless. Instead of coffee, bacon, and tortillas, he wanted water.

"You look a little peaked," Floyd said, eyeing him. "Better have some tequila."

"I've had a drink."

"Then have another."

"Oh, I'll be all right," Jesse said as they packed to leave.

They formed by the stream, fewer than three hundred patriots while their anxious families stood by watching. Some would ride. Most would walk, all in handmade sandals. Some would not return. Poor as these men were, Jesse thought, they were better shod than the shoeless Army of Tennessee, singing and marching toward its deathblow at Franklin. Poorer than poor Mexicans? True. Which was a commentary on the state of the Confederacy. One Spencer company was mounted, half horseback, half muleback. There was much smiling and good-natured gibing in the ranks, which Jesse knew was expected from young men who thought they would live forever.

Floyd gave the command to move out, and as they did, a weary depression settled upon Jesse. He knew what had raked it up. It was the marching again, the dust again, the tramp of feet again, the thin column of twos again, another rehearsal of the past. The never-ending sense of moving into a confrontation whose ending he knew not. To shake the feeling, he caught up with Floyd and Father Garza at the head of the column. The *padre* thanked him for his presence with his eyes and his quick warm hand. Nothing was said. Nothing needed to be said.

The advancing day brought them to a rib of hills overlooking the town by the river. At this early siesta hour the town seemed to doze. Hardly anyone stirred in the plaza. The white bell tower of the church, high against the bright sky, seemed to rise above all the prevailing violence and evil in force there. Farther back from the plaza, on this side, the tricolored French flag flew over a high-walled, three-story building.

"We'll have to draw 'em out somehow," Floyd said. "Their headquarters is like a fort. What do you think, Father and Jesse?"

"That seems wise," Garza agreed.

"We could make a running pass by the gate," Jesse mused. "Shoot it up. They might give chase. Or we might snipe at 'em from a distance. That should ruffle their feathers enough to make 'em come out. The gate's closed, but I see a few sentries on the wall. Anything but a massed infantry attack. We've seen too many, Cullen."

"Need you remind me, brother reb? Meanwhile, the boys need rest after their march. Gives us time to make some strong medicine for Colonel Dubray and his intrepid Legionnaires."

They rode back, and Floyd set out pickets to watch while the command rested in the pines. Taking a stick, Floyd drew a map on the ground. There was a wash here. The timber ended here. An Enfield company could snipe from there and fall back, firing as it did so, to draw the enemy out. A Spencer company could take cover in the wash, holding its fire until the pursuit neared the pines. That would catch the enemy in an enfilading fire and cut them off from the fort. Reserve companies could be posted here and here. They ruled out making a dash by horseback and shooting up the gate. The Juáristas might look stronger than a handful of mounted peasant guerrillas on a hit-and-run raid. If so, the enemy might not venture out. Better to give the impression of a few poor foot soldiers harassing the place. So the battle plan took rough shape. All three men agreed the walled bastion would have to be taken to make victory complete. But how? By laying siege? Nobody liked that choice. Garza pointed out the Juáristas had only enough supplies for a few days. They talked on.

When the time came, Father Garza rode along the line of soldiers, many truly just boys. He talked to them in a firm voice while leveling a stern forefinger, then pointing in the direction of the fort.

"He's telling them to be brave and to follow orders," Floyd interpreted for Jesse. "That today they are going to fight for something sacred—their country. That God is on their side. I just hope he's right. You never know what green troops will do the first time under fire. They might skedaddle. But I don't really think so. What more could they fight for?" He checked himself and looked at Jesse, a touch of dry irony in his voice. "Like it used to be."

Now, lifting his hands, the Father blessed his men, as they uncovered their bowed heads, his rich voice both gentle and compelling,

The moment passed, in its wake a burdensome silence as grim faces turned toward the fort. Every man also carried a machete. Garza joined the two advisers, and Floyd posted the mounted Spencer company in reserve with all but one of the Enfield companies. He sent the foot company of Spencers ahead first, to slip into the cover of the brush-choked wash, then the Enfield company that would serve as sharpshooters to entice the garrison.

Floyd dismounted and tied his horse. The Mississippian was frowning hard. "I'd better go along with the Spencers. If they start firin' too soon, they'll ruin the whole plan." He too carried a repeater.

Jesse and Garza would stay with the reserves, the Father to pass on any commands.

Presently it was time once more. All the pieces of the gamble in place. The Spencer company hidden in the wash, and the last of the Enfield riflemen in position among the pines, under orders not to fire all at once, but now and then at the sentries on the wall. To pull back deeper into the timber if the French pressed in close. So Floyd said he had told the young Juárista captain and lieutenant.

The first crack from an Enfield shattered the afternoon stillness like an unexpected thunderclap out of a clear June sky. Jesse, seeing the puff of white smoke, felt the old tensions start up, forgotten in this moment the nagging malaise burning his eyes. A scattering of shots followed. Just enough to give the effect of a few snipers bent on devilment more than any threat. The sentries on the walls had disappeared. A lull set in. Jesse could see the riflemen reloading. He was on the verge of ordering them to fire a little faster when a bugle sounded in the fort.

They're coming now. Probably amused that some mere Indians would dare interrupt their siesta. Nothing like a little skirmish to relieve the boredom of occupaton duty. Voilà!

A rifleman fired, then another and another, until the pines seemed to sprout blooms.

Enough. Enough. Not too much. Draw them in. Make it look easy.

His cautioning thought died at sight of the broad gate in the wall swinging open and infantrymen filing out in twos. They made a colorful array there against the dusty wall, clad in red trousers, flashy shell jackets, and smart kepis. They formed rapidly in two ranks. Jesse could hear an officer's hurrying voice.

A company. About seventy-five men, when I thought in their contempt for peasants they'd send only a platoon. Never underestimate the enemy, which I was about to do.

Another sharp command, and the Legionnaires formed in a column of fours and advanced on the pines at the double-quick, a jaunty officer, sword drawn, on the right flank. Veterans, all right.

The uneven sniping continued, the riflemen, some flat, others behind trees, masking their strength. On Jesse's right the Spencer company lay hidden. Waiting. Rifles ready. Floyd watching. *Wait. Wait. Not yet. Let them almost reach the pines.* It was as if Jesse could read Floyd's mind. Everything was going as planned. Another few yards and the red-trousered infantry would reach the edge of the woods, their entire flank raked with fire from the repeaters.

The enemy came on confidently. A splatter of musketry greeted them from the pines. Several stumbled, went down. The rest did not falter, too professional for that.

Watching the Enfield company, Jesse pulled at them impatiently with his mind. *Fall back. Don't wait. Now, damn it! Now! Get the hell back!*

Instead, yet another ragged volley. Instead, yelling like fiends, the Juáristas rose and charged from cover, Jesse shouting, "No! No! Get back!" while vainly motioning them back. The front squad of the Legionnairies slowed step as if astonished. The officer's alert command broke the confusion, and the company began forming a front.

Machetes swinging, the Juáristas hit them before they could, a wave of white-clad bodies literally hurling themselves against the milling bright line. A melee now. Machetes clashing against gun barrels. The enemy had made the mistake of not fixing bayonets.

There was a shudder of sound on the right. The Spencer company men had opened up, furiously working the levers of their repeaters. The last half of the Legion company seemed to melt all at once in heaps. Bit by bit, grudgingly, the lead red trousers gave ground. In the confusion there, the Spencer company suddenly ceased firing for fear of hitting their own men.

Jesse could only watch, his main attention on the hand-to-hand fighting, which could have been avoided. Green boys against veteran campaigners. The brave young always eager to fight, always scorning death. He could see bodies in cotton white on the ground among the red. But the boys were forcing the enemy back. In moments the Legionnaires would be on the run. In fact, they were breaking now.

A bugle's shivering notes rose above the yells and the crash of battle. Jesse glanced up. Like a released torrent, more infantry came pouring through the fort's gate, forming rapidly. The bugler kept blowing the alarm. Not one company, Jesse saw, but two. Bayonets fixed this time. Now three companies.

He turned to Garza, who had watched in entranced silence. "Father," Jesse said, fast, "send a runner to the Enfield company to break off. Come back at once! They must or be swallowed up! You see what's coming! Tell 'em it's your order!"

Garza nodded, understanding, and called, spoke rapidly, emphatically, and a runner went bounding away.

Now. . . . Jesse watched the field. Sun flashing on bayonets. The three Legion companies ready. . . . There was so little time left. . . . The impetuous Enfield company was finally disengaging, finally drifting back, still full of fight. Good! . . . What he saw before him was like pieces in a puzzle, and of a sudden, as if remembered out of the past on other bloody fields, the pieces seemed to fall into the right places. Turning again to the *padre*, Jesse said, "Send a runner to Cullen. Tell him to hold his fire until we open up. The plan is the same as before. Hurry, Father!"

It was done. The field was quiet.

Through Garza, Jesse dismounted the other Spencer company and deployed it in the pines where the first Enfield company had been, and placed the other companies in close reserve. Looking toward the wash, he saw the riflemen posted again, waiting. Catching Floyd's eye, Jesse waved, and Floyd waved back that he understood. Hurrying, Jesse tied his horse and Garza's behind a tree.

Unsheathing his Spencer carbine, he said, "Let's stick close together, Father," and they took long strides down through the thinning pines and stationed themselves to watch.

Jesse knew the enemy would not delay. And they did not, swinging along in perfect unison, column of fours, bayonets at the ready, a hardened arrogance about them, showing an infuriating air of superiority, these brightly uniformed veterans of many wars from many countries, despising the peasants who dared oppose the Emperor of Mexico and fire upon his majesty's troops.

But the attack would not be as before, Jesse saw, as two companies formed separate fronts, one to attack the wash, the other the pines. They charged the wash in splendid style, shouting, firing and reloading as they came, and Floyd's men could not wait. A ripping volley struck the front rank, sending it reeling. Men behind stepped into the gaps. Still they advanced. The fire from the wash was now a continuous sheet of flame.

The other enemy company struck in a rush, on the run, holding fire for the moment. Jesse sensed why from the past. The enemy figured that after one volley from the Juáristas' muzzle-loaders there wouldn't be time to reload. Then the Legion would be among them with bayonets.

He didn't have to order the Spencer riflemen to fire. They let go a volley just as the enemy fired. The oncoming red trousers faltered, stumbled, some dropped, and then, raising shouts, they came on. Along the line of Spencers Jesse could see men down. The acrid stink of gunpowder was stifling. The repeaters banged again. This time the attackers halted in midstep, a bewilderment seemingly upon them. Another volley so soon? Levers worked again, and the crashing line flowered with smoke. The charge died abruptly in its tracks. Only a confused milling now. The survivors turned. Another volley cut them down. Then they broke. The same over in front of the wash. It was finished here except for the pursuit.

But the third Legion company—where was it? It hadn't come up in support of the others.

Jesse jerked about on seasoned instincts. There they came on the double-quick, aiming for the Juáristas' left flank, between the Spencer company and the river. Pointing, Jesse yelled at Garza, "They're tryin' to outflank us. We need two muzzle-loader companies over there quick. Come on!"

The Juáristas jumped up at the *padre*'s shouting and waving, and some yards on, at the edge of the pines, Jesse placed them in two kneeling ranks, barely in time.

Instead of a wide front, this Legion company moved in fours, its intention plain. Coming fast, it would swing in, pivot, and then form a front to roll up the flank. Old stuff. But well-timed and would have been effective seconds ago had the patriots in the pines had muzzle-loaders instead of repeaters. A pincers movement.

Father Garza stood up behind the crouching infantry to see. Jesse pulled him down roughly. "Get down, *padre*. Your people can't afford to lose you, least of all. Now stay down!"

Jesse's eyes blurred as he watched. Everything seemed to sway. He shook his head and, forcing the vertigo aside, took a hold on himself.

As through a burning haze, he saw the enemy halt and wheel smartly to form a broad front.

"Tell the boys to start firing by rank, Father."

The initial volley blew gaps in the moving line. As the veterans steadied, still in the swinging pivot, the second volley roared and the gaps widened. An officer ran shouting from a flank. Before he could rally them, a third volley struck. They didn't run, but they began to back away, firing as they retreated. The officer was shrilling curses at them when a fourth volley crashed. That broke them suddenly, some toward the fort, some toward the plaza.

Jesse feared what was likely, if not inevitable, to follow with undisciplined troops filled with battle lust. It came in a burst of motion. Whooping like wild men, they gave chase, machetes swinging. When a knot of Legionnaires paused to fight, they charged them like savage bulls and cut them down and charged on, looking for more. No semblance of order. Father Alberto's little army of boys, as he called them, tasting their first heady intoxicant of victory, had turned into an avenging mob. A Legionnaire of fair skin and yellow hair below his kepi dropped his rifle and held up his hands in surrender, so close Jesse could see the fear bulging the man's pale eyes. Howling like wolves, these peasants of Indian blood cut him down as well and rushed on.

Jesse had seen enough. "We've got to stop this, Father. The boys are running amuck."

Garza's elation likewise had ebbed at the sights. Together they brought up the remaining reserve companies and marched them fast for the gate, picking up both Spencer companies on the way.

Floyd was jubilant, the light of battle still on fire in his eyes, his slouch hat at a rakish angle. "By God, suh, we whupped 'em good! Our Johnny Reb Indians did! You should've seen the surprise on the foreign bastards' faces when our repeaters kept up the fire after the first volley."

The battle was dwindling to scattered shots around the fort and over in the plaza. Shortly, the shooting pinched off, and the muzzle-loader companies that had charged the flanking Legionnaires so ferociously came stringing back. Floyd entered the fort with a platoon of Spencer riflemen, braced for trouble.

Jesse stayed behind with Garza, bringing order to the returning companies after their merciless chase. As he moved about, the ground seemed to sway crazily under his feet. He had to steady himself. His eyes and face burned. He felt a hand on his shoulder.

The *padre* asked, "You all right, Jesse? Not wounded?"

"I'm fine," Jesse said. Long ago, ages ago, on the never-ending, footsore marches, in heat and cold, his lank belly growling, he'd grown to detest complainers and whiners. More than anything else right now he longed only to go down to the river and bathe his face and rest in the shade of the trees.

Floyd and his men soon returned, herding a few surly prisoners. "The damned place is all but empty," Floyd reported. "No staff officers. But there's a big passel of guns and ammunition. Even a fieldpiece we can take along. A twelve-pounder Napoleon, complete with caisson, no less. Plenty of shells. It's a big victory for Mexico, *padre.*"

Citizens began showing themselves, expressions of relief and gratitude on their dark faces, mixed with horror at the strewn battlefield. Garza went out to them. They started talking all at once. The *padre* listened patiently and, turning, said, "Colonel Dubray and his staff left with the Hussars during the last stages of the battle. The citizens saw them leave the fort by a rear gate and ride across the plaza. They're grateful to us for ridding them of the oppressors. Life has been very cruel here. I, in turn, am grateful to you, Floyd and Jesse. I see now that victory requires more than the fire of patriotism, more than love of country. It needs experience in battle and leadership. Without you today we would have been massacred, boys against wily veterans."

After giving the people his blessing, he moved back a way with Floyd and Jesse. "Another garrison is south of here. So we should linger only long enough to pack up the arms and ammunition. The citizens will tend to the burial of these poor misled mercenaries. I—"

Shouts and gunfire interrupted. Startled, the three swung to see. Jesse saw a squad of Juáristas, rifles smoking, and the prisoners crumpled before the wall of the fort. He stared in utter disbelief. Executed!

He looked openmouthed at Garza. "No, Father, no! This can't be allowed! You don't shoot prisoners!" He was furious, raging. "Who gave the command? Who?"

Shaking his head, Floyd just threw up his hands in disgust. Father Garza, too stunned to speak, could only rivet his gaze on the execution squad. He strode over there. His lashing voice carried back like a whip. A rifleman replied in a meek tone. Head down, Garza walked slowly back.

His voice was like a lament. "They did it because Dubray's troops have been shooting prisoners. However, it is no excuse. It will not happen again, I promise."

"We're acting like barbarians, not soldiers," Jesse raged, appeased not one bit. He was shaking uncontrollably, sick through in mind and body. The figures of Garza and Floyd seemed to sway and flicker strangely before his eyes.

"The Legion has been carrying out Maximilian's Black Decree, which calls for conscription and execution of armed patriots found guilty by a military court," the *padre* said evenly. "Maximilian has issued some pardons, which shows the man has compassion, but Dubray has ignored them to carry out his own decree. Other patriot bands have retaliated in kind. Eye for an eye. That's what's behind the executions, what brought this about today."

"Then both sides are barbarians," Jesse cried, his voice venting still more outrage. "I won't be a part of this anymore, Father. I'm finished here. I can't go on. I will advise you no longer."

Taking with him the shocked hurt in Garza's dark eyes, he turned his back and, still carrying his carbine, stumbled across the littered battlefield to the river. There he bent down and drank and bathed his face and lay down under a tree, completely miserable and exhausted. Inside he was burning up, and the turquoise sky was spinning like a great blue ball. It looked so tantalizingly cool up there, so longed for, so peaceful, he wished to go there. His life seemed to stop as he closed his eyes, in his ears the soothing murmur of the river.

He did not move until he heard Floyd's easeful voice. "Time to head back for camp, Jesse. I know how you feel about what happened." He held the reins of the red horse.

"I don't think I really care anymore. I'd just as soon stay here. I don't give a damn."

"You've got a fever, probably from bad water, and you're goin' to camp," Floyd said firmly, pulling him to his feet. "A shot of tequila might help."

Jesse shook his head no. He tried to mount and, failing, clung to the saddlehorn until Floyd gave him a leg up. Thereafter his awareness was a series of flashes of consciousness, of Floyd and Father Garza often at his side, of calling for water, of hanging on, of the steady motion of his horse. Once he fell from the saddle, and he remembered dimly how his horse stood waiting until hands lifted him back up. He wanted to speak out but could not. And, finally, he seemed to fall into a black world where nothing registered.

11

This nebulous place where he wandered on foot, if he could call it a place, had no form, no meaning. No beginning, no middle, no end. He was adrift and virtually powerless to help himself. It occurred to him eventually that this nothingness could be what death was like, yet if so, strange that he could see about him, strange that he could realize his state of being. Therefore, he was not dead, a conclusion that cheered him for a while. Simply put, vaguely remembered, he had become lost while on a distant journey toward a peaceful shore, because he longed for peace of mind more than anything else. More than riches, more than fame, said to be a young man's passion; more than power. But the journey had left him lonely and extremely weary, and the slightest movement burdened him even more, so all he could do was drift helplessly among the misty currents, lost and doomed forever unless he struggled and found a way out. Somehow he must keep on. He must. If he did not, then he would surely die. He knew that without doubt.

A long time seemed to pass, yet nothing changed where he was, always drifting, always lost, always weary as he struggled on, step by step. Sometimes he crawled. He would know no inner peace until he reached that invisible shore.

Was that a voice? He strained to listen, but the voice, if it was a voice, had fallen silent. He stumbled on. His footsteps seemed somewhat steadier, despite his pathetic weakness. After a while he thought he heard sounds, muffled across the vaporous distance. Crying out, arms reaching, he wheeled into a staggering run and fell flat, too weak for such impulsiveness. Determined, he pushed up on his knees. But like the voice, the sounds had vanished. However, he knew one certainty: The sounds he'd heard were not the thunderous battle crashes of his old nightmares; they were the gentle movements of people at peace. He called out with all his strength, but no one answered. He was still alone, far from the shore. He almost gave up then, and fell back, turning his face to where the sky should be and was not, willing to die where he lay. Presently, like a nagging, he heard the voice again. Sometimes a man's voice. Sometimes a feminine voice, sweet, haunting. It was calling him, he thought, even though he couldn't make out the words. Maybe just his name. That was it. Somebody was calling him. He started crawling that way. Damned if he was going to die in this shrouded world of no meaning!

Not long after that he caught sight of the first glimmer of light. Going at a reeling step, he realized that the fire that had burned unchecked inside him for so long had gone out. A voice reached him again. And although he could not see the person, the voice . . . or was it more than one voice? . . . continued to call him on, leading him toward the obscure light.

When he broke through, there was light shining down everywhere. And there were faces. They seemed unreal at first. Cullen's . . . Father Alberto's . . . Doc Pedro's. . . . And there was a Mexican girl he'd never seen before. He heard their warm voices, but when he tried to answer he could not. Yet he knew that finally he had made it to the peaceful shore. This was it. He felt grateful with all his heart, because it was life itself. At that point he slipped into a deep, dreamless sleep.

When consciousness stirred in him again, he saw that he was in a large tent. He turned his head curiously, and there was the Mexican girl. She smiled at him, a sweet smile of encouragement, like a ray of light across her Indian face. He managed to crack a dry grin, no more, and went back to sleep. Afterward, whenever he woke up, she was always there, either smiling at him or feeding him or drawing blankets about him. In between, he was aware of others passing in and out. Cullen, Alberto, or the indefatigable Doc Pedro. It was they who took him outside in the cold to relieve himself, for he was too weak to go alone. Little was said. He still existed in a kind of vague world, half real, half imaginary, pulled both ways. In his weakness it was so easy to drift away.

One day he woke to dawning clarity, feeling strength and hunger. The girl was close by as always. It struck him that her skin was the color of earth, that her eyes, set big and wide and deep, were the blackest he'd ever seen, and her long hair, as black as a raven's wing, was knotted on the back of her neck. Her high-boned features held an expression of happiness. About sixteen, he guessed, and grown up. Mexican girls matured fast. One of Father Alberto's *soladeras,* women soldiers or fighters. Who as yet had not fought in the rifle companies, but served in the camp. And who would not carry rifles, if Jesse had any say. But wait. Hadn't he resigned as an adviser? He had, back at San Juan, after the savage executions. That seemed long ago, and he wouldn't think about it just when he was beginning to feel better.

He sat up with hunger gnawing at him, and he pointed to his mouth and rubbed his middle and rolled his eyes, once again damning his lack of practical Spanish.

She burst into a laugh of high amusement that brought a hidden prettiness to the Indian features. "Hungry, you are, *señor?*"

"You speak English!" he said, astonished that she did and embarrassed at his own crude sign language.

"Some I speak. Father Alberto teach me since I was leetle girl after Apaches keel my family. He say he want education for young ones so we won't become like *burros* for foreigners. So our Mexico make free we can."

It was the same sweet voice of his wild dreams. The discovery delighted him. "What is your name?"

"Ana—you are Jesse." She pronounced the *j* like an *h*.

"Well, Ana, I'm happy to know you, and I thank you for taking such wonderful care of me." He took her hand. "For saving my life."

"Everybody pray for you. Everybody care. Not just me. Long time you sick. Fever. Everybody afraid you die. You very weak. Bad dreams. You rave."

"No doubt," he said, shaking his head, still holding her hand. "I feel like I've been on a long journey to a faraway land." Speechless for so long, he sensed a banked-up store of words being released. "There was no light where I was. . . . Whenever I tried to get out, I fell down. But voices kept calling me toward the light . . . and when I heard them I got up and went on a little way . . . till I fell down again. But every time I felt like giving up, the voices called to me. And one of the voices was yours, Ana. I know."

"Others call you, too. Father Alberto, *Señor* Floyd, Doc Pedro."

He regarded her with increasing interest. She wore a long-sleeved white cotton shirt and a brown skirt and the inevitable sandals. No frills, since there were few if any in a Juárista camp. She wore no silver or turquoise necklace or earrings, which indeed would look becoming against her dark skin. Her earth-brown face was scrubbed clean, and her smile was even and white. Glancing around, he saw a cot on the far side of the tent. So she had been here night and day. The realization humbled him. Father Alberto had kindly arranged for her to nurse him through the fever. Also, perhaps, a sort of machination in hopes he would find a pretty Mexican girl attractive and desire to stay and serve as an adviser? Ashamed, he dashed the thought as ungrateful.

"Now, Ana," he said, letting go of her hand, "some food, please. I'm ravenous."

Her smile was quick, but not one of passive assent. "First we wash." She left him and vanished outside the tent. He could smell a pungent juniper fire. Returning with a brass bucket of steaming water and cloths, she sat them beside the bed and began helping him pull the odorous gray flannel shirt over his head. She wrinkled her nose at its smell and gasped when she saw the ugly red scar down his upper left arm. "How this?"

"Apaches."

Her face clouded instantly in understanding, in memory.

"Doc Pedro healed it with prickly pear," he said.

She scrubbed him from head to waist, then had him lean over the bed above a pan while she washed and soaped his long yellow hair with what he thought was yucca roots. Drying his hair, she found the strip of naked scalp left by the minié ball and, touching it gently, exclaimed again. "How this?"

"Long ago in the American war."

"Father Alberto tell us about it. Your Civil War."

"We Southerners call it the War Between the States. Cullen Floyd was in it, too. We're survivors."

"It was very bad."

"It was and lasted a long time."

His hair dried, she went to his pack across the tent and took out a blue shirt and trousers and underwear and helped him slip into the shirt. He thought she was finished with him, but she motioned for him to take off trousers and underthings, hardly more than thin rags by now, and handing him the wet cloth and towel, said, "You wash now," and left the tent.

After some minutes he saw her peek around the tent flap and note that he was dressed. Forthwith, she brought a bowl of warm beans and a wooden spoon and one tortilla. He wolfed that down and looked at her for more. All he got was the Indian smile, which could mean anything, he was fast learning. "Enough now," she told him, and took the bowl and spoon away.

To his disappointment, she did not come back, and he lay down, feeling weak but wonderful. The last he remembered was the rejuvenation of being washed and the feel of clean clothing and the comfort of warm blankets. He couldn't have been more grateful. Life was good again. Another beginning was at hand.

Voices. Not of his dreams, but real, broke his slumber.

He opened his eyes to see Floyd grinning down at him, and with him Father Garza and Doc Pedro. "Ana brought us the good news," Floyd said, taking his hand. "Welcome back, Johnny Reb."

"I feel good," Jesse said. "It's been a long journey. What month is it?"

"January. Late January."

"I thank you all," Jesse said, and held out his hand to the others. "Ana makes a wonderful nurse. And as I just found out, is strict as a country schoolmaster who's whipped all the big boys."

"Many prayers were said for you," Garza said, "and Doc Pedro searched far and wide for the herbs you needed."

"He must have found them," Jesse said gratefully, looking at the old Mexican. "As I told Ana, I kept hearing voices calling me back. Urging me on. Whenever I lost hope and wanted to quit, voices seemed to rally me . . . like in battle. . . . I was trying to reach a shore, and then there was a far-off light. The voices, the shore, the light. Strange."

Garza kept jogging his head, his intent face alight.

"The voices were yours, all of you, and Ana's. When I served on the Plains an old government scout, badly wounded in an Indian fight, wasn't expected to live, but had a miraculous recovery. He told me that while he was gone, as he called it, he found himself on the other side of the greatest canyon he'd ever seen. No horse, no food, no water. He was lost. He kept looking for a trail back and found one. The other side of that canyon looked a mile high. He started climbing. There was a wind, and when he couldn't go on, a voice in the wind would call to him. It led him on till he was safe. When I looked skeptical, he said, 'Strange, you think, soldier? Well, I've been there.' " Jesse paused. "So have I, Father, Cullen, Doc."

No one spoke. They just looked at him, believing.

He was getting drowsy again. His pent-up talk, finally released, was tiring him. His last thought as he drifted off was Garza's blessing in Latin and the touch of the Father's hand on his head and the faces dissolving.

Sleep. He couldn't get enough of it. He would wake up, always finding Ana there; then he would eat and drink a little and fall into depthless sleep again. At times Floyd took him out and back.

Something began to bother him. It started slowly at the back of his mind and, gathering momentum, raced to the forefront of his awareness. He woke up in alarm, filled with guilt, shouting, "My horse—where is my horse?"

Ana was beside him in an instant. "Safe is your horse. Show you I will." She helped him to the door of the tent and said, "Wait here."

In less than a minute he heard hoofbeats. Ana rounded the corner of the tent leading the red horse on a halter. He looked sleek and well-groomed, his alert head high, his blood-bay coat brushed bright, his forelock combed down between his ears. A pretty red ribbon adorned his black mane. She led him in close. Jesse thought the horse's eyes seemed to quicken at sight of him, and he stroked the blazed face again and again. When he stopped and stepped back, the horse moved in and smelled of Jesse's shirtsleeve and nuzzled his arm.

Jesse chuckled. "Guess he wants to make sure I smell the same as I did on the trail. Not as strong, but enough the same, I reckon. He was a wild horse once and is suspicious of man, rightfully so. Always will be. Is there a handful of corn I could feed him? I used to give him some as a treat."

Leaving him the halter rope, she went around the tent and returned with shelled corn cupped in both hands. Jesse held the feed out, and the red horse took to it eagerly, to the last kernel.

"Guess I'm back in good standing now. You've taken extra good care of him, Ana. I'm mighty obliged to you. He even looks fat."

Jesse slanted a deviling grin at her. "Maybe even a little spoiled and lazy."

She differed at once. "Not spoiled, this horse. Some boys tried to ride him bareback, and he threw them high," she said, describing an arc with one hand.

"I would suggest that you be careful around him. I doubt that he'll ever be completely tamed. But I like him that way. You are welcome to use my saddle gear when you want to ride him. Though I'd better be along and help you mount him. He likes to dance away."

Her response was to take the halter rope and leap to the horse's back, as nimble and quick as a cat, unmindful of her skirt pulled above her slim brown legs and thighs. Using the one halter rope as a rein, she somehow put the horse through a figure eight, then another, and another, the horse never resisting or taking a wrong step. Taken aback, Jesse saw that she was also using her knees to guide the horse, that undoubtedly the two had practiced this before. She rode back and slid down nimbly, but instead of conceit at her surprisingly impressive ride, he read overcoming shyness and, perhaps, the guilty fear that she had been showing off.

"You ride like a Plains Indian," he congratulated her, still aghast, "using your knees to turn your horse. A very pretty ride. And the red horse seemed to like it."

Suddenly apologetic, she said, "he looked so lonesome when you sick, so I rode him . . . but only after we acquainted. He like to go fast and turn quick. I use your bridle and saddle and blanket." The last was a timid question, a late confession.

"Glad you did. Did he throw you?"

"Only two times." She held up two fingers. "In corral, so he never run away. And I never get mad and mean to him. Friends we are now. I love him, that horse. He is wild but kind. And much savvy up here." She tapped her head.

"You're quite a girl, Ana." As he looked at her, marveling, the insight turned over in his mind that some Indian or *mestizo* would be getting a fine wife before long. A resourceful one. A pretty one, too. Mexicans married young. His chronic weariness caught up with him at that moment, and he turned to go back to his bed.

Her voice, still tentative, checked him. "You have name for your horse, Hesse?"

"I just call him red horse. In my mind I think of him as that. Yet every good horse should have a name. Do you have a name for him?"

Her eagerness spilled out. "Father Alberto tell me your horse how brave is. In many battles." Her eyes flashed.

"Well, he's fought the Apaches and the Hussars . . . been under fire from bandits . . . been chased by the U.S. army . . . and he was at San Juan with the bullets flying all around. I found out early, against the Apaches, that he won't panic and bolt under fire. He's brave, all right. I think a lot of him."

She reached out and touched his arm, looking up into his face, her head coming only to his chest, her eyes like a child's. "I have name I hope you like. *El Soldado*—the soldier. You like?"

How could he say no? But he pretended to weigh the matter while she waited, holding out hope, the expectancy filling the high-boned face. A still longer, teasing wait, and suddenly, as if coming to a decision, he said, *"El Soldado* it is. You've named him. I like it. It fits."

She squealed with delight and, catching him by surprise, leaned up and kissed him on his bearded cheek. The next he knew she was leading the red horse, rather the battle-hardened *El Soldado,* away.

Exhausted from his little venture, he went back to bed.

A scratching on the tent flap woke him, the old "official knock" in the army by a superior officer before entering a tent where other officers were present. Floyd entered in march step, displaying a sheathed sword. He drew the sword and waved it around.

Jesse sat up sleepily. "Where in the world did you get that parade ground ornament."

"One of the boys gave it to me, picked it up on the field at San Juan. Said he thought I ought to have it as an officer of the revolution, y'know. Look, Jesse, there's gold on the handle. Imagine!"

Jesse's response was a tired smile. Sometimes Cullen reminded him of a little boy, though always a refreshing one and always likable.

"Don't you think it's a handsome piece?"

"I think it's about as useless as tits on a boar hog."

"Whoa, now, brother reb. You know our cavalry carried sabers. Van Dorn's outfit and Forrest's."

"I remember, and I also remember we seldom saw a dead cavalry-man, unless he'd been kicked by a horse."

"Aw, posh, Jesse. I just wanted to show you some of the spoils of war in Mexico, scarce as they are."

Relenting, finding his humor, Jesse said, "All right, it's a very handsome piece and proper that it be carried by Mr. Cullen Brad-ford Floyd, at last receiving the sword of honor unfairly denied him for so long."

Floyd's long face broke into a loose grin. Sheathing the saber, he pulled up a makeshift chair and sat down. "I hoped maybe, as an article of interest from San Juan, it would give you a lift after all you've been through."

"I'm just weak. But mighty thankful to be alive, and I haven't forgotten the people who pulled me through. What's going on?"

"Things are quiet now. The French didn't come back into San Juan. It was a big victory for Mexico. Father Alberto got word yesterday they've pulled out of Chihuahua City, on down to Tor-reon. There's a slow movement to the south, toward Mexico City. Spring and summer will tell the tale. . . . Alberto was right when he said the word would go out if we won at San Juan. A hundred or so new recruits have joined us. I'm working them in with the old boys."

"That's better than forming a new company or two. They'll learn fast from the others. What about arms?"

"We picked up more than enough ordnance off the field, besides what we found in the fort. Mostly muzzle-loaders of Belgian and Austrian make. Plus plenty of ammunition for the twelve-pounder." He turned his head a little, and Jesse caught an oblique hopefulness in his eyes. "If we don't drill and keep discipline," Floyd said, "the old boys will fall back to where they were. They're pretty cocky after San Juan. On top of that, we've got the new ones to train. What I mean is, Jesse, two reb drillmasters sho' beat a lonesome one." He closed his plea with his characteristic carefree smile.

Silence settled between them and hung. Jesse couldn't find the exact words he sought, because his feelings seemed distant, not of much consequence. "I know," he said wearily. "I know. Right now it's hard to say."

"Sho'. You rest now. Rest good."

12

It was February now, and winter gripped the high country with a firm gray hand. After all the time that had passed, he was still weak. When could he ride again, even walk to the edge of the pines surrounding the encampment? For days he had heard Floyd drilling the Juáristas. The familiar sounds called to him. Floyd's strident voice. The tramping. The slap of hands on rifles doing the manual of arms. The crunch of sandaled feet marching at the double-quick. At times he longed to be out there; most times he wasn't certain. Discouragement rode him hard. Why, when his fever was long gone? But he knew why, in a way. It was because of his gnawing indecision—whether to stay and resume duties as an adviser, or go? Go where? He was miserable, and his weakness deepened his misery.

His friends came and went like pleasant dreams. Floyd with news of the camp and what little was known elsewhere of the war, which seemed at a standstill. Juárez was quiet. Even Father Alberto didn't know his whereabouts. Floyd always in good humor, his breath smelling of tequila. "You're not drinkin' enough, Jesse." Quick-moving Alberto, his hands shifting restlessly, eyes flashing with emotion when he talked about the revolution. "You have been very sick, *amigo* Jesse. Time will heal you, yet time is a laggard. Have faith. The Lord hasn't forgotten you. Now sleep." Nothing ever said about Jesse's outburst after the San Juan executions. Nothing would be said, Jesse sensed. A murmured blessing. A hand gently pressing his head. A hush. Then slumber.

Today, as usual, he was dressed as if for outdoors and lay on top of the blankets. But he swore to himself that today would be different. He had given in to weakness and troubled doubts too long, each abetting the other. He must get up and regain himself, strengthen his unbelievably wasted and feeble body. He must. Digging deep within himself, he pushed up from the bed and sat on its edge until his head ceased whirling. Rising, he pulled on coat and hat and on protesting legs made his way to the tent flap, his heart already pumping hard. He threw back the tent flap and struck out grimly, his objective the corral where El Soldado was. He would go see his horse. He would, despite his trembling legs and the spinning gray sky. At first his walk was steady, but after several steps he began to weaken. He kept on. He saw the red horse wheel at his approach and come to the corral fence. That was the last he remembered until the pine-needled floor of the forest flew up and hit him.

Hands grasping his body drew him toward consciousness. And Ana's voice calling, "Hesse . . . Hesse." She took him by the shoulders and pulled him to a sitting position.

"Ana," he said. "What would I do without you? But that I must get strong enough to do."

She helped him to his feet and, an arm around his waist, walked him back to his bed. He dropped down, sighing, "I have to get my strength back. Can't do it staying in bed. You can't nurse me forever."

Her Indian smile said she didn't mind. At least that was how he took it. Or was she just being nice? She wasn't submissive and he didn't want her to be.

"Next time," she said, "we walk together. Side by side. Pretty soon strong you will be."

Her inverted sentences, fewer now as her English became more fluent with practice, always amused him. "I should've started days ago," he said.

"No. You too weak. I watch. You just not able, maybe. Maybe not."

Looking at her, he suddenly remembered what he had found in his pack for her yesterday. He had wanted to give her something, to show his appreciation for all she'd done. This sweet, childlike Indian girl, yet not too childlike at that after what had happened to her family, who as far as he could tell had nothing but the clothes on her back and a few blankets, or maybe a *rebozo* to throw around her shoulders. Getting up, he went to the pack without staggering, rummaged a moment and turned with a new bandanna figured in white on blue.

"This is for you," he said, holding it out for her, folded in a small triangle.

She didn't seem to understand. She froze.

"It's for you, Ana." By now he had learned to pronounce it as she did, AH-nah. "A small thing. I wish it was a necklace or some earrings. Something much nicer."

Still, she didn't take it. Her face changed. Her big black eyes seemed to fill and grow even larger.

He got it all at once. She wasn't used to gifts, if any. She didn't quite know how to accept it. "For you," he stressed, and took her hands and placed the bandanna between them. Her lips were trembling. He kissed her then as he would a child, on the forehead, and embraced her lightly, his body stiffly away from hers, and drew back. He did it because, for all her competence, for all her hard-won maturity, she was still a child in years, still an innocent. But gazing down into the brimming black eyes, he glimpsed something more, and he could not resist kissing her on the mouth. Her lips, in the first moment unresponsive as if not used to being kissed, turned sweet and giving. He was the one who pulled back, in surprise and guilt, rather shocked at himself.

She unfolded the bandanna and held it out, her eyes dancing. "Oh, *gracias, muchas gracias,*" she said, and hugged him. "How wear it? Like this, yes?" And she arranged it over her shining black hair like a hood and held the ends under her chin, as an old woman might, he thought. No. He shook his head from side to side. "You no like." And she drew it around her throat and tied it. "Now you like, yes?"

"I like that much better," he assured her.

Murmuring, *"Gracias, gracias,"* she ran outside and, shortly, he heard her exclaiming voice among the women of the camp.

He was left with a warm feeling, but his old fatigue claimed him, and he lay down, thinking he'd never seen such a small and simple gift bring such pure enjoyment and appreciation. On that observation he slept.

It was one of those teasing days in early March when spring paid an early call and the warm breeze was like a caress and the glory of the sun in the flawless sky made all things seem possible, this day in March, this early day, this bountiful day.

She stuck her dark head inside the tent and asked, "You like for walk, yes?" She was always heedful of his privacy. Had Father Alberto also taught her that? More likely, Jesse reasoned, it was inherent. In her blood. Her Indian breeding. Did a Mexican have to be part Spanish to show the finer niceties? Of course not. Mexico had had its civilization centuries before the Spaniards had raped and sacked the country and imposed their religion.

"You bet." He was sitting on the edge of his bed after a midday nap. He was much stronger now, gaining a little each day. Before long he would be himself again. The decision that he would have to face eventually, which seemed not so critical as his health improved, he had shelved in the farther recesses of his mind. He sensed that he would not be asked again to serve as an adviser, not after what he had been through. The decision would be his alone. He was utterly sick of war and its terrible realities, its miseries, but war, here, meant he was with friends. And now there was a new complication: Ana, who was growing on him each day.

He joined her and they skirted the edge of the noisy camp and made for the piny forest, strolling slowly. Patches of snow lingered stubbornly in the shady places. But the brilliant sun was almost everywhere, like a golden glow. He inhaled the keen, cool incense of the pines. After a while she stopped. "You all right, yes?"

He nodded. They strolled on, Ana beside him. She wore the bandanna tied at her throat. She picked up a big pine cone and tossed it at a gray squirrel and missed. The squirrel, seeming more puzzled than alarmed, didn't run. Jesse pitched a pine cone a bit closer, and the squirrel scampered up a pine trunk, hastened out on a branch, and barked defiantly at them.

They laughed and went on. It was good to laugh at little things. A sign of his improved being. There seemed no end to their aimless wandering, Ana running ahead sometimes, now close, her watchful eyes never straying far from him, silently asking was he all right. She made him rest awhile before going on. Up a long-running ridge through oak and juniper brush and towering ponderosa pines and tiny piñons, struggling toward the true spring and down the ridge to a brash and garrulous little stream born in the high sierra.

Puffing, they stooped to drink, mouths dripping, and started across, stepping from rock to rock, holding hands, Ana in front. She slipped, squealing alarm, and was falling surely when he caught her and held her, laughing in turn at her helplessness. Something was happening. He saw it in her eyes and sensed it all through himself.

Happening on this special day of self-renewal, this day of finding himself again. He was still holding her fast when he slipped and they both toppled laughing into the stream.

Drenched, still laughing, the stream laughing with them, they got up and, to show his newly found strength, he picked her up and carried her to the bank and a little way beyond. Out of breath, they plopped down on winter-gray grass. Discovering that he still held her, he released his arms and sat back to dry out in the sun.

"You have any relatives?" he asked her.

"One uncle in Chihuahua City."

"Could you go there and live with him and his family?"

She smiled. "He is mule driver with many children. Better I stay here with the *padre* and people I like very much. There I become burro for uncle, you see."

"Instead," he said, chuckling, "you have become a burro for Jesse, yes?" mocking her a little.

"I like very much what I do for you. Is no work."

"Thank you. You are generous. I was thinking if you went to Chihuahua City you could go to school."

"But I have school. Father Alberto teach me."

"I know. You have learned much. You're a very fine girl, Ana. Very fine. Very bright. Be proud you're an Indian. You're hardly more than a child, yet you're not a child. You have lived. You've experienced much sorrow. I just wish life offered you more opportunities than here in camp. It is also dangerous. There's a war going on not far from here."

The clean-cut Indian features did not change one whit.

"What I mean is, that you would like more schooling. You would find it exciting." He tapped the side of his head as she had about the red horse. "You have *muy* savvy, like *El Soldado.*"

He was teasing her and she knew it. "More than burro, yes?" she twitted him.

"Much more."

And they laughed. Then, looking at her, he discerned the pensive look he saw sometimes creep into the depths of the rich dark eyes. This near, he caught the scent of her, elusive and pleasant. It was not perfume; she had no perfume. It was not soap. Maybe something primitive she put on her straight black hair. Or it was just

Ana. Her youth. Her cleanness. Even her fingernails were clean. Her smile was white. He was beginning to distrust himself around her.

He looked away. "I'm talking too much. But it is good to talk to you. To let go, to discuss. You're a good listener. I was sick at San Juan, and when the boys executed the French prisoners, it was too much. I broke down. Went to pieces. Said things. Said I would not be an adviser anymore to Father Alberto. . . . I was already long sick of war. . . . My life seemed to fall apart right there. Any hold I had on myself. I just wanted to lie down and die somewhere close." He smiled, faintly sardonic. "Guess I almost got my death wish. Would, if it hadn't been for Cullen and Father Alberto." He turned to rise.

Before he could, her staying hand brushed back the long hair from his forehead. There was that wistful look on her face again. He started to get up, but she said, "Your family before very bad *Americano* war. What they like? Your family, you love?"

"Oh, yes. My father, my mother, my sister, my brother. My father was a farmer. Raised mostly good cotton mules, which he sold to plantation owners in the South. You would say he was well-to-do. I went to school. I became a country schoolteacher. I liked that. Then the war came."

He would have ended the narrative there, but she asked more questions, childlike in her interest. He skipped all but the necessary details about the war and the prison camp, his wearing the Union blue in the West, what happened when he returned home, and his decision that led him to El Paso and Mexico.

"Now you know all about me," he said gently. "It's not a pretty story, Ana. Mostly war and what it does to people." He'd spared her his nightmares.

She hadn't moved during the telling. "Is true story," she said, smoothing his hair again. "Is sad story. I understand why you here. Why *Señor* Floyd here. In Mexico we understand. Much sadness here, too, sometimes."

He took her hand and held it, his way of thanking her. She spoke then, her voice picking up a new tone. "Was girl back there long time ago?"

That broke his somber mood. "You are a keen one, Ana."

"Was girl there?"

"You are also persistent." He had to grin at her serious mien.

"Yes, there was a girl. We all had girls back there. That was one reason why we marched off to war, the girls and the bands playing 'Dixie.' "

She was puzzled. " 'Dixie'?"

"A very popular song."

"I understand. You love girl?"

"I guess I did. I thought I did. She was pretty. But no prettier than you." *In a different way,* he thought.

"What happen when you come back from West? She there for you?"

"She had married another man."

Her eyes flashed. "I don' like girl like that. Why she no wait for you?"

"I don't know. Maybe she thought I was dead."

The black eyes were still flashing. "She wait till find out, no? I don' like that girl."

"It just happened that way. It wasn't her fault."

"I don' like that girl."

"It doesn't matter. It happened long ago. We'd better go now. I see dark clouds moving in." He still held her hand. It was time to go. He drew her up, sensing her reluctance to leave. He held her for a moment, then abruptly started off toward the stream.

"Wait. You go wrong." She pointed down the stream.

He struck out, but she caught him and took his hand. Hand in hand, they idled along, content, neither speaking. After a while he noticed that she was leading him on a roundabout way toward camp. Smiling to himself, he said nothing. Neither did he wish for the afternoon to end. The sun was still strong, despite the hint of weather in the slowly changing sky.

No words had been exchanged for some distance when Ana stopped and let go of his hand and asked, her tone containing more than mere curiosity, "What her name, this girl who no wait for you after war?"

His mind elsewhere, he was a moment answering. "It was Sally."

"Sal-lee," she said, musing over the name. "Is pretty name. Is."

"But no prettier than yours."

She regarded him suddenly with a searching, even-lipped gravity, her face altering softly. In that moment she was not a child anymore, he saw, she was a woman. She said no more, but she caught his fingers in her hand.

They strayed on in silence through the cool pines, to the low chanting of the wind in the treetops, and reached the edge of a sloping meadow, aglow with sunlight. She gave a little cry of delight and darted away, daring him to catch her. He gave chase. The grass was slick from the last of the melting snow. Just when he felt his boots begin to slide, she fell with a laughing shriek. He tried to save her, just managing to catch her arm, when they both went down. They landed rolling and came together in each other's arms. They lay like that for a panting instant, startled, as if uncertain. Then he kissed her, feeling her arms slipping around his shoulders, while he gripped her so close he feared he might be hurting her. She said nothing. Easing his arms, he lifted his head. "Dear Ana," he said. He'd never seen the Indian face so smooth, the black eyes so soft. She drew his face down to hers and kissed him and held him, and when after some moments he looked at her again, her eyes were closed, and in the slanting sunlight her face seemed cast in bronze.

All at once he was afraid, stabbed by a swift guilt, swept by the desire to protect her. He sat up. "We'd better go," he said. "It'll be dark by the time we make camp."

She opened her eyes but did not stir.

"Ana, we've got to go now," he said, sounding firm about it. When still she did not sit up, a teasing behind her procrastination which he did not miss, he took her hand and very gently raised her to him. There he embraced her, kissed her forehead, the child's kiss, and lifted her to her feet, the moment now gone.

Again hand in hand, they made for camp. Their stroll soon became a walk, their walk increasing to a fast walk, because the sky was darkening and there was a bite in the high country air. Neither spoke. Jesse seemed to move through a haze, his mind wonderfully at ease, his principal awareness only of Ana at his side, her body touching his at nearly every stride.

Sundown wasn't far off when they reached camp, just ahead of gusting winds freighted with cold. Jesse built a quick juniper fire, and she warmed their supper of beef and beans mixed with red chilis. They were eating like wolves when Floyd walked up to the campfire, holding a bottle of tequila.

"Where've you two been?"

"We went for a hike," Jesse said.

"Some hike, all afternoon." He was teasing them.

"It was a long hike. Any news?"

"Some more recruits volunteered this afternoon. Gonna have to hire me a drillmaster, looks like."

"About how many men do you have under arms?"

"I figure around four-fifty or so. Way they're comin' in, be five hundred or more before long."

Jesse left the question of the drillmaster in abeyance. It was as if he ignored for the moment what would come up in the future.

"You're feelin' better," Floyd said. "That's good." Giving them another teasing look, he started off.

"Don't go," Jesse said. "Eat with us."

"I've already dined at the festive board of Doc Pedro's. Now I have a rendezvous with my friend here," he said, eyeing the bottle. "Don't want to disappoint 'im. Good night."

Howling and blowing snow, the storm struck moments after Jesse had lit the lantern in the tent. Then, remembering his horse with a sharp pang of guilt, he rushed out to find him standing at the corral gate, facing the tent in equine anticipation. Jesse pulled down armfuls of feed from a high mound of wild hay and scattered them inside the corral. There was no cover at all for the red horse, not even a brush windbreak, which Jesse regretted. But, he thought, going back, a wild horse wouldn't expect any.

"I should've fed *El Soldado* before I satisfied my own appetite," Jesse said in a blaming voice, guiltily shaking his head. "Generally I do better than that. But I guess he forgave me."

She sat on the cot, huddled in a blanket, her feet drawn up under her. She had let down her raven-black hair, which fell straight and thick below her shoulders. The effect, he saw with approval, was striking. Contrasting the ebony of her hair against her earth-brown skin. Framing the high-boned structure of her face, and the luminous black eyes, and the straight nose with just the hint of an arch to it, a near-Roman nose, just enough to show pride and bearing. Not forgetting the full mouth and the sweet smile therein for him. She also looked cold.

In concern, he draped his coat around her and sat down beside her. She leaned her head against him. "Tell me," she said, "about how you grow up in what you call Ten-naw-see, you say."

He did at length, rather verbosely, covering the pros and cons of the slavery question, how even Southerners were split over the issue, until he reached that stage of his life where he met Miss Sally and squired her around and attended dances at the Jamesons' home and their good-night kisses on the veranda. Skimming that period to such an extent that Ana turned to him and asked, "You no tell me much about Sal-lee. Why you no tell me?"

"Oh, there isn't much to tell."

"So you say." She tilted her head just so, and her eyes sought much more, sensing much more. "Maybe so you tell me about the bad *Americano* war you call the War Between the States?"

"I don't like to talk about it, Ana. I lost all my boyhood friends. Too many good men died."

Penitent at once, she gave him a hug. "Then maybe so you tell me about *Yanqui* prison where you almost die?" Childlike, he thought, she was interested in events which, viewed from far away, seemed less brutal and, veiled by the passing years, had even taken on an adventurous hue.

"We lived like animals. We died like animals. I survived is all. Many good men didn't."

Sadness rose to her face and she laid her head against his shoulder. Drawing the blanket tighter about her, she also moved her feet from beneath it and he saw that they were bare. She had no shoes or boots, only sandals. Instantly he went to his pack, dug out a pair of gray woolen socks, and pressed them into her hands. "Put these on right now," he told her.

Amused at the order, she pulled on the socks, which came halfway to her knees, and gazed up at him. "You like, yes?"

"I like. Now you tell me about your childhood. Your growing up." He paused, abruptly remembering. "But not if it makes you sad about your family."

"Is sad, yes. But Father Alberto say when pray for your family the sadness you can bear in your heart and God will bless you and love you and love is strength. I do that and always I feel better. Not so much sad, yes? You understand?"

In that seeking face, so full of honesty and trust, how could he answer other than, "I understand."

She poured out her story then. Growing up on a big plantation in Sonora where her father labored for the *hacendado*, who did not cheat her father and let him work a corn patch and keep half the crop. Ana the youngest of nine children. One of her earliest memories was of her mother telling her the heathen Apaches would get her if she didn't mind.

Although she obeyed her mother most of the time, the Apaches came anyway, when Ana was eight. They came like a fierce hot wind out of the north, on foot and horseback, streaks of white painted across their savage faces, screeching like demons. She remembered their faces because she was playing with a sister in the mesquites, where they then hid while the Apaches struck down her mother and brothers and sisters and her father when he ran from the cornfield with a hoe. The sister with Ana started crying loudly. When the Apaches heard and started toward the mesquites, Ana ran and hid. But the Apaches did not kill her sister. Instead, they took her away on a horse, and Ana supposed she became a captive in the mountains far to the north to grow up like a heathen, which was worse than death.

Jesse had put his arm around her while she graphically told the story. Shaking his head in sympathy, he asked, "What happened to you after that? You were all alone."

"I lived in the hacienda of the *hacendado*, who had many little ones to feed. One day Father Alberto come, and when he heard what had happened, he talked to the *hacendado* and I went to live with the *padre*'s people, and he give me this, which I wear with thanks to God the Father for sparing my life." Opening her shirt at the throat, she showed him a tiny cross on a slim silver necklace. "That was eight years ago," she said.

So she was sixteen, Jesse thought, still hardly more than a child. Moved by her story, he kissed her on the forehead and tightened his arm around her.

"You are *simpático*," she said, looking up at him.

"I am," he said, "and you are a very brave girl."

Afterward they sat in silence for some time, drawn together, listening to the howling wind flapping the tent like the wings of a giant bird, Jesse lost in drifting thought, conscious of a lulling contentment. Presently, taking notice of the growing cold, he got up and took a blanket off his bed and gave it to her. "You'll need this tonight."

As usual, he turned his back while she undressed, and when she was in bed, he drew the extra blanket over her.

"Be snow in morning," she said. "Very cold." The black eyes were intent on him; otherwise the Indian face was unreadable.

"False spring," he said. "Just like Tennessee sometimes." Denying the impulse to kiss her good night, he blew out the lantern, undressed down to his underwear, and got into the cold bed.

As if that was a signal, the storm kicked up to a higher crescendo, its howl rising to shrieks. He endured that until the tent started flapping and tossing even more violently, until he questioned whether it could withstand the beating. In sudden concern for her, he said, "I think you'd better come over here, Ana. I'm not sure this tent is going to stand." Getting up, he stood by the bed.

In a moment he sensed her warm presence beside him in the total blackness. She handed him a blanket. "You take back," she said in a shaking voice. "We need."

"You get in first," he said.

She did, and he spread the blanket over the bed, and slipping in beside her, he pulled all the blankets over them. He could feel her shivering. He turned toward her and found that she faced him. "Ana," he said, and wrapped his arms around her. Her shivering ceased after a bit.

"I wonder why you wait so long," she whispered in his ear. "You think Ana is child. But is no child. I woman now for you, Hesse. I love you. I never love before."

13

There was a dreamlike quality to the swiftly passing days, so filled with laughter and the fulfillment of lovemaking. Time held little meaning for Jesse. He could not recall such peace of mind and happiness, even as a boy. They hiked the woods and took turns riding *El Soldado*, amused at his displays of equine independence. They cooked and relished their simple fare as if it were beyond compare. She wore his shirts and socks. She washed his clothes and cut his hair. Their drafty tent, flapping in the night wind, was a refuge against the outside word. All this, while aware of the eyes of the camp upon them.

As they lay in bed one night, Ana asked, "Was this long-ago girl, this Sal-lee, make better love than me."

His laughter pealed out. "Why, I never kissed her but a few times. How would I know? You are a little pry, Ana."

She was stubborn, the tone of her voice on the brink of doubt and perhaps pouting. "But maybe so you think her better than me?"

He laughed some more. "No woman could be better than you," he said, gently turning her over while her arms slipped around him.

Yet he could not get it out of his mind that she was hardly more than a child. He noticed that when he woke up before she did and saw her mouth grown soft in sleep, her lips barely parted, like a child's. Sometimes he caught it in the timbre of her voice, the voice of a small girl whose childhood had been violently interrupted.

He often thought of marriage, but Father Alberto was gone much of the time, and when in camp busy with Cullen training the recruits. Where the Father went, not even Cullen and Doc Pedro always knew. But there would be marriage in due time, after which Jesse would take her to Texas to make their home. A plan, however, which he hadn't broached, for fear she'd be unhappy leaving her *padre* and his people and her beloved Mexico.

By now, Jesse thought, he felt that he could put his past behind him and go on with his life. At last!

This day, like so many others, had been perfect in all respects. Spring was truly here! He and Ana had groomed the red horse and taken turns riding him to the stream where they had fallen in that never-to-be-forgotten day that had led to their avowal. Afterward, Jesse mused again of Texas with Ana, removed from the violence of strife-torn Mexico. A home. First of all, a home. He swore to himself they would have that. Their family was already assured, for Ana was with child.

It happened again as it had on the trail with Cullen, when he had not the faintest warning. The nightmares swarmed out of his peaceful sleep. Flashes of the man-to-man death grapple around the Carter House. So real Jesse could see the powder-blackened faces of the Union boys through the roiling smoke. So real he could taste and smell the bitter stink of gunpowder and hear the shrill shouts. One stood out above all the rest, savage and horrible in his ears: his own, it was. He'd gone berserk, clubbing, thrusting, slashing. . . . By God, the Yankees were on the run! . . . No—they were rallying! . . . He saw Lacy and Drake go down. And, as always, before he could help them, the old, ripping pain struck him down and blackness rolled over him.

Someone was patting his face. "Your face is cold with sweat and you make groans," a voice said. "You sick?"

He felt an immense weight lift from him. It was Ana's sweet voice. Staring up at the gray ceiling of the tent, he had the sensation of emerging from the depths of his private hell into a cathedral of streaming light. For a while back there he had been in the Yankee hospital in Nashville and Pat, the nurse, was trying to rouse him to take some soup. Pat, his good friend. Jesse knew he'd been there because the hospital's stench of death still lingered in his nostrils.

"You sick?" she asked again.

"Just bad dreams," he mumbled groggily.

She kept patting his face. Now she pushed hair away from his forehead. "Is cold, your face. Afraid you sick."

"I'm all right now. Just bad dreams from the war. I never know when they're coming. But I am cold. Keep me warm."

Murmuring, she snuggled closer and cradled his head in her arms. He slept then.

Cullen joined them that afternoon, full of good-natured teasing. "As healthy as you look, don't believe you need any more of Doc Pedro's magic herbs," he told Jesse, his eyes giving Ana his meaningful approval.

"I'm lucky," Jesse said. "I didn't know a man could be this lucky and happy. To have a girl who'll soon be his wife and such good friends." He actually felt regret for his solitary friend. "Reminds me, Cullen. Did you ever go back to see that girl you told me about?"

"I did."

"What happened?"

"As I rode toward the house, I saw her on the porch, rockin' a baby."

"Didn't you stop? Maybe it was her sister's baby."

"About that time a young man came out of the house, picked up the baby, and kissed 'em both. I just pulled my slouch hat lower and rode on by."

"I see. Sorry it happened that way."

"I don' like that girl." Ana spoke up. "She no wait for you."

"I guess it was just as well," Floyd said. "No respectable Southern girl would marry a galvanized Yankee."

"But glad I am Sal-lee no wait for Hesse," Ana said brightly, going over and putting her hands on his shoulders. "I like that girl now."

"I told her about going back home," Jesse explained, smiling.

They talked on about trivial things, as if by mutual agreement skirting any pressing questions: Jesse silent on future plans; Floyd on progress of the revolution; when the camp might move. Until Floyd, clearing his throat, said, "Father Alberto wants to take most of the command south tomorrow where a villager's reported a big camp of Hussars," and Jesse knew then why he had come. "We'll leave a company here," Floyd continued. "I'm not askin' you to ride with us. Just thought you ought to know, because you'd wonder at the pullout."

Jesse nodded. "Reckon I would, it's been so quiet lately."

After Floyd had gone, Jesse grew thoughtful and sensed the same in Ana. A war was going on not far away and they were still a part of it, bound to it by blood and obligation. He put his arms around her, kissed her tenderly, smoothed the raven-black hair, and said nothing. But the rest of the day and evening drew by in somber reality, their thoughts heavy. She clung to him throughout the night, while the feeling redoubled in him that he ought to go with the command in the morning. At least, as an observer, now that he was able-bodied again. Let them know that their cause was still his. Offer an opinion, if asked. In that event, he would be an adviser again, only a limited one. This once, this last time, before he took Ana to El Paso, which as yet he had not told her.

When morning came, he said, "I've decided to go with the boys. This will be the last time. I feel I ought to. They won't expect me to fight, if it comes to that." A lie, for her sake. If a fight developed, of course he would pitch in if needed.

He expected her to object. She did not speak at once. But the the black eyes in the Indian face betrayed her. Behind them he read dread and mounting fear.

"I know you go," she said. "I know last night. I no want you go. I afraid for you. But you go. You man. You fight for Mexico."

When the red horse was saddled and the Spencer sheathed and he came to the front of the tent, she regarded him for a long time without speaking. He held her and kissed her again and again. There was nothing more to be said.

"Go with God," she said then, and he felt her arms release him.

He mounted and rode out to Floyd and the *padre*, and when he looked back, she was watching. He waved. She waved. A picture he took with him, that stayed in his mind. Already the day had turned forbidding.

As Floyd formed the Juáristas and gave the command to move out, Jesse estimated some two hundred men rode good horses. Finally some needed cavalry. All the infantry companies marching in good order. One company of muzzle-loaders left to guard the camp. Cullen and Father Alberto had improved discipline since San Juan. These men moved with purpose and there was no grumbling. Jesse, thinking of Ana, willed himself to concentrate on the coming work at hand.

As they marched along, Floyd pointed to a little man at the head of the column. He was dressed in peasant white and wore a wide straw sombrero like the others; in addition, he fancied a broad, silver-studded belt supporting a holstered pistol. And black boots instead of sandals. A gnomelike, wizened man, he rode hunched over, remindful of a jockey, his attention never wavering from the trail.

"There's the villager who brought the news about the Hussar camp. He's guiding us back."

They passed through up-and-down country fissured with deep canyons down into pine-clad hills, everywhere burgeoning signs of spring. After two hours of marching Floyd called a halt.

"Well," he said to Jesse, "what do you think of the boys now?"

"Much improved. No straggling, such as we had before San Juan."

Floyd's deep brown eyes twinkled. "Although I've drilled and marched their tails off, I'm glad to give the credit to Father Alberto. He gets after 'em hard. Shames 'em. Then inspires 'em. When you combine the word of God with personal magnetism, you've got a leader. He can make a man feel no bigger than a piss ant one minute, then make 'im think he can move mountains the next. Believe us Johnny Rebs could've used some more like him back yonder."

"He's the reason you've stuck, isn't it?"

"I can't think of a better one," Floyd replied, with a half grin. "And why you've come today?"

"One reason. Also you and the boys. I'm showing my colors."

"You didn't have to come, you know."

"I know. . . . This is my last ride with the boys, Cullen. I'm taking Ana to El Paso, though I haven't talked to her about it yet. Be hard on her at first. She'll get homesick. We'll settle there for a while."

Floyd's mouth fell ajar and Jesse saw his swift surprise, akin to gloom, replaced at once with warm approval. "Sho'. Get her out of this damned war. I wish you happiness, old friend. You bet."

They left the hills and came down into the thorny desert, scouts out, cavalry on the lead, the infantry keeping up, going at a swinging dogtrot, like Apaches, Floyd pointed out proudly. "They can cover fifty miles a day at that trot," he told Jesse. "After all, they're Indians, too."

Now the sun read late morning.

When the low clutter of a small village appeared in the distance, like an island on the sunbaked ocean of desert, Floyd halted, only the second rest of the day for the hard-marching foot soldiers.

The hunched guide drifted over, his leathery face gullied and parched by the sun. He spoke in Spanish to the *padre* and Floyd, his eyes quick-moving as he picked up a rock and drew a map in the grainy soil and made a circling motion, which Jesse interpreted as meaning around the village. He looked at them for approval. They nodded and he left.

"The Hussar camp is about two miles beyond the village, posted around a big spring just off the road," Floyd explained to Jesse. "We'll halt for half an hour. I want the boys rested before we tie into 'em."

"What is your plan?"

Floyd looked first at Garza, who said, "We've discussed it at great length, at the same time taking into consideration that the enemy may not react as we should prefer. I've left the details up to Cullen."

"It's simple," Floyd said. "I'll take the cavalry way around and we'll come in from below, in the hope they won't be expecting attack from that quarter. One company of horse will carry Spencers. Father Alberto and the infantry boys will spread out in a half-moon from this side, Spencers on each flank. They won't fire until we open up. If the other people fall back this way, our infantry should have 'em boxed and cut off from the town, where they could fort up."

"What if they don't break this way?"

"That will mean they're making a stand. Then the infantry will charge the camp. The red trousers will be caught in a pincers, like the old feller betwixt a rock and a hard place."

"Sounds feasible."

"Any suggestions, suh?"

"None a-tall."

"Like I said, Jesse, you don't have to get into this."

"Indeed not, Jesse," the *padre* affirmed. "You stay out of it. You've done enough. Just watch from a distance."

Jesse was touched. "Thank you, Father. I thank you both. But since I'm here and mounted, I can't just stand by. I'll ride with Cullen."

Garza withheld any words, but his Zapotec eyes burned like coals.

Soon it was time to go, and Floyd took the cavalry on a wide loop around the village, traveling at a trot, the humped guide ranging ahead. Beyond it, he swung in behind a screen of thick mesquites. The Hussar camp now lay to the southwest, Jesse reckoned. Onward they crossed a broad passage of horse tracks headed northeast, so fresh the walls of the prints were still crumbling. Floyd cut the tracks a glance and rode on without pause.

Less than three quarters of an hour had gone by when the guide flung up a hand and pointed northwest. In that direction, he signed, was the camp. When the column closed up, Floyd rode quickly ahead, the horsemen following in double file. Coming out of the mesquites, he formed a column of fours and spurred forth at a canter. They moved in this order for some three hundred yards, toward a swell of land, tangled with spiny brush, which blocked view of the desert and the village.

Here Floyd halted to let the hard-used mounts blow a bit. He divided the column into four companies, the Spencer outfit behind him, and struck out. Over and down the rise they moved, and there he swept them into a gallop. The camp would be near.

Before them Jesse saw the desert unfolding and beyond it the disarray of the village—but the desert was empty of movement.

He pulled rein at the same instant Floyd did, causing a crowding of oncoming riders.

"What the hell!" Floyd snarled. He rode on at a slowing trot, viewing as Jesse did the litter of a recently vacated camp: the black circles of campfires, some still smoking; the orderly rows of manure where the picket lines had been; the clean squares where the tents had stood. Floyd waved the guide over. For an interval they traded hot Spanish, climaxed when the guide, humping his shoulders, spread both hands and said, *"Quién sabe, señor?"*

"I'll be damned," Floyd said, venting disgust. "Claims he has no idea where they went or when. But from all signs they broke camp not long before we got here. Let's take a look-see, Johnny Reb."

With his words, he reined left, Jesse with him, and they began tracking. They crossed the south-going road, which showed no recent heavy travel, circled to the west and around, which showed only a few tracks, and to the north toward the town, which revealed heavier prints, but the telltale horse droppings were old and dry. Riding on, they swung eastward and found fresh tracks.

"Hell," said Floyd, looking to the northeast, "these hook up with what we crossed comin' down the east side."

"They do," Jesse agreed.

"Let's tell the *padre*," Floyd said, "and follow these. I don't like this." He was beginning to scowl, a sign of trouble, which Jesse shared.

A short parley followed with the *padre;* afterward, trailed by the dog-trotting infantry, the riders set out on the fresh trace. It wound back into the piny hills, climbed eastward where the footing was easier. From the broadness of the chopped trail, Jesse estimated that they followed no fewer than two or three companies. He told Floyd. But the principal concern remained: Where were the Hussars headed? Again, the guide shrugged with a *"Quién sabe?"* It was now midafternoon. They waited for the foot companies to close up and went on.

An hour later the tracks veered sharply northeast, into the sierra, the horses grunting at the climb. They rode hard for a time, the trail's general direction unchanged, Floyd still scowling, Jesse uneasy. Floyd halted the column and said, "There's a smell about this that won't go away. Could they be linkin' up with another outfit?"

"Not up here," Jesse said, "unless they know the mountains better than we do."

They rode on. When the tracks shifted north, they followed on only a little way before both reined up as if of the same sudden inkling. Pinning a look on Floyd, Jesse said, "I hope to God I'm wrong, but there's only one place they could be headed for this way now—our camp," chilled at his words.

"Where's that *no-sabe* guide?" Floyd snarled, biting off his words, and whipped around. The guide, who had been riding behind them with the advance of the next company, wasn't there. "He must've quit us before we turned north," Floyd said, his lips forming a tight line. "We've been duped, Jesse. Our guide paid to draw us off. Let's ride!"

They tore out, Jesse's mind closing on how it had happened: while the guide ("Money can buy anything in Mexico, Jesse") led them to the empty encampment, the companies of Hussar horse slipping by, guided toward the Juárista stronghold in the sierra. He tried to shut out the consequences at the camp, guarded by one muzzle-loader company. His dread grew.

Time seemed to mock them, to lag, to dawdle, the day locked in its flaunting of springtime, while their mounts, worn down by now, labored over the up-and-down trail. Another hour slipped by.

A shudder of sound reached Jesse—that was a volley—after it a flurry of ragged shots. Filled with foreboding, he spurred the red horse, and the pines flew by in a blur.

Floyd waved his arm for the trailing column to come on faster.

Another volley swelled above the drumming rush of the horses over the pine-needled carpet of the forest. Then more sporadic firing, then an ominous quiet.

The red horse was going at a dead run when Jesse, Floyd a few jumps behind, burst into the clearing. Before him a scene of wild confusion and high wailing: men and women immobile in shock, others dashing aimlessly about, a woman, hands to her face, standing over a downed rifleman. The shapes of other soldiers strewing the campground. A man holding a lifeless child, his tearful face turned beseechingly to the sky. Two girls aided an old woman.

He jerked the horse to a sliding halt at his tent and came down running. The tent's flap was closed, which gave him hope. He flung the flap away and tore inside and stopped short.

Ana lay on her back, a great smear of blood on her shirt—his shirt. The calm Indian features set in earth-brown marble, the enormous black eyes staring heavenward to God the Father.

"My God—no!"

He took her in his arms. She didn't move. Numbing shock swept over him. Next, tearing grief. Gasping, choking, heaving. She was gone, he knew. Gone, gone. While he fought to deny it. He'd seen too much not to know. He couldn't leave her. He would not. . . . Gentle hands disengaged his arms, and he felt himself being drawn to his feet. Someone covered her face. Others lifted her to the cot. . . . Unable to rest, he was only vaguely aware of the passing of day into night and night into day, which brought upon him another crushing reminder: Once again he was the survivor. Why, why? *Why Jesse Alden Wilder again? Why not sweet Ana?* It was so cruel, so beyond his limited understanding of how life worked. Would she be alive if he hadn't gone? She hadn't wanted him to go. Had she, in her primitive Indian intuition, sensed something? *She knew.* That tore even deeper. There was no end to his self-torture.

He walked the woods in grief, weeping, unable to lift his head to the sky, which, fittingly, was overcast today. Walking, walking, head down, hands locked behind him. Restless, ever moving, he came to the corral. The red horse's head lifted, the mustang eyes alertly on him.

Guilt seized Jesse. Poor, neglected, faithful, once-wild creature! Jesse did not remember unsaddling and penning him. Someone had, but he was without feed. In shame, Jesse led him to the stream and back, and threw down mounds of hay. As the red horse lowered his head to feed, Jesse saw the red ribbon in the black mane. It was sacred now. Her hands had woven it with loving care. It would remain there till it wasted away, untouched. Overcome, he threw his arm around the bent neck and wept into the black mane. The horse quit feeding, turned, and nuzzled Jesse's arm. Moved, Jesse thought of the solace noble animals gave in times of grief.

At the rosary and mass for the victims, some thirty soldiers, women, and children, Jesse stood woodenly, Father Alberto's words a meaningless chant in his ears, until the Father sprinkled holy water on Ana's plain pine casket, then taking a tiny wooden crucifix from the top of the casket amid the wildflowers, the *padre* kissed it and presented it to Jesse. By now the rituals seemed spectral.

After the burials on the slope above the camp, Jesse returned to the silent tent, empty of the past, its laughter and love. Her scent still lingered here, like a soft, sweet rain. Over there her few belongings, clean and neatly folded. He bowed his head, thinking he could sleep here no longer.

He was sitting on the cot, staring into space, still holding the crucifix, when Floyd entered, laid a long arm around his shoulders, set a bottle of tequila on the floor, and started to leave. Instead, suddenly, he stared at Jesse with a shock close to horror, his eyes sprung wide. He opened his mouth to speak, but his lips seemed to lock.

"What is it?" Jesse asked dully.

Floyd made an uncertain motion toward his own head, hesitated and looked away, as if powerless to speak.

Puzzled, Jesse rose. His head, his face? He moved to a tiny mirror hanging on a tent pole and glanced into it. He saw a stranger's face: lined and drawn, the embers of the eyes, the mouth warped in bitterness—and the long snow-white hair. With a gasp, he threw up a warding-off hand and slumped down on the cot.

"It's all right, Jesse. It's all right." Floyd's arm was around him. Floyd held out the tequila. "Drink this. That's an order."

Jesse drank.

"Now another."

Jesse obeyed and put the bottle down. "Y'know, Cullen, I remember an instance where a man's hair turned white from fear in battle. But not this."

"This is worse. No man could lose more."

"I'm all right now, old friend."

Floyd left and Jesse, taking another pull on the bottle, caught himself sinking into deeper bitterness.

A rustling at the tentflap registered on his consciousness. But he didn't look up. He didn't care. Head still bowed, he felt a hand rest lightly on his head. Still, he didn't look up. Whereupon, he heard the *padre's* healing voice:

"You have suffered so much, *amigo* Jesse. In your long, terrible American war. Now in ours. . . . War comes from the freedom of choice which God gives man. And man suffers. But God understands. He is not without compassion. . . . I felt the same bitterness as yours when Apaches killed my dear mother and father . . . my dear brothers and my one precious little sister, Lucía—my entire family. One day a happy family. The next wiped out. Man's cruelty to man." Jesse sensed the *padre* was selecting his words carefully. "But God understood my grief. He touched me as he touches you now through me . . . in love and understanding, which you will feel, I promise you. He will dry your tears. He will raise you up. He will not forsake you. He cannot heal the hurt, but he can take away some of the pain."

Jesse felt the hand press down, now lift. There was a faint rustling, and then the *padre* was gone.

Eyes closed, Jesse found himself drifting off into blessed rest.

14

Daylight dried his tears, left him shaken and exhausted. But he had slept most of the night. Rising, he stepped out of the tent into a sun bold with promise of another day. Before he could build a cooking fire, Floyd was there so quickly to stop him that Jesse knew his friend had been watching for him.

"You're eating with us," Floyd insisted, and Jesse did not demur.

The affable Doc Pedro had outdone himself this morning: deer steaks and gravy, fresh tortillas, red beans, and coffee. After a slow start, Jesse ate with relish.

"I have a piece of interesting news," Floyd said after breakfast, over more coffee. "Some of the boys who lost family in the raid slipped off to the village and paid the guide a call. They tortured him. Just before they put him out of his misery, he confessed to taking fifty pesos to mislead us. He also said the notorious Colonel Dubray led the raid. The order was to spare no one, women or children, as a means of discouraging any more volunteers from the village."

Jesse nodded. "It seems to fit his reputation." It was also war, he thought, feeling no surprise.

"Late spring or early summer should determine the outcome of the war," Floyd said. "President Juárez will win. How soon depends on how much longer the bishops and Mexican aristocrats stick with Maximilian. How great the sacrifices of the Juáristas. Father Alberto senses this. He is impatient. . . . Tomorrow we move camp again to the south." His tone and his eyes on Jesse as he said the last were matter-of-fact. No more, no less.

"I'll be riding with you," Jesse said.

"God knows nobody expects you to." A vast understanding deepened in Floyd's long-jawed face.

"Where else would I go?"

Floyd looked beyond Jesse, his eyes devoid of any persuasion, one way or the other. The decision was up to Jesse.

"So I'm going," Jesse said.

He went to the tent and began putting a pack together. Until now this war, like the first one, had been largely impersonal. Bad as it had been back there, you didn't shoot women and children. Now Jesse Alden Wilder was going to do something about that. This Jesse, who knew all about killing, because he'd done a heap of it, starting as an apprentice killer, like thousands of other boys wearing the blue and the gray in the dew-wet woods of Shiloh. Boys killing boys. He was because this was personal. It was also a matter of duty and honor.

On the afternoon of the third day he observed a mixed column of infantry and Hussars in escort moving snakelike on the narrow road below. Under him the blood bay stirred restlessly, fox ears twitching. The enemy had been foraging, a euphemism for rape, robbery, and murder, Jesse thought, noting the driven cattle and the loaded mules. Some Mexicans had been impressed as drivers.

Scouts had spotted the column that morning as the Juáristas marched and rode south from their new camp in search of battle. The rolling terrain and the gap through which the enemy had to pass had suggested the simple tactic. So now with the *padre* Jesse waited for the signal of gunfire from Floyd's Spencer-armed cavalry, which had raced around to seize the gap, behind Jesse infantry and horsemen formed in fronts of fours.

The head of the column was within rods of the gap when Jesse heard the first rattle of gunfire and saw big mushrooms of powder-smoke puff up.

He turned to the *padre*. "Let's go, Father!" and waved everybody forward.

They dashed down the rocky hill in a wave and hit the road at a run, the sprinting infantry not far behind the riders. The marchers in the column, faced toward the firing at the gap, weren't aware of the new threat until the Juárista cavalry was nearly upon them. When they turned, it was too late. One crumpling volley and the avenging patriots were upon them, machetes out, yelling like wild men. After them closed the hard-charging infantry. A deadly milling began.

Jesse fired twice, seeing the uniformed figures jerk from the impact of the bullets. After that he was like a piece of flotsam swept along on the swift current of the charge, the eager Juáristas rushing around him to join the hand-to-hand fighting. Suddenly he had to hold up in order not to hit his own men. Pulling up, he noticed the *padre*. He held a revolver, but he wasn't firing it. He held it out before him, the barrel pointed upward, as if it were foreign to him. He wasn't fighting. A kind of terrible sadness enveloped his thinly cast, sensitive face.

As the firing slackened, Jesse saw arms raised in surrender. Fearing another repetition of San Juan, he yelled at the *padre* and pointed, and Garza understood, and they began herding the prisoners off the road. The firing died completely. The battle was over.

Jesse felt spent, glad it had ended so quickly. Somehow the sense of triumph and gratification he had expected to feel was lacking. He spent the next half hour directing the gleaning of the battlefield, while Garza questioned the prisoners in French. Jesse and Floyd were discussing the battle, the Mississippian pleased with the command's discipline, when the *padre* joined them.

"These soldiers," he said, "are from the Presidio Montaña, sent out by Colonel Dubray to pillage the countryside." He looked down at his sandaled feet. "I fear other things also happened. It is always that way. Believe me, I've just heard more than one battlefield confession. Interesting, how when a man is close to death or has felt its hot breath, he wants to clear his soul. These men expected to be executed as they have executed our men taken prisoner."

"The presidio will be a tough nut to crack," Floyd said. "I've seen it. High stone walls and towers."

"It has to be taken if this is to stop," Garza said. His eyes seemed to flame.

Floyd nodded. Jesse silently concurred.

They moved on, the prisoners in tow. In the middle of the column the mule-drawn, twelve-pounder Napoleon waddled along on two wheels like a tethered bulldog, trailed by its caisson of ammunition.

"A man don't capture many fieldpieces like that," Floyd said to Jesse, putting on a bit. "My first, suh. I have named it Old Betsy."

"Goes nicely with your sword," Jesse said, smiling.

The battle had gone well, and possibly this would all be finished before long, Jesse mused, wondering why his anticipated elation had failed him. Justification alone wasn't enough. He felt only weariness, but he would stay through the finish.

They bivouacked that evening without fires. The hardy Juáristas' daily rations now consisted of pinole—a mixture of ground corn and mesquite beans—half a pound of dried beef, and half a pound of coarse brown sugar called panocha. They stirred the pinole with water and sweetened it with the panocha. Simple, Floyd pointed out, and a man could march on it.

Morning light revealed the Presidio Montaña as a bold bastion standing above the arid plain, with a village crouched at its stone feet. The picture of an Old World castle rose to Jesse's mind. He and Floyd and the *padre* circled the village and presidio, which had north and south gates in a quadrangular perimeter wall flanked at each corner by cylindrical towers.

"We sho' can't rush the place," Floyd said when they rode back to the command, "and we can't knock it down with cannonballs."

"We can snipe and see what happens," Garza said.

"Dubray bit at San Juan. I don't believe he will again, Father, but we can try."

So they posted sharpshooters with muzzle-loaders in a half circle within two hundred yards of the north gate and began sniping at the sentries. Other than an answering shot now and then, nothing had changed after an hour.

"They won't take the bait a second time," Floyd said. "We've got enough rations for three days to figure out what to do."

"Can the cannon be elevated enough to lob shells inside the presidio?" Father Garza asked. "Perhaps on logs?"

"The recoil would throw the gun back on itself, and I wouldn't vouch for the accuracy. Any notions, Jesse?"

While Floyd and the *padre* talked, Jesse had observed the presidio, the village and its plaza and its rather large church with a broad, tall tower, a white dove of peace hovering high above all else. In his weariness, he saw the forthcoming battle more as a field problem to be solved by coolness and analysis than one of impassioned bloodletting.

"There is . . . a field of fire into the presidio," he said, his words halting. "Beats building ladders—which we have no means to do— scaling stone walls and losing many men. Or bombarding the north gate with the twelve-pounder, then rushing the fort across open ground and losing many men."

"What is it you see, Jesse?" the *padre* asked.

"A wild idea, maybe. The belfry of the church tower overlooks the presidio. Range not more than a hundred fifty yards or so. If we could tote that gun up there, we could fire right down into the compound. They'd have to come out and fight or surrender."

"Hmmm . . ." Floyd said, casting a skeptical look at the tower. "Tote it up there, you say?"

"Do it like we do everything—muscle and sweat. Rush the gun up to the tower, unbolt it, take it up the stairs in pieces. . . . We'd have to reassemble the gun carriage up there." Once proposed, the plan seemed almost too improbable to Jesse. He rubbed his chin.

Floyd slapped his leg. "Let's do it." And Garza jogged his head.

All went well until they reached the door of the church. There a priest in black cassock, crucifix in hand, blocked the way. His eyes and gestures said this was desecration. Garza began explaining, and while that was going on, the sweating Juáristas toiled up the narrow staircase, muscling the gun pieces and the carriage. Behind them came Floyd, urging others on with powder and shell. He carried a bucket of water and a sponge.

After the fieldpiece was assembled and pointed out a window, Jesse stopped in abrupt frustration. Although he knew the rudiments, he'd never fired a cannon, wasn't certain that Floyd had, and of course the Juáristas hadn't. "Cullen, you ever fire one of these little monsters?"

Floyd was all assurance. "It's easy. All you do is load, fire, and swab with a sponge."

"Know how to set the range?"

Floyd blinked, stumped. "I reckon you just point it in the general direction." Taking a rammer from underneath the carriage, he pushed home a bag of powder and a can of canister.

"Wait," Jesse said. "Let's see what we're shootin' at."

They could look down into most of the presidio. Within the quadrangle Jesse saw a two-story wooden building, obviously the barracks. An adobe building with a patio, which he guessed was Colonel Dubray's quarters. And corrals for horses and mules and sheds for storage. Sentries moved on the walls.

They aimed the gun, then Floyd pulled the lanyard cord and a deafening boom shook the belfry as the gun's recoil flung Jesse and Floyd and three Juáristas upon the steps, the gun hanging precariously above them.

"Believe I forgot about the recoil," Floyd drawled.

"I think we overshot the presidio."

Floyd sent for rope to be tied on each wheel for a man to hold against the recoil. With the gun barrel depressed, the next shot exploded inside the quadrangle. Now they had the range. They poured another round into the quadrangle. A bugle's scrambling notes sounded. When red-trousered companies started forming, Floyd said, "I'd better get down there if they bust out the north gate. Come on, Father!"

"Send me some sharpshooters," Jesse yelled.

Another blast of canister tore the formations. Another round struck higher and smoke curled up from the barracks. Jesse lowered the hot barrel. Floyd's sharpshooters piled into the belfry and fired from the windows, adding to the choking powdersmoke. The bugle down there called again, brassy and frantic. Before Jesse's crew could get off another shot, the companies ran for the north gate, bayonets flashing. As the crew swabbed and reloaded, the gate opened and the companies rushed out.

A furious roll of musketry greeted them, Jesse catching the familiar *bang-bang* of the Spencers. One company of fours wheeled on the double for the churchtower. Jesse swung the barrel around and yanked the lanyard and with the bellowing *tom* of the Napoleon, canister shredded the ranks. Sharpshooters joined the killing. A second round of canister checked the charge, sent the company staggering brokenly back toward the gate. The other companies, still under continuous fire, were also falling back, milling in confusion at the gate. Jesse glimpsed men throwing down their rifles and raising their arms in surrender. The battle was virtually over there.

He glanced down into the presidio. The barracks were burning. A clump of horsemen was forming in front of the adobe. Yet it was too late to help at the north gate. His mind turned on only one possible meaning and caught: San Juan again? Looking at the powder-blackened faces around him, he gestured for the gun crew to keep firing into the quadrangle and motioned for some sharpshooters to come with him. They ran down the stairs. Mounted, with the riflemen flanking him, he rode hard for the south gate.

It was closed. Then it opened outward on five horsemen, in obvious command an officer in a gold-braided uniform and a plumed helmet, astride a bay. He shouted and they all charged, sabers out. Jesse eared back the Spencer's hammer and fired. The bullet struck the officer high in the chest. As he swayed, but still came on, slashing with his saber, Jesse drove another bullet into him that knocked him from the saddle. The sharpshooters were firing. All the riders were down, and the whooping Juáristas dashed in, grabbing for the reins of blooded horseflesh. Beyond the gate through the smoke Jesse could see white-clad infantry pouring into the quadrangle. The gun crew held its fire.

While the red horse danced, Jesse just watched, feeling relief and the old after-battle numbness, his ears ringing, his mouth bitter with the taste of gunpowder.

Floyd and a horde of yelling cavalry stormed around the wall and pulled up. He read the story here, his eyes raking. He looked down at the gold-braided officer, whose mustached face showed arrogance and cruelty even in death.

"You and the boys got Dubray and his staff," Floyd said, his satisfaction grim. "Caught him pullin' out same as he did at San Juan." He seemed to wait for Jesse's show of triumph.

"It's done," Jesse said, and that was all. In that moment he could think only of her and what had been.

May wind cooled his face. Ever southward the Juáristas marched now, a growing tide of patriots, sweeping all before them as they skirmished with the retreating red trousers, their ranks swelled daily by volunteers. Passing through the plazas of the dusty villages, where pretty girls in white waved and tossed flowers, and there was plenty of beer and tequila, and the people shouted, *"Viva Mexico! Viva Juárez!"*

Eyes followed Jesse as he rode by, white hair streaming to his shoulders. He discovered also that he was being shouted at.

"They have a name for you," Floyd confided, clapping him on the shoulder. "They call you *El Soldado del Pelo Blanco*—the Soldier of the White Hair. How's that for a po' Johnny Reb?"

Jesse could only shake his head. With some amusement he noted that Floyd wore his saber every day now, that when riding through the villages he carried himself more erect than usual. *Well, my good friend, why not? You've earned it and more.* Only yesterday, with due formality, Floyd had brought news from the *padre* of their promotion to Citizen Generals, "commissions approved by no less than President Juárez himself, suh."

Jesse had to banter him some. "At last, Cullen, the commission so unfairly denied you for so long. Is it brevet?"

Floyd drew himself up. "Hell, no. This is permanent. I can't wait to get to Mexico City and have my uniform made."

"Go easy on the gold braid, will you? We've seen enough of that."

"I was thinkin' of something in green with yellow epaulets. A double-breasted frock coat, maybe. How's that strike you?"

"A little too showy. I prefer something conservative. Maybe black with silver buttons the size of 'dobe dollars, four stars on each shoulder strap, and loops of silver on the sleeves. Worn with crisscrossed bandoliers trimmed in silver. What d'you think?"

"I think a certain Johnny Reb is about to get hisself ducked in the crick."

Jesse was aware that events were moving fast. With the prisoner count increasing, Father Garza had established a camp at Zacatecas. The general expectancy was the prisoners would be released within a few months, because the war couldn't last much longer. Juárez's forces had driven Maximilian's garrisons from all major points except Mexico City, Puebla Vera Cruz, Querétaro, and San Luis Potosí. Only scattered detachments remained north of San Luis Potosí. It was these in stubborn retreat that Garza's peasant army now pursued.

His Juáristas were resting this day, waiting for provisions to catch up with them, when Jesse saw the column approaching the bivouac. Only one rider, the rest on foot. More volunteers, he thought. Pickets halted the rider, who gestured emphatically, imperiously; cowed, the pickets waved the column on.

Curious, Jesse saw the *padre* soon walk out to greet the new arrivals. The rider, mounted on a high-headed gray Arabian, gestured to his men as if they were a bountiful gift; in turn he awaited the *padre*'s bow of gratitude. Garza nodded and pointed toward the camp.

"Now who the hell could that be?" Floyd asked, walking up.

"No doubt some *hacendado,*" Jesse said.

"An *hacendado* with his army of peons. Each man treated like a dog."

"We won't have to wait long. Here comes Father Alberto now."

The *padre*, his usual gracious self, said, "I want you to meet Don Enrique Sedillo, who has just come to us with a hundred good riflemen." As they walked away, he added, "I must say that he has been somewhat slow joining the cause, but now is better than never."

"There's nothing like victories to attract fair-weather patriots," Floyd said, and for that drew a frown from the Father.

Sedillo's spacious tent of several rooms was already up. He stood before it, arms folded, a tall, slim man dressed in skintight *ranchero* pants set off with silver down the seams, and a brown military tunic. Under the great gold-embroidered, dove-gray hat the face was an inscrutable mask: quick black eyes busy sizing up the two Americans; goatee, long black sideburns, and a clipped mustache. A long, curved nose and a tight, haughty mouth. He had an air of command, of reserve and dignity. Two ivory-handled pistols hung on his bony hips.

When Garza made the introductions, Sedillo shook hands formally, briefly, and the *padre* added proudly, "Both *Señor* Floyd and *Señor* Wilder have been commissioned Citizen Generals by President Juárez. Without them, we would not be where we are today, but fighting a guerrilla war in northern Chihuahua."

Sedillo said, "So you are *Yanquis?*" and his lean face stiffened.

"We are not Yankees," Jesse corrected him mildly. "We are Southern Americans. We served in the Confederate army."

"In Mexico all *Americanos* are *Yanquis, señor.*"

"There's a big difference in the United States between Yankees and Southerners," Jesse said. "That's why we fought a bloody war not long ago."

The jet eyes snapped. Sedillo clapped his hands, and a servile peon brought out a small table, and another brought a bottle and glasses, tinkling them so in his nervousness that Sedillo shot him a damning glare. The man fled. Sedillo poured the drinks and, with the manner of a practiced host, invited his guests to imbibe.

"To victory," he said, holding his glass high. "I look forward to holding some command in your army, Father Garza."

They all downed their drinks. It was hot cognac.

"First, we are grateful that you and your brave men have joined our ranks, Don Enrique," the *padre* said, not to be outdone. *"Señor* Floyd and *Señor* Wilder are my advisers. Because of their invaluable experience in war, they plan our strategies and decide who will carry out various duties. I know they will find a fitting place for you, Don Enrique."

That, Jesse saw, brought everything to a mollifying close. As they strolled back to camp, Floyd said wryly, "The good Father is one slick politican, the way he stroked the Don's fur. Passed the hot iron to us. What are we gonna do with that vain son of a bitch?"

"Maybe we could put him in charge of a four-company battalion and call him colonel."

"That wouldn't be enough rank. Notice how his hackles went up when he found we're Americans? He hates all Americans. Now that most of the fightin's over, he wants to ride in the victory parade when we hit Mexico City. Only reason he brought in his ragtag gang of peons. I feel sorry for the poor bastards. Notice how they groveled?"

"You talk like you've run into this hate before."

"I have. And it was always from some lordly *hacendado* who held himself above his peons because of his claimed Spanish blood. Wouldn't touch an Indian's skin unless it belonged to some poor little Indian girl too afraid to cry out when he took her to bed."

Next morning Jesse led the red horse out and brushed and curried him. After all the hard riding of late, the red ribbon still graced the black mane. On impulse, Jesse mounted bareback and rode beyond the camp. He was coming back when, from the corner of his eye, he saw the gray Arabian bearing down on him at a run. He pulled up.

Sedillo waved a leather crop. "I happened to see you taking care of your horse, *señor*. Excellent. You have pride. Would you like to race a little? Say to that big mesquite yonder?" He pointed with the whip.

Jesse looked. The mesquite was about a quarter mile away. He waved back and said, "Why not?"

When the horses were even, both riders shouted and they were off. The warmed-up Arabian jumped to the lead. After a hundred yards the red horse began taking to the uneven ground, closing the gap. He loved to run, and Jesse sensed a change in the rhythm of his mount. All at once the red horse charged to the Arab's hindquarters.

He was flying now. For a time they ran head to head. Sedillo was lashing his mount. Jesse clapped his heels and his horse shot ahead. He had half a length on the gray when they flashed past the mesquite.

Sedillo could not mask his chagrin, nor Jesse his elation, when they reined up. *"Señor,"* said Sedillo, "you surprised me with the speed of your horse. May I ask his breeding?"

"He's a mustang. I bought him off a trader in El Paso."

"Mustangs are descended from early Spanish stock, which carried strong Arabian blood."

Jesse felt like saying, "You mean if it's not Spanish, it's just common stock."

"Would you consider a longer race tomorrow?" Sedillo asked. "For two miles down on the flat? We could mark the track."

Jesse saw through the two miles. Arabians were distance runners. "I don't know if my horse can run that far, but I'll race you a mile."

"Agreed, *señor.*" Don Enrique was eager. "And a wager?"

"Oh, I might bet five pesos."

Sedillo jerked. "That is for peons. I won't bet less than fifty."

Jesse's excitement still held. "I'll bet you fifty."

Next afternoon Jesse rode a light saddle fashioned from a wool blanket cinched with rawhide and another wide strip of rawhide looped at the ends for stirrups, thanks to Doc Pedro's handiwork. The circular track, marked by stakes, was approximately half a mile in length, so they would have to go around twice. Father Garza would act as both starter and finish-line judge. Approaching the track with Floyd, Jesse noticed groups of Mexicans gesturing and talking excitedly.

"Doc Pedro tells me Sedillo's boys are bettin' down to their drawers," Floyd said, amused. "The Arab has never lost a race."

"Neither has *El Soldado,*" Jesse said, feigning boastfulness. "But I wonder how he'll take the turns."

Sedillo was already on the track, erect on a light leather racing saddle with iron stirrups. Garza, smiling, for this was like a fiesta, a break in the campaigning, motioned for the riders to come to the starting line, marked by a post.

Sedillo took the inside position at once. Too late, Jesse realized that, unwittingly, he had been outmaneuvered. The inside would be an advantage on the turns. He should have called for a flip of a coin. He rode up and crouched in the saddle.

At the *padre's* shout Jesse jumped his mount out and they took the lead, held it going into the first turn. There the red horse drifted wide. By the time Jesse brought him around, the Arab was winging two lengths ahead. The bay drew even on the back stretch, but again the Arab gained ground in the turn. Jesse could hear his boys whooping as the red horse moved to the Arab's head in the stretch.

Just before they entered the third turn, Jesse began reining his mount a little to the inside. They lost less ground this time. The red horse was learning. Again they closed. Going into the last turn, the gray hugged the inside and opened up only half a length. At the top of the stretch Sedillo started whipping, and the Arab seemed to find wings in his feet. Daylight opened between the horses.

Jesse clapped heels for more speed, and the red horse dug in. Suddenly the daylight vanished. Jesse was whooping at him. They came to the Arab's hindquarters. Now his girth, his shoulders, his neck, his head. There they seemed to cling, unable to forge ahead.

Some instinct beyond thought moved Jesse. From his depths he called up the shrill rebel yell, "Yee-haaa! Yee-haaa-haaa-haa!" and the red horse laid back his ears and flattened out. He broke clear. Half a length, then a length. A wild horse again. They sprinted past the post like that, and in Jesse's ears the roar of the boys was like music he'd never heard before.

His eyes were wet with pure joy when he reined in well past the turn and jogged back under tight rein, for the red horse still lunged to run. Sedillo was waiting at the post, his haughty face a tight mask. He motioned. A peon handed him a leather purse and he passed over fifty pesos. As Jesse nodded his thanks, a kind of bewilderment broke through Sedillo's face and he said, "I do not understand. A range-bred horse beating my purebred Arabian."

Jesse couldn't hold back the retort, "I reckon it's his Spanish blood, *señor.* "

On the dusty road to San Luis Potosí the Juáristas came upon a straggling enemy supply train. Floyd sent two companies of cavalry on a flying sweep, and they cut off the wagons. A sharp fight ensued. Jesse observed that Sedillo's hundred-odd infantry, as yet not assigned to any of the original units, moved in aggressively. Floyd had decided it would cause less friction to let the lordly *hacendado* operate independently without rank. The fighting tightened to around the wagons. Jesse, with the *padre*, sent in more companies, and they overran the escort. The firing all but ceased. Hands went up, stayed up. It was over, Jesse saw, riding forward. He had kept out of this, content to direct and observe at a distance.

Floyd rode up, a wild excitement in his eyes. "There's some Johnnies with the prisoners!"

"The devil you say!"

"Eight or ten. Part of the escort. Gave us hell for a while."

Jesse spurred off. Not far, he slowed, shocked to see prisoners lined up against a wagon. Sedillo strutting about, forming a firing squad. By God, he was! Jesse kicked his horse into a run, shouting as he came. He yanked the Spencer up and fired one shot into the air.

Sedillo turned at the report. The firing squad lowered rifles.

Furious, Jesse rode between the squad and the prisoners. He shouted at Sedillo, "We don't shoot prisoners in this army, Don Enrique. Disperse your men!"

Sedillo didn't move. "The French shoot our prisoners."

"We're not barbarians like the French. I say disperse your men."

The lordly head tilted higher. "I refuse, *señor.*"

"That's an order from a Citizen General commissoned by President Juárez. You will obey orders as long as you're in this army."

Sedillo stood even more erect. "I refuse the order."

"You will obey or I will shoot you here and now for insubordination," Jesse said flatly, sighting on him.

"I still refuse."

Jesse eared back the hammer. It made a distinct click. He was going to shoot the man, conscious of a dead silence and of hundreds of men watching. Sedillo was beginning to twitch. In another moment he'd break.

Floyd and Father Garza rushed in, waving and shouting in Spanish. Jesse lowered the carbine as the *padre* spoke sharply to Sedillo, who bowed formally from the waist. Fixing piercing black eyes on Jesse, he said, "We Sedillos are not ones to forget wrongs imposed on us, *Señor Southern Americano,*" and strode off with his men.

Jesse faced the prisoners. It was easy to pick out the expatriates, in worn civilian clothes and the slouch hats of old, men with their past like print on their gaunt faces. He snapped them a salute. "At ease, you Johnny Rebs. What was your outfit?"

A slim, tobacco-chewing man drawled, "Bate's Brigade, 37th Georgia, and Bushrod Johnson's Brigade, 17th Tennessee."

"Fine. You-all fought at Hoover's Gap. Now march to the rear, boys. You have nothing to fear. Before long this war will be over." He warmed to these men, ached for them, understood why they were here, as homeless as he and Cullen. As they filed by, one said, "Sho' much obliged to you, suh. That turkey-cock struttin' feller was mighty wrathy to shoot us."

Jesse doffed his hat to them all.

That evening a serious-faced Floyd told Jesse, "Listen to me, ol' reb. You humiliated Sedillo in front of hundreds of men. You should've shot 'im. He's a vain bastard and full of hate for all Americans. Like he said, he won't forget." Floyd handed Jesse a pistol on a gunbelt. "Wear this wherever you go. Quicker to get to than your Spencer. So be on the lookout. I'll watch, too."

"I think he's all bluff."

"Don't fool yourself. I know his kind."

Jesse heeded the warning and strapped on the gunbelt in the morning. But the fast-moving events of the day soon shuttled the threat to the back of his mind. San Luis Potosí fell without a shot, the French evacuating and retreating toward Querétaro. Surging crowds greeted the Juáristas with cheers, flowers, food, drink, and music. The victors marched on to the outskirts to camp. Father Garza relaxed discipline for the day, and soon the boys were streaming back into the city. Floyd needed to replenish his tequila supply. Would Jesse care to go along?

Wearily, Jesse declined. He fed and tied his horse and, enjoying the luxury of a tent for the first time in weeks, he stretched out to rest. He had become more thoughtful of late, nearly withdrawn. His mind dwelled constantly on Ana and that shattering day that never seemed to end; without appeal, he considered less frequently his delayed future. Just before he dropped off to sleep, he heard the distant voices of the revelers blending with spirited music. The sounds of victory, he thought, of a poor nation freed of invaders.

A sibilant voice jarred him awake. "Wake up, *gringo!*"

He sat up at once, blinking, knowing. His gunbelt lay uselessly out of reach on his pack.

"Stand up, *gringo!*" Sedillo pointed a rifle at him.

He stood and looked into a mask of consuming hate and the certainty of death.

"We Sedillos never forget an insult. You are going to die for that, *gringo*. Let's see if you can die like a man, like the *Southern Americano you claim to be.*" He spat out the last words.

One last instinct took over. It wouldn't save his life, but he was going to dive for the rifle.

The next he knew there came a blast of gunfire, but strangely he felt no pain. Utter astonishment erased the hate from Sedillo's face as his eyes sprang wide and he dropped the rifle and collapsed at Jesse's feet.

Father Garza moved from the open door of the tent, a smoking pistol in his right hand. Even now it seemed awkward and foreign to his grasp. He said, "Mexico is not about to forsake a friend sent us by God the Father in our time of dreadful need. Are you all right, *amigo* Jesse?"

"I'm fine, Father. Do you want me to take the pistol?"

Garza looked down at the weapon. His hand was shaking. "No. We still have a way to go."

15

The victors pressed on next morning, trailed by a swarm of eager recruits, which caused a great deal of confusion and noise, until Floyd halted the column and scattered the new men throughout the companies.

"Let this go on very long," he told Jesse, "and we'd turn into an armed mob. Hangovers are no excuse. I've got one myself."

After drawing the command up in double-ranked company fronts for inspection at order arms, he and the *padre* and Jesse rode slowly down the line. Now and then Floyd would halt and point to a man and order him to straighten up or to hold his rifle properly.

Coming back, the three halted, front and center, and Father Garza began addressing the command. He was still the same unaffected little man Jesse had first met dressed in peasant white, handmade sandals, and small gray hat, astride the same brown mule. His pleasing voice carried passion today. Jesse caught part of the meaning. He was telling them to be brave and dutiful, to love God and country and honor their president, Benito Juárez. Then, riding along the long line, he blessed each company as the men bared their heads and kneeled.

Front and center again, he raised his right arm and shouted, *"Viva Mexico!"* and the Juáristas shouted back, *"Viva Mexico!"* And the *padre* shouted, *"Viva Juárez!"* and the patriots roared the words in turn.

The command moved off with a jaunty air. When Garza dropped back to question a machete-armed boy who looked no older than ten or twelve, Jesse said, "Cullen, I want to ask you something. I know you marveled at what Father Alberto did yesterday. So did I. Another second and I'd been blown away." He paused. "Have you ever seen him fire a gun?"

Floyd reflected. "Come to think of it, I can't recall that I have.

He's always carried that pistol, but I've never seen him use it . . . no, I haven't."

"Then I believe that was the first time he'd ever fired a shot."

"I marvel again," Floyd said, awed.

The day passed without alarm. But next midmorning scouts clattered in, greatly excited. A large force of the enemy waited ahead, drawn up for battle.

The three rode out to reconnoiter. Before them Jesse saw infantry in place across the road to Querétaro, one flank anchored against a rocky ridge, the other flank guarded by a deep arroyo. Behind the infantry, wagons formed a second line of defense. The broken nature of the terrain made bringing cavalry in on a flank or their rear virtually impossible.

"It's the San Luis Potosí garrison," Floyd said. "They knew we'd catch up pretty quick, so they decided to make a stand. Couldn't have picked a stronger position. I don't like the looks of this. How do you-all size it up?"

Garza, ranging his eyes back and forth, said, "It's evident that we can't outflank them. Yet I shy away from a costly frontal attack."

Jesse nodded. "I would never agree to a massed infantry assault across a field of fire like this, Father. Neither would Cullen. We saw too much of that foolishness in our war back home." Of a sudden his mind seemed to do a flip-flop. His voice thickened. "Boys marching shoulder to shoulder. Raw boys, going into battle for the first time, used to talk about 'seeing the elephant'—meaning their first ordeal of battle. Many times all that we gained was a little piece of ground—and a field of slaughtered boys." He put a hand to his forehead. He was getting weary again. "But somehow we'll have to fight these people here."

Floyd broke Jesse's inertia. "I don't see a fieldpiece on their line, and we've still got my Old Betsy. What's the range of a 12-pounder Napoleon, reb Jesse, or thereabout?"

"For canister—and I think that's what we've got the most of—I figure it's about four hundred yards . . . that close. Would put our gun crew under rifle fire."

Floyd laughed dryly. "Our gun crew, you say? That means you and me and the country boys who served the gun in the belfry. Well, come on, Jesse, and remember the recoil!"

There was more to it than merely bringing up the twelve-pounder and collecting the old gun crew. As they deployed the Juáristas in company fronts behind the Napoleon, bullets from the red trousers began to hum and whine overhead, followed by the steady *crack-crack* of rifles.

The first projectile fell short. The second was high. The third blast of little iron balls tore gaps in the line. They had the range now. *Load, fire, swab.* A storm of missiles. Firing from the enemy fell off. Jesse could see tangled milling clumps of men falling back. By God, they were breaking!

A mighty chorus of primitive, high-pitched yells soared up behind Jesse. The Juáristas saw the breaking line as well, and here they came on the run, unrestrained, on their own, wild to fight.

Floyd, his mouth smeared with black powder, whipped a look at Jesse. Now! They ran to their horse holders and flung themselves onto their saddles. The red horse danced.

Floyd drew his saber with a flourish, caught in a torrent of charging foot soldiers. He spurred ahead of them and Jesse. Waving his saber, he yelled, "Come on, boys! We've got the goddamned Yankees on the run!" and spurred faster, still waving the saber.

Despite the headlong moment, Jesse had to grin. Floyd's impulse was so natural.

High in the saddle, Floyd appeared to be carried away on the rushing tide of men and boys in peasant white, their peaked hats bobbing.

Looking toward the enemy, Jesse saw the disorder again. But with the twelve-pounder no longer firing, officers were frantically trying to reform the broken line. A splatter of musketry sounded there. To Jesse's dismay, he saw Floyd lurch and, swaying, start to fall. He dropped his saber.

Rushing up, Jesse caught him and held him in the saddle till he could bring Floyd's plunging mount under control, aware of the Juáristas charging ahead without letup.

Jesse eased him to the ground and held his head. Floyd's face was already ashen. "Long way from home, Jesse," he said, a going-back in his eyes.

"Home is where we are, Cullen." Jesse took his hand. "I'm right here with you. Hold on." He'd never felt so ineffectual.

Floyd groaned. "Don't leave me."

"I won't. I promise." Jesse glanced around helplessly for Doc

Pedro. He gave Floyd a sip from his canteen, but the water only ran down his chin. "I'll get you some tequila from your saddle pack."

Floyd's lips hardly moved; even so, his eyes held a glint of his old mockery. "Nevah . . . waste good liquor. . . . Remember that . . . ol' reb."

Tearing at the pack, Jesse found a bottle and held Floyd's head up for a drink; that, too, driveled away. Jesse looked around again for some sort of help, though sensing little could be done. The Juáristas had reached the line. It was hand-to-hand now. Machetes flashed.

Suddenly Floyd strained to sit up, but fell back, coughing blood, a wild light in his eyes. "How'd the charge go?"

Jesse wiped Floyd's mouth with a bandanna. "Fine. The boys are driving 'em back. We're winning."

"One war we won . . . eh?"

"You bet."

"Ah . . . that's good. Don't leave me, Jesse. Ah . . ."

"I won't. You know I won't."

Floyd was fading fast. His breathing was ragged. He didn't seem to see Jesse. Jesse continued to hold him, wishing for Doc Pedro. And before long Doc Pedro ran up with Father Garza. Jesse looked at them appealingly. Doc Pedro opened Floyd's bloody shirt, looked for a moment, turned his eyes quickly away and closed the shirt and stood by, grieving in silence. Floyd hadn't moved.

"Cullen!" Jesse said sharply, as if calling him back. "Cullen!" His voice broke.

"I'm afraid he doesn't hear you anymore," the *padre* said softly. He bent over Floyd, murmuring in Latin, rose and bowed his head, hands clasped.

Jesse got it. Last rites. He squeezed his eyes against the tears.

Everyone seemed frozen. In the distance the battle was lessening, down to shots here and there; in a short time even those sounds faded.

Jesse held Floyd a while longer, reluctant to let go, refusing to accept this; rising, finally, he kissed Floyd tenderly on the forehead and drew the rebel slouch hat over Floyd's face. Gazing down at him through streaming eyes, he said, "He was like a brother to me. He was my brother."

Beneath a brassy June sun the red horse carried him steadily along the winding road to Querétaro, riding beside Father Garza. A somberness weighed on them both. Again Jesse was the survivor. Why? He had asked it many times before and he asked it again. There was no ready answer. It was life. It was fate. Glib responses. A man could say that and feel no comfort or understanding. The *padre* had expressed it best. "It is God's will, *amigo* Jesse. Accept that and you will feel better in the days ahead, I promise you in God's holy name, and God does not lie." So he had accepted it, yet his pain and guilt seemed no less with his rooted weariness.

They rode more like travelers now, sending scouts ahead as usual, followed by the command raising streamers of chalky dust, but apparently no enemy forces existed between them and the city. This morning riders had brought news, some weeks old, that Maximilian, under siege in Querétaro, had surrendered and was held prisoner with two native generals. President Juárez was there. Maximilian's other forces had either surrendered, the messengers said, or were retreating toward Vera Cruz. All fighting had ended. The war was over.

"There is disturbing bad news with the good," Garza passed on to Jesse. "Each prisoner's cell has a large crucifix and two silver candlesticks."

"Meaning . . . ?"

"A clear warning that they must prepare for death. I am disappointed. I thought our president possessed more humanity than that. Still, it is also the law. His decree of '62 threatened death to all who opposed our independence, meaning natives who favored an emperor, and death to aliens who fought us, which includes the Austrian. Execution is the strict letter of the decree, not the spirit, which is God's way."

Querétaro lay in a valley fringed by low hills. Father Garza camped the command outside the city and rode in alone. It was late before he returned. His face was troubled.

"There is much tension and sadness in the air, Jesse. Maximilian and the two Mexican generals will be executed by a firing squad at three o'clock tomorrow afternoon. The people want to spare the prisoners—even petitions have been passed. But the president is adamant."

He regarded Jesse sadly. "This brings us to the end, doesn't it, *amigo*? Tomorrow I shall disband our tough little army, send the boys back to their bean and chili patches with hopes for the future. The raw boys you and Cullen so generously and nobly trained and made into soldiers. Proving that victories demand more than passion." All at once his gray mood passed. "But you don't have to leave. Mexico has a home for you. I will find one for you."

Moved, Jesse looked up at the flawless blue sky before he answered. "I am grateful, Father, but I feel I should go back to the States. Exactly where, I can't say at this time."

"You have finished what you and Cullen set out to do. Mexico will not forget. You can always come back to us."

This was pulling Jesse down into the tricky currents of deep emotions, and he was having mixed feelings about going. He took a hold on himself and said, "However, there is one unfinished thing, based on what I know about war, and then I'll be finished with war, God granting. I will go to President Juárez and plead for the lives of Maximilian and the two native generals."

Garza was startled. "He won't change his decision. He is a very stubborn Indian, honest and good as he is."

"But Mexico needs to change this eye-for-an-eye, this endless bloodletting."

"Then try," Garza said, pleased.

"But will he see me?"

"He will see a Citizen General, I assure you. I will send word ahead."

Juárez's headquarters, befitting the citizen president, was in a small adobe house over which flew Mexico's flag, three vertical stripes of green, white, and red. Two lines of sentries guarded the door.

"I am Citizen General Jesse Wilder to see President Juárez," Jesse said, addressing a stern-faced boyish captain, who jerked his head in immediate understanding. Jesse held up his arms, inviting inspection. "I have no weapon, Captain. Nonetheless, search me."

The captain complied. The ensuing delay was lengthy, also befitting the busy citizen president, before Jesse was escorted inside.

Jesse saluted smartly. Behind the plain wooden desk sat a short-

set, solidly built man in a dark suit. His black, Indian eyes, set wide
in the taut, strong-boned face, projected an intimidating quality.

The man spoke. "So you are Jesse Wilder—Citizen General Wilder, I should say—formerly of the Confederate army—now in the
patriot army of Father Alberto Garza?" His voice, lacking the vehe-
mence of Spanish, was like him: deliberate and keenly observant,
though pleasant in tone.

"Yes, *Señor* President."

"Why do you come here? Do you seek land or a post in my
insolvent government?"

"No, sir. I want nothing like that. I've come to plead for the
pardon of Maximilian and the two native generals."

The Indian face tightened. "Why? They've been found guilty by
our courts."

"It's barbaric, sir, to execute prisoners. Mexico must rise above
that as a nation. The trials were hardly more than a mere formality,
since the death penalty was fixed at the time of their arrest."

Juárez stood, his eyes like points. Although he couldn't be more
than a little over five feet in height, Jesse saw, he created the impression of a much larger man. His black hair, cut short, danced with
the motion of his head as he spoke. "The execution of the invader
and the two traitors is the law of Mexico, written in a decree. Your
plea is denied, General Wilder."

"Sir," said Jesse, "with all due respect, I remind you that as
bloody as was our War Between the States, which the Yankees called
the Civil War, neither side shot prisoners."

To Jesse's surprise, the president did not interrupt. His attitude
was more that of a patient listener.

Now Jesse's words came in a flood. "There's been so much killing,
Señor President, that Mexico runs red. I've lost my beloved Indian
wife and unborn child and my best friend in your war. What Mexico needs now, sir, is mercy and forgiveness to build on." He bit his
lower lip, primed for an outburst.

It did not come. Instead, Juárez considered him intently, yet
without anger. In his low, inflexible voice, he said, "You are dismissed, General Wilder."

Jesse saluted, did an aboutface, and walked out beyond the sentries where Father Garza waited. "I know what the president said.
But he heard a voice raised in forgiveness . . . and one voice

speaks and another until they become a multitude of voices crying out for righteousness."

Not long afterward the three-o'clock sun beat down upon them like a fist. Jesse had the red horse packed. He waited with the Father, their faces turned toward where the sounds would come. A volley crashed. Jesse tensed, saw the *padre* flinch. They faced away.

"I know you will find peace of mind somewhere, *amigo* Jesse," Garza said. "because you believe in God, and God always provides in some way. . . . *Un abrazo, amigo.*"

They embraced. Impulsively, Jesse hugged him again and stepped back, seeing Father Alberto's face swimming in a green mist. Jesse turned to go. As he mounted, the red horse danced a little, and then they set out on the dusty road leading north.

EPILOGUE

There's a story passed down in my family about my paternal great-grandfather, Jesse Alden Wilder, who served four years in the Army of Tennessee during the Civil War. Wounded at the bloody battle of Franklin, Tennessee, he woke up in a Union hospital; upon recovering, he was faced with two choices—serve in the Union army on the western frontier, where men were sorely needed, or go to a Yankee prison camp. He chose the latter. There he saw friends die of starvation and ill treatment. With others, he tried to escape and failed. Knowing that he would probably die if he remained much longer in prison, he reluctantly took the oath of allegiance and wore the Union blue on the Plains for nearly two years. Mustered out, he returned home hoping for reunion and understanding. Instead, old neighbors turned their backs on him and walked away. His own family disowned him. It was total rejection.

I never quite understood this until I came back from Vietnam, when my homecoming became much the same as his. Although my family didn't throw me out, neither were they proud of me. I've felt the same self-imposed guilt Jesse did for having survived the war when close friends and many others did not, the same isolation and alienation. Sometimes I have nightmares about the war, like Jesse had. Sometimes I've wept and drunk too much. But Jesse left me a legacy. I've learned how to endure and live with my demons and move ahead. I won't run. Thank you, Great-Grandfather Jesse, for helping me to understand myself.

ABOUT THE AUTHOR

Fred Grove has written extensively in the field of Western fiction, from the Civil War period to modern quarter-horse racing. He has received the Western Writers of America Spur Award five times—for his novels *Comanche Captives* (which also won the Oklahoma Writing Award and the Levi Strauss Golden Saddleman Award), *The Great Horse Race,* and *Match Race,* and for his short stories, "Comanche Woman" and "When the Caballos Came." His novel *The Buffalo Runners* was awarded the Western Heritage Award by the National Cowboy Hall of Fame, as was the short story "Comanche Son." He also has received a Distinguished Service Award from Western New Mexico University for his regional fiction, including the novels *Phantom Warrior* and *A Far Trumpet.* He is a contributor to anthologies, among them *Spurs West* and *They Opened the West.* This is his twentieth novel.

For a number of years Mr. Grove worked on various newspapers in Oklahoma and Texas as a sportswriter, straight newsman, and editor. Two of his earlier novels, *Warrior Road* and *Drums Without Warriors,* focused on the brutal Osage Indian murders during the Roaring Twenties, a national scandal that brought in the FBI. It was while interviewing Oklahoma pioneers that he became interested in Western fiction. He now resides in Silver City, New Mexico, with his wife, Lucile.